There he
and khaki cargo shorts. He looked undeniably like the bad boy next door. More like the billionaire bad boy. Whatever the title, she regarded him as positively handsome, dangerous, and lethal. She focused on his face. His mouth slipped into a sexy smile that flashed a desire he was having trouble hiding. She found herself stepping away from him.

"You look…" Her thoughts jumbled in her head. *You look great. You look fantastic. You're a fine specimen of a man. Kiss me now.*

"Yes?"

She swallowed her foolish and untimely feelings. "You look just right."

He cocked an eyebrow and gestured to his clothes. "That's it?"

Her heart hammered against her chest. "Is there something you need, Mr. Knight?"

He boldly stepped closer to her. "You, Ms. Cavanagh. I need you."

Love Changes Everything

by

Suzanne Hoos

This is a work of fiction. Names, characters, places, and incidents are either the product of the author's imagination or are used fictitiously, and any resemblance to actual persons living or dead, business establishments, events, or locales, is entirely coincidental.

Love Changes Everything

COPYRIGHT © 2019 by Suzanne Hoos

All rights reserved. No part of this book may be used or reproduced in any manner whatsoever without written permission of the author or The Wild Rose Press, Inc. except in the case of brief quotations embodied in critical articles or reviews.
Contact Information: info@thewildrosepress.com

Cover Art by *Diana Carlile*

The Wild Rose Press, Inc.
PO Box 708
Adams Basin, NY 14410-0708
Visit us at www.thewildrosepress.com

Publishing History
First Champagne Rose Edition, 2019
Print ISBN 978-1-5092-2841-6
Digital ISBN 978-1-5092-2842-3

Published in the United States of America

Dedication

To Helen...
fellow writer, mentor, and friend...
Rest in Peace

"The weak can never forgive.
Forgiveness is the attribute of the strong."

~*Gandhi*

~~

"There is only one happiness in this life,
to love and be loved."

~*George Sand*

Chapter One

"This position is not for the weak or the faint of heart, Ms. Cavanagh. You will be expected to work at least sixty hours a week, and that includes most weekends as well as traveling both here and abroad."

Hallie Cavanagh tried not to squirm in the metal folding chair. Sixty hours a week? Most weekends? Traveling? Her head spun as she listened carefully to the criteria she was expected to meet if hired. And that was a big "if." The conditions sounded severe, if not impossible. No matter. Right now, she needed to stay calm and make a good first impression. She had to show Aaron Knight she was a good fit for this job.

Questions about her business acumen came fast and furious for thirty minutes. She handled herself professionally, but there was nothing professional about this interview. In fact, most interviewees would deem it downright weird. Aaron Knight, the CEO and president of this multi-billion-dollar conglomerate was asking the questions from a computer screen as she sat in a cramped windowless room. She could only assume most successful people like Aaron Knight had their quirks.

"You must be at the beck and call of ARK Enterprises whenever you're needed. That means you'll make yourself available to me at all hours of the day…and night, if necessary." His deep voice boomed over the speakers and bounced against the innocuous beige walls.

Hallie swallowed the hard lump forming in her throat. His words caused her to flinch.

"I understand." Did she wanted to hear any more stark rules she would have to follow if she was going to be part of this international corporation?

"I hope you do."

Stay focused, Hallie. You need this job. The reason hovered over her like a storm cloud. Her mother deserved the best care she could offer. Still the question lingered. What was she getting herself into?

"I can assume then you know what you're getting yourself into?"

The gruff voice brought her back to the moment. "Excuse me?"

"Ms. Cavanagh, are you all right? We can end this interview now if you're—"

"No, sir." She sounded like a fledgling soldier in the army. Was he frowning? She couldn't tell by his silhouette. He sounded like he was frowning. "I'm fine." Her otherwise common sense and control were taking quite a hit. She rubbed her hands on her navy-blue skirt.

Was that an intimidating sigh?

"You will be given five weeks' paid vacation, which is unheard of in other corporations, but you'll need every bit of those weeks to regroup from procurement to procurement. The salary I'm offering is more than generous, but I warn you, no amount of money was enough to keep my last executive director of acquisitions from quitting after seven months. The job was clearly too much for her."

Her?

Though her heart beat double time, she remained calm. She wasn't about to give away any inkling of apprehension.

You will make yourself available to me at all hours of the day...and night, if necessary. His ominous words reverberated in her brain.

His intimidation made the job seem a veritable pressure cooker, but was that the real reason the last director had left the company? Or was there something else that drove the executive away? *Stop it. I'm always thinking the worst.* Aaron Knight was known to be a player when it came to women. Had he come on to the executive? Mentally, she shook her head and forced the dark, if not foolish thoughts to disappear.

"You will earn every penny with your blood, sweat, and many tears, but I would appreciate you keeping your emotions to yourself. No matter how browbeaten you might feel, unrequited sentiments have no business in the workplace."

"I understand." Squashing sentimentalities wouldn't be a problem. She hadn't felt anything in the past year.

"And, Ms. Cavanagh, I cannot stress enough that with any sign of faltering, any breach of confidentiality, or the smallest mistake that costs my company money, you will be let go without so much as a blink of an eye. Have I made myself clear?"

"Yes, you have." She stopped, quickly assessing her flippant tone. She had struggled all through the interview to keep her voice steady, and now she sounded dismissive. Should she be worried?

Aaron Knight apparently caught it, too. His

shadowy figure leaned back and stiffened.

What had she done? *Ignore it. Pretend it never happened.*

"Excuse me?"

"Sorry."

"Are you mocking me?"

Shit. "No. Mr. Knight. I'm just trying to take in the enormity of the job."

"And you don't think you can handle it." It wasn't a question.

"No—" She squared her shoulders. "I mean, yes, I'm sure I can."

"But?"

"No buts. If you give me a chance, I'm sure—"

"This interview is over, Ms. Cavanagh. You'll hear from my—"

"No, I want to hear it from you." *What am I doing?* Silence.

"You have my résumé, Mr. Knight. You know what I'm capable of. If I have the job, I want you to tell me." *Stop talking. Stop talking!*

The computer snapped to black. She sat back, stunned. She'd really messed up this time. Damn it. Why hadn't she kept her big mouth shut?

The door opened suddenly, making her heart flutter. The tall, attractive, willowy woman who had introduced herself before Hallie's interview as Lavelle Andrews, Aaron Knight's administrative assistant, was now here to personally throw her out.

Even though her face burned with embarrassment, Hallie stood, gathered what was left of her dignity, and tried not to make a show of her disappointment. "It's been nice meeting you, Ms. Andrews. Thank you for everything. I'll be going now." She sidestepped the table and headed for the door.

Lavelle put out her hand to stop her. "Just a moment, Ms. Cavanagh. Your interview isn't over."

"But I thought that—"

Lavelle adjusted her stylish, black-rimmed glasses. "It seems Mr. Knight wants to meet with you—in person."

****

Thirty-year-old Aaron Russell Knight stared out the window of his posh yet sterile office high above Manhattan. The several large panes of spotless glass that dominated one wall allowed him to drink in the panoramic view. He loved New York. His connection to the city was something he prized. Its energy and everything it had to offer ran through his veins and ignited his senses. But he liked the anonymity of it even more than its vitality. The millions inhabiting this concrete island made it quite easy for him to get lost among the crowds, even though he cut a high-profile figure.

A city boy, born and raised, he had learned how to become independent at a young age. While suburban brats were learning how to balance on a bicycle, he was already riding the subway to school before the age of eight. While those same kids spent weekends running through the wet grass on soccer or Pop Warner fields, he was making a buck or two delivering pizzas from Romero's on a beat-up scooter to downtown patrons. And later, when teenage boys fought their angst over who to ask to prom, he was ducking his father's punches while trying to deflect the physical abuse away from his younger siblings and long-suffering mother.

Living in a dysfunctional family taught him early on that no one was going to help him through life. He'd struggled for things he'd wanted, fought for things he believed he deserved. No one had ever handed him anything on a silver platter. Maybe that was why he was so prosperous now. Maybe that was why he felt so alone.

Wasted feelings aside, he'd had no idea that seven years ago his insignificant start-up company would be a success. Who knew that buying, selling, or lording over others' companies and properties was something he'd excel in? Something that drove his ambition. Like his hard-nosed grandfather, Malcolm Clark, he had a head for business and a heart for no one.

Or at least he thought.

But moments ago, much to his chagrin, he'd been blindsided by this latest applicant, and now he struggled to understand why. Why was this insignificant woman making him feel things he hadn't felt in years? Maybe his whole broken life?

Over the last month, he'd conducted at least a hundred interviews for the position of executive director of acquisitions. The job was challenging on all accounts. Acquiring the right companies for profit was his religion. Rebecca Strauss, his last director, had run out of the building screaming and cursing his name. He couldn't blame her. He was a bastard when it came to ARK Enterprises. He demanded hard work, loyalty, and confidentiality from his employees. He was as exacting and exhausting as the work itself. But being a hard-ass made him the success he was. Being in control was what he did best.

But so far, those many interviews he'd conducted

only exposed the lack of competence and absence of work ethics in many of the candidates. There were some prospects, far and few between, that showed possibilities, if trained correctly, but who had the time?

What was that old adage? "Time is money." Yeah. He liked that. He lived by that rule. He was prepared to interview a hundred more candidates if he were sure that the perfect one was among them. But today, fate had dealt him another hand, and as intrigued as he was, he couldn't help but wonder why.

Hallie Cavanagh's insistence that he let her know if she was hired on the spot was downright blatant. Would he call her attitude insubordinate? Maybe not. After all, she didn't work for him. Yet. If she expected a yes or no answer, she had severely underestimated him. He wanted to know much more about her, and it wouldn't be all about business.

A quick knock on the door drew his attention. He walked around to the front of his sleek, glass-and-chrome desk, leaned against the edge, and folded his arms over his chest. He crossed his ankles, being careful not to scuff his Italian oxfords. The unexpected pinpricks along his body surprised him. Images of high school and first date jitters rose to the surface, chipping away at his self-assurance. The sensation was annoying at best. What was going on? He was the one with the upper hand. He took a breath and rolled his shoulders, relieving the unwanted tension. "Yes?"

Lavelle peeked around the edge of the door. "Mr. Knight, Ms. Cavanagh is here per your request."

"Send her in."

Lavelle nodded and opened the door wider.

Aaron's heart lurched, and all his thought

processes ceased when Hallie Cavanagh entered the office.

With purposeful intent, she walked up to him and held out her hand. "Hello, Mr. Knight. It's an honor to meet you."

An honor? Her overly confident demeanor amused him. Was it an act? Inside, she was undoubtedly vibrating with dread, wondering what he'd say to her—do to her.

"Thank you, Ms. Cavanagh." He took her hand, shook it, and gave her face a raking gaze. "It's a pleasure to meet someone who challenges my authority." He enjoyed seeing the instant blush on her cheeks. He detected a little tremble on the bottom of her curved, parted lips. Her scent, soft, subtle, vanilla, and something exotic, wafted in the air and drifted into his senses.

But he was getting ahead of himself. He didn't want to scare her off. Why did she dare question him when she damn well knew she was interviewing for a lucrative position in his company?

"I'm sorry, Mr. Knight. I didn't mean to—"

He was disappointed she'd broken away from his hold so soon. He could have held her silky, warm hand all day. He caught himself before his hardened emotions became too maudlin.

"That will be all, Lavelle. Thank you." He looked away from Hallie. Was that his wobbling voice? *Get hold of yourself, man.*

Lavelle closed the door.

The anonymity of the computer screen had done her a disservice. With a calculated eye, Aaron assessed the young woman. She cut quite the striking figure.

Maybe five seven. Slender but not skeletal. [obscured] that. Shoulder-length, shiny brown hair, the color [of a] strong cup of coffee. A girl-next-door kind of face, whatever that meant. And those eyes. Blue? No, green maybe. Whatever the color, they were mesmerizing, and despite her embarrassment, not shying away from his.

She remained ramrod straight in her four-inch black heels probably purchased at Marshall's. Her light-gray, knock-off designer suit showed very little skin, just a shapely pair of legs. He could tell by her stark body language she had some control issues. *Who doesn't?*

He gestured to a red tufted leather chair across from his desk. "Please have a seat, Ms. Cavanagh."

She remained standing. Had she heard him? Was she that nervous being in his presence? Or was she that arrogant?

"Ms. Cavanagh? A seat. Please." He folded his arms across his chest. He kept his face expressionless, his amazement hidden by a slow breath. Imploring, no matter how slight, wasn't something he ever did. How had she manipulated him into giving an order twice?

"Yes, of course." She perched on the edge of the chair, crossed her legs at the ankles, and folded her hands in her lap. Though her straitlaced behavior charmed him, he had a feeling that beyond her proper mannerisms beat the heart of a rebel. "Do you have trouble with authority, Ms. Cavanagh?"

"Excuse me?"

"Let me put it in a way you might understand better. Are you always so impulsive?"

She opened her mouth but then hesitated.

...an aware that his scrutiny was ...rtable. "You were about to say...

...ning as most would do when he ...sition, Hallie straightened her ...e. "First, I don't appreciate you belittling my intelligence." She tilted her head. "Second, is impulsiveness a job requirement?"

Feigning a cough to cover his surprise, Aaron composed himself. Now she was bordering on insubordination, and yet he couldn't help but be intrigued. What else would she say? What else would she do? He was curious if not determined to find out.

"I might add it to my list, if you think it's a viable attribute." His teasing broke the tension, and the corners of her mouth lifted upward in a smile he found utterly charming.

She tucked a strand of that shiny dark hair behind her ear. He noticed the diamond stud in her lobe. Probably fake.

Instead of reeling in his arrogance, he surmised it was time to catch her off her guard. See what she could handle. See if she could handle him. *I really am a bastard.* But damn, it was fun. "Tell me something about yourself."

She blinked. "What do you mean?"

The edge to her voice made his groin tighten. *What the hell is that?* "It's not a difficult question." He caught himself. Was he belittling her again? In this PC society, he often argued that people were way too sensitive about every little thing. Was this Hallie Cavanagh's MO? Was this how she would secure this position? Crying mental abuse of power?

But this time she didn't seem flustered or annoyed. "I graduated second in my class—"

"No, not like that. I want to learn something about you beyond your résumé. Something personal. More…intimate." Much to his chagrin, he found himself fantasizing about slowly unbuttoning her jacket and revealing her assets. Again, he was off to a place he had no business being in. But the twinkle in her eyes and her lion-like confidence urged him on. "Am I making you uncomfortable?"

"Not at all. It's just that my life isn't all that special. There's really nothing to tell."

"You know what they say about the unexamined life."

"Is not worth living, I know." The corners of her mouth twitched upward. "Do you ask all your employees to divulge their innermost secrets?"

"You're not an employee."

She struck a cool pose. "Not yet."

He grabbed onto the edge of the glass top of his desk with both hands to steady himself from her sharp comeback. Beautiful, brazen, and totally bigheaded. What was he going to do if he hired her? What didn't he want to do? On the outside, he remained collected. Inside, he was dying to touch her, smell her, and taste what she had to offer. He wanted his mouth exploring every inch of her. He wanted to whisper his wants, his desires, and his longings to her. He wanted Hallie Cavanagh in every way. "I do respect the privacy of my staff, if that's what you're asking."

"Really?" It wasn't a question.

Jesus. He cocked his head. Was she mocking him? Did she realize being impertinent could cost her this job? Did she care? "You don't believe me?"

"I don't know you well enough to believe you."

"Touché." He eyed the outline of her breasts as they rose and fell with the deep breath she took. A small sigh escaped her lips, and his heart responded, thumping hard against his chest. What in the hell was happening to him?

"I have an exorbitant amount of student loans—"

"So does one quarter of the country. Try again." He was being a royal pain in the ass. He couldn't help himself. She was making it so easy.

"I'm a Starbucks fanatic."

"Boring. Let me make this easier. Tell me something that you…" He paused, frowning. "Something you believe in."

She bit her bottom lip, squared her shoulders, and looked thoughtful. "Love, Mr. Knight." The force of it the word nearly knocked him to the floor.

"Love?"

"Yes. I believe in love."

The air in the room became charged with electricity, and its jolt shook every muscle in his body. He eyed her curiously. Of course she believed in "love." She was young, not naïve. Impressionable, perhaps? Probably searching for her Prince Charming. But princes were few and far between in this world. Happily ever afters were found in kitschy romance novels. He silently wished her luck.

"Did I say something wrong?"

Quickly, he reined in his jumbled judgments and pulled himself together. "No. I just wasn't expecting that."

She tilted her head. "What *were* you expecting?

That I believe in power? Money? The stock market?"

"No one believes in the stock market, Ms. Cavanagh."

She smiled.

An unfamiliar emotion made his stomach clench. Awkwardness. He wasn't used to the sensation, couldn't explain it if he wanted to. Suddenly, all those fantasies of desire and need disappeared in a puff of gray smoke. Now what he wanted was her—gone. Yes. Gone. Gone from his office, gone from ARK, gone from inside his head. She was actually causing him discomfort. Discomfort led to mistakes. In the corporate world, make enough mistakes and businesses collapsed. He hastily made up his mind that Hallie Cavanagh wouldn't be the best candidate for this job. The words "This interview is over. Good day, Ms. Cavanagh" were on the tip of his tongue, and yet he remained mute, trying to make sense of what was going on, indulging in an impossible craving to hear what she would say next.

"What about you, Mr. Knight?"

He blinked in surprise. Being caught off guard again wasn't a good look on him. "What about me?" His brow wrinkled. What was she doing? How did she turn the proverbial tables so quickly?

"I think it's only fair that you offer the same information that you ask of your employees." Her voice was quiet and thoughtful.

Her brashness excited him. The light in her blue eyes—yes, they were blue—was unsettling. Her gaze met his with a stinging force as though he were wrapped in a live wire.

He changed his mind. He didn't want her gone.

What he wanted was to yank her out of that chair and have intense sex with her right on the top of his desk in front of all of Manhattan.

"Tell me something *you* believe in."

What the hell? To cover up his astonishment, Aaron uttered a soft, husky laugh. *All right. I'll play along. And then I'll dismiss her.*

She waited, looking eager. Looking beautiful. Looking like his next conquest.

"It seems that we're quite the opposite when it comes to beliefs."

"How so, Mr. Knight?"

Why was his chest constricting? Damn it. Was he having a heart attack? He took a breath to release the tightness. The air sputtered in his lungs. Her focus was on him, and he had to say something.

"You see, Ms. Cavanagh, I don't believe in love."

****

She got the job!

Exiting ARK Enterprises, Hallie kept pace with the city crowd and basked in her success. She had no idea how she'd done it, but the position of ARK's executive director of acquisitions was now hers. After their strange encounter in his office, Aaron Knight had offered it to her. Just like that. Just like she'd known he would.

In the moments before she'd been ordered to his office, she'd thought she'd really blown her interview to smithereens. Acting so smug, so superior was a stupid thing to do. But in reality, it'd turned out to be a brilliant move—or at least the right move.

Their conversation, though, was strange. Asking her to tell him something personal bordered on an imposition. No. Intrusive was more like it. She'd go so far as to call it disturbing. Was that the great Aaron Knight's way of intimidating people? Catch them off guard and see what happened? Ask personal questions and expect answers? Could she work for a company—for a man—who thought nothing of coercing his employees? The butterflies in Hallie's stomach had become pterodactyls.

She was making too much of this. In a megacompany like ARK Enterprises, she and Aaron would hardly cross paths, except probably in staff meetings and—if she cost the company money. She wasn't going to think that way. She couldn't. The important thing was she had been hired for a very lucrative job that would change her mother's life for the better. That was where she needed her focus.

After the interview, Lavelle had escorted Hallie to HR to fill out paperwork. She was issued a password, a company cell phone, and a thick binder filled with information on the corporation's regulations and day-to-day procedures. Lavelle pointed out the importance of reading all the material before starting the job. Hallie smiled. The speed-reading course she'd taken in college would finally pay off.

"You're now part of the ARK team, Ms. Cavanagh. Mr. Knight expects you to be prepared, not only for your department, but company-wide."

"I understand, Ms. Andrews."

Lavelle seemed satisfied. "Please, it's Lavelle."

"All right, Lavelle." A wave of ease washed over her. "And I'm Hallie."

"Then we'll see you on Monday morning, Hallie." She'd walked Hallie to the lobby and wished her a good day.

Even now, an hour later, her head spun, her heart raced, and her body tingled with exhilaration. It was time to celebrate. She headed for the nearest Starbucks to get her favorite—an iced coconut mocha macchiato. She hoped the drink would soothe the red-hot sensation wreaking havoc inside her.

She ordered her specialty coffee and added the slice of lemon pound cake calling her name from behind the glass dessert case. Finding an empty table in the corner, Hallie leaned back in the chair and blew out the shaky breath she'd been holding on to since she left ARK Enterprises.

It was still hard to fathom she was the actual director of ARK's acquisition team. It wasn't like her to second-guess her decisions or her abilities, yet thinking about the enormity of the position gave her pause. Working for Aaron Knight was daunting at best. But the rewards would be endless. If she lasted more than a few weeks. Her brow creased with worry.

No amount of money was enough to keep my last executive director of acquisitions from quitting after seven months.

That wouldn't be her. She wasn't a quitter, no matter how bad life got.

Now, knowing better days were ahead, Hallie raised her coffee in a self-congratulatory toast. A silly gesture, but she was proud of her accomplishment. Taking a well-deserved sip through the straw, she savored the cold, sweet coffee as her mind drifted.

I don't believe in love.

Out of all the things she could have recalled about the interview, and there were many, his words lingered.

Her mind whirled in bewilderment. Was he just trying to catch her off her game? Teasing her? Did he say it to mock her personal opinion about the lofty emotion? Or was he really as callous as the media made him out to be? It was quite possible she'd never know, and that was all right with her. She was hired to do a job, not to be Aaron Knight's shrink.

The information was intriguing, though, if not sad. Of all the things he could have said, why had he chosen to tell her his feelings about love—or lack of them? What *did* he believe in? Money? Power? Sex?

She stopped. Maybe his words were just that—words. Maybe they meant nothing. Maybe he'd said them to get a rise out of her. Strangely enough, he had. But that's all he'd do. The last time she trusted her emotions to someone, she'd been in love. Truly in love. Her heart twitched. What a disaster that had turned out to be.

Concerned, she pursed her mouth. Could the so-called ruthless CEO be playing her in some way? This job meant everything to her. Independence. Experience. Money. Especially money. Especially now.

She drummed the tabletop with her fingers. She wasn't about to abandon her mother—even if her mother was slowly abandoning her. Finances and her own severance pay from her previous employment, the now-defunct advertising firm Sawyer & Company, were quickly dwindling and would soon not be enough to give her mother the care she required. For that to happen, she needed money. Before her thoughts spun out of control, she reeled them back.

Breaking off a piece of the lemon pound cake and tossing it carelessly in her mouth, Hallie took in her surroundings. Most of the clientele in the coffee shop were college-age students with laptops humming and earbuds stuffed in their ears, listening to the latest alternative rock music. She was reminded of her own college days. Exams. Internships. The late nights. The impossible mornings.

Digging deep in her tote, she fished out her cell phone. But it wasn't hers. It belonged to ARK Enterprises.

You will make yourself available to me at all hours of the day…and night, if necessary.

The idea that this phone might be her techy ball and chain was worrisome. But she would deal with it. She had to. The dark screen lit up with a ping, startling her. Was Aaron Knight already tracking her down? A message flashed. *Welcome to ARK Enterprises.* She could almost hear Aaron's no-nonsense voice. The next message prompted her to add her fingerprint and password for identification. She didn't, figuring she'd do the setup on Monday morning. The screen faded once again to black.

She stuffed the phone in a side pocket in her tote and found her own cell. She checked her texts, calls, and emails. Nothing important except a quick *good luck with the interview* text from her best friend and roommate Sophie Fletcher. It made her smile. She wanted to text her back about getting the job but stopped herself. She'd rather tell her friend the good news in person.

Now if only she could stop typing Aaron Knight's name into Google. Didn't happen. Instantly, a gazillion hits popped up, along with pictures. She tapped one of them, and his image filled the screen.

Pictures did him no justice. In person, he was so handsome with his bedroom eyes and roguish demeanor. Even clean-shaven, he had that bad-boy scruffiness she found attractive. The primal aura of masculinity she'd experienced in his office today exuded his charismatic power. Now, with his face staring up at her from her phone, she feared she'd lose control. In the image, his light brown hair was groomed meticulously like it had been today. His tailored and subtle pinstriped suit didn't hide the well-muscled and tapered body underneath. She breathed in deeply. His scent that filled his office still lingered on her skin.

She swiped to another picture. This time he was dressed in a dark-pink polo shirt and body-hugging jeans. She liked pink on a man. To her it showed he wasn't afraid to embrace a softer side of himself. She almost laughed out loud. A softer side? Aaron Knight? Who was she kidding? Maybe for other men less powerful, less intimidating than he was, but there was nothing soft about the mogul.

His hair was tousled as though he'd just finished a whirlwind tour on his yacht, if he had one. Of course he had one. Didn't every billionaire? His lips were firm and sensual, and she wondered what they would feel like against hers. And his eyes. Those midnight blue eyes filled with vibrant and unswerving sinfulness, staring into her soul.

She had to come back down to Earth—and now. She sucked down the rest of her macchiato and gave herself brain freeze, which was just as well. She shouldn't be thinking about him in that way. He was her boss, and that was all he was going to be.

Finished with her coffee and half of the slice of

cake, Hallie dropped her phone in her bag, cleared off the table, and headed out the door. Today was Friday. She still had two days of freedom. She was going to make the most of it.

And she'd start by sharing the good news with the most important person in her life.

****

An hour had passed. Or maybe two. He didn't know, nor did he care. Still in his office, Aaron shook his head in disbelief. How had he allowed the interview to get so out of his control? All right, maybe out of control was a bit severe, but the newest employee of ARK Enterprises certainly had his head in a whirl. So much so he didn't think twice about hiring her on the spot. For him, these interviews were more of an art form than a mad dash. After the impersonal albeit unapproachable conference conducted via computer, he usually scrutinized the potential employee's résumé and found out what he could by Googling said person.

With Hallie Cavanagh, he had skipped over all his methodical minutiae and hired her straightway. Why? Maybe because he hadn't counted on taking one look at her and getting slammed in the chest with what felt like a sledgehammer. What was so different about this woman to make him second-guess his customary approach?

She was bright. No doubt about that. Graduated second in her class at Harvard Business School. Worked for Sawyer & Company advertising. She'd held the important position of account executive until the company closed its doors. Thinking about it, he could have saved that company from going under, but then he might not have met Hallie. Most times, he liked to clean house of the businesses he bought. Hell, he could have fired her sight unseen.

Standing at the window, he took in the cityscape and thought about her hurrying along the sidewalk with others like her. What was going through her mind right now? Excitement about being hired? Anticipation? Was she thinking about him?

A muscle twitched in his jaw. No doubt, she was easy on the eyes. Not that that should matter, but she had an ethereal, otherworldly air about her. Muscle and grace etched her lithe, lean body. Her dark hair was her crowning glory. Her full lips, high cheekbones, and teasing smile all added up to—well, someone he'd like to get to know better. And her eyes. Soft and blue and reflecting too much pain.

Pain from what? Surely she was too young, too unsophisticated to experience any real pain. His insides tightened, and a bitter taste touched the back of his throat. He turned to gaze out the window. Who was he to make that judgment call?

Her words reverberated in his brain. *I believe in love.*

The thought was laughable. He had to be careful, though, not to demean her belief. Not to belittle her, as she had pointed out. He thought of his own life—his father in particular and all the mental, emotional, and physical pain that bastard had caused his family. And then that terrible day found its way into his thoughts. The day he kept locked up in the back of his dark mind. The day he'd decided to stand up to his father. In that moment, he'd realized he was no better than that scum. Love? Not a chance in hell.

He sat at his desk, keeping his negative thoughts at

bay. It had been so long ago. He had more pressing issues. Issues like Hallie Cavanagh. No matter her foolish beliefs, he somehow knew she was going to be a good fit for ARK Enterprises. Strangely enough, he'd never been so sure of anything in his life. In the brief time they'd been face to face, he could tell she was ready for the challenge the job entailed. She would keep him on his toes. He liked that. It would keep things interesting. Her assertive nature would work well in procuring acquisitions.

Maybe it would serve him even better in his bed.

Jesus, man! What am I thinking? He shut that thought down immediately—or at least tried to.

He reached for the pen on top of a small stack of folders and began drumming it against the glass top of his desk. As they'd sparred in his office today, he knew it was wrong, but he couldn't help imagining her naked. He guessed her neck and shoulders would be downy and supple, her breasts just enough to fill his hands and mouth easily. Her hips curvy and her thighs smooth. His groin jerked in greedy expectation.

Was he crazy? He hired for a job, not for his pleasure. For him, that was a hard and fast rule. Never bed, date, or even entertain the notion of having a cup of coffee with an employee. Plenty of other women out there would fulfill his needs if he wanted them.

Women flitted in and out of his life all the time. All shapes, sizes, colors, and ages from the clingy and not-so-virginal twenty-one-year-olds and up. He especially enjoyed those in the forty to fifty age brackets. These women knew themselves and knew what they wanted, and what they wanted was a good lay with no strings attached. He had experienced all kinds of sexual tastes, too, from the missionary position to remote-control orgasms and everything in between.

But that had been the younger, impressionable, inexperienced Aaron. Though he had his choice of companions, now he very rarely ended his nights rolling around in bed with these women. Most of the time, they only accompanied him to charity events or political gatherings. He enjoyed giving the media fodder for gossip. "A different woman every night" became the blather for the society pages.

Lately, though, he'd dropped out of that gilded group. He'd absorbed everything he could from those people at the top—their connections, their expertise, and their advice. His penchant for women had declined as well. He frowned. Sometimes, that part of his life seemed so pointless.

He was on his own now, making his own decisions and becoming very wealthy from them. What else did he need?

So what was he doing fantasizing about Hallie Cavanagh? He pushed himself away from the desk and got to his feet. His brain was numb. He needed a vacation. At the very least, he needed to see his therapist.

One thing was surprising, though; she hadn't commented on his "I don't believe in love" remark. She hadn't even flinched. She probably thought him a bit crazy for sounding like a badly written romance novel. After all, who didn't believe in love? He winced. Aaron Russell Knight, that's who. He had learned the hard way that love was a waste of time and effort. No one experienced love without realizing the pain it brought. And he'd had enough pain for a lifetime.

Chapter Two

Golden Living Nursing Home, situated on the Lower East Side of Manhattan, was more tarnished than golden and more "walking dead" than living. Compared to the other nursing homes in and out of the city, Golden Living was old and tired-looking. The rooms were small and stuffy, the common areas needed fresh paint and new furniture, and the food service was flat and unsavory. But it was the only place Hallie's mother, Donna Cavanagh, could afford with her health insurance.

On the positive side, the staff was knowledgeable and welcoming, and the caregivers were kind and nurturing to their patients. Joanne Allen, the head administrator, went out of her way to help the families of the infirmed in any way she could.

One subway stop and a taxicab ride later, Hallie walked through the automatic doors of the rehab building. The lobby was crowded with visitors and patients. Joy, the therapy dog, a huge golden Labrador, was sitting in the middle of the green and pink flowered carpet being petted by several children, probably here to visit Grandma or Grandpa. The acrid smell of disinfectant mixed with the aroma of a prepared but unpalatable lunch assailed her senses.

She followed a long hallway and stopped in front of Joanne's opened door. She knocked.

Joanne, her eyes blurry behind her red-framed glasses, turned away from her computer screen, saw Hallie, and smiled. "Hallie, it's good to see you. How are you?"

The usual cloying sweetness of Joanne's perfume hung heavy in the air. "I'm very good. And you?"

Joanne shrugged. "You know the routine. Too much to do and too little time in the day to do it. But otherwise, I can't complain."

Hallie took a breath, hoping for the best and fearing the worst. "How is she today?"

Joanne pushed back her rolling chair and got to her feet. "She's a bit more lost in the past than usual, though one of her nurses said she called out your name."

A touch of release soothed Hallie's nerves. It wasn't the best news, but it wasn't the worst either.

"I'm sure she'll be glad to see you." Joanne tilted her head. "You seem anxious."

Hallie sighed. "I know I'm late with her payment, but I came to tell you I was hired today for a very well-paid position at ARK Enterprises. I'll be able to pay this and next month's expenses once I get my first paycheck."

"No wonder you're beaming. That's wonderful news." The genuine excitement in Joanne's voice felt like a warm hug. She came over and wrapped her arm around Hallie's shoulders. The gesture was comforting and kind. "I'm sure you want to tell Miss Donna all about it."

Hallie forced a smile. *Miss Donna.* The nurses and health givers at Golden Living were famous for referring to the patients by those "cutesy" names, probably to make their lives seem warmer and cuddlier. For Donna Cavanagh, those sweet terms didn't matter. She barely reacted to life around her, much less to being called Miss Donna. She might as well be called Santa Claus or Minnie Mouse.

"Thank you, Joanne. I don't know what I would do without your support."

Joanne sloughed off the compliment. "Go. Share your news. If you need anything or just want to talk, you know where to find me."

Breathing a well-deserved sigh of relief, Hallie left Joanne's office and walked toward the double doors at the end of the hall. Her muscles began to tighten again as she stared through the wire-reinforced glass panels. Beyond these secured barricades were those patients whose memories of family and friends were quickly fading, patients whose eyes were cloudy with confusion or blank with forgotten reminiscences. They faltered between the names and faces they should recall and stammered with anger when they couldn't.

An emptiness entered Hallie's heart. Her mother was one of these patients.

She'd noticed the change close to two years ago when her mother, in the middle of baking her "famous" chocolate chip cookies, held up an egg and stared at it.

"What's wrong, Mom?"

"Hallie, what is this? What's it for?"

"It's an egg."

"An egg? What do I do with it? How does it work?"

Though concerned, she discarded the lapse, chalking it up to a motherly prank. But when a disoriented expression clouded her mother's face,

Hallie became worried.

Troubled but not wanting to upset her, Hallie gently removed the egg from her mother's grasp. "Like this, Mom." She tapped the shell on the mixing bowl and broke the egg open.

Her mother smiled, pooh-poohing the momentary memory loss as insignificant. "Of course. It's an egg. I remember now."

But in those few moments, she hadn't remembered.

And life went on—only not as Hallie expected. Every day, her mother said things and did things that made Hallie question her mental capacities. She was argumentative one moment, talking gibberish the next, and forgetting the simplest facts she'd known only days before. She lost her keys. Everyone did that, right? She couldn't find her glasses. She walked into a room and forgot why she was there. Hallie was sure that had happened to her many times.

But when Mrs. Gilbert, one of her mother's neighbors, called in a panic to tell her Donna was found by the police wandering the streets dressed in only her nightgown, the magnitude of what was to come forced Hallie to conclude what she already suspected.

Several examinations from neurological doctors confirmed the diagnosis. Her mother was suffering from stage three of Alzheimer's. And there was no cure—only meds that might slow the progression. The disease would gradually eat away her mother's memories, take away who she was, and make her slip slowly into dark places that were becoming more and more difficult for Hallie to reach.

In those two years, her mother had become more demanding to handle. For the most part, she could no longer function on her own. Hallie had some tough and heartbreaking decisions to make. Though she'd put up one hell of a fight, her mother finally surrendered to selling her house and living in a facility, where medical professionals could care for her.

Now Hallie closed her eyes, centered her thoughts, and pressed the buzzer on the wall next to the doors. The loud, obnoxious noise made her throat close with dread. One of the nurses at the station recognized her. Immediately, the lock clicked, and Hallie pushed one of the doors open.

"Your mother's in the common room," the nurse told her.

"How is she?"

"A bit confrontational this morning. Accused one of the patients of cheating at cards. She's calmed down, though."

Hallie sighed and nodded. "Wish me luck."

The nurse smiled and crossed her fingers.

The common room was a gathering place for patients to socialize, play games, or watch movies on a big screen TV. Tables, chairs, and couches filled the space. The blinds were opened, allowing the sunshine to spill through the dusty beige slats. The brightness brought light and warmth to the otherwise dingy place, almost making it pleasant but revealing dust and debris in the corners. She scrunched her nose against the acrid odor.

Standing in the doorway, she squinted until her eyes became accustomed to the late-afternoon glare. Once her sight adjusted, she could see the remnants of a tiny garden outside the window. The view of the budding trees and sturdy shrubbery almost made her forget that the Golden Living Nursing Home was surrounded by the big city, until the wail of an ambulance siren shattered the repose.

Only a few patients, men and women, were sitting about. Some were sleeping in wheelchairs. Others seemed comatose. Two women were playing cards. One of those women was her mother.

"Hi, Mom." Hallie's voice was a cautious whisper.

Her mother ignored her. She was too busy pulling out the cards and rearranging them in her hand. She watched her mother's frantic moves. Was she really that lucid that she knew what she was doing?

"Mom? It's me, Hallie. How are you today?"

She was wearing the pink robe Hallie had bought her for her birthday last month. Someone had painted her ragged fingernails with a pale pink polish. Her graying hair had been pulled back and styled in a long braid.

This time her mother looked up. "Hallie?"

The tremor in her voice tightened Hallie's throat, and tears stung the back of her eyes. She *had* recognized her.

"Yes, Mom. It's me." Elated, Hallie took a seat in the chair between her mother and the other woman, who was staring intently at the cards in her shaky hand.

"Did you get permission to be here?"

"I don't need permission, silly."

"Why are you here?"

"I wanted to see you."

Her mother stared at her, her face turning to stone. "You came at a very bad time. Can't you see I'm busy?"

"I have good news, and I wanted to share it."

"Put down a card," the other woman ordered. "You can't have six cards. One of them has to go."

Her mother looked away from Hallie and turned to her partner. Hallie stiffened and prepared for the worst. The nurse had mentioned her mother's aggressive episode earlier. Was it about to get ugly again?

Snatching one of the cards she was holding, her mother threw it down on the table. "Satisfied?" she hissed.

The other woman grunted but nodded her approval. Hallie's mother speared her friend with another glare. Hallie held her breath, but the confrontation settled down quickly.

Forgetting about the card game, her mother gave Hallie her full attention. "Do you remember when I used to take you to the park to play?" Suddenly, the harshness in her voice changed to something light and safe. "You used to love the monkey bars and swings."

Hallie nodded, smiling. It was a memory from the past, but that didn't matter. She'd go along with it. "Of course I do."

She'd been told her father had died in a motorcycle accident when she was two years old. Her only recollection of him was a man who was always laughing. Widowed and working two jobs, her mother, no matter how tired she was, had always made sure she had time to spend with her daughter. The park down the block from where they lived had been Hallie's favorite place.

"Oh, yes. You were very young." Her mother patted Hallie's hand. "We used to have such fun back then."

"Tell me about those days," Hallie encouraged,

figuring any recollection would stimulate her mother's brain.

Donna squeezed her eyes shut. The delicate skin on her forehead crinkled.

"Mom?"

Her mother drew in what sounded like a frustrated breath and opened her eyes. She said nothing, just stared blankly ahead. Her card-playing partner had left the table, but she hadn't reacted to her absence.

"Mom, you were telling me about our trips to the park when I was little. Remember?"

Her mother locked gazes with Hallie. Storm clouds seemed to hover over them. "What are you talking about? What park? There was never a park." Her usually frail voice heightened with irritation once again.

"You said I liked to go on the swings." The hairs on Hallie's arms tingled.

"Who are you? Are you one of those nurses who forces me to walk and eat and shower?"

"It's me. Hallie. Your daughter." Hallie mentally closed the door on the what-ifs of the day. What if her mother remembered names and faces? Phone numbers and addresses? Birthdays and family events? But today wasn't unlike every other day she'd spent with her. She arrived hopeful and left hopeless.

A shadow came over her mother's face. "I have no daughter. I'm all alone."

Hallie's heart sank, her body collapsing. The memory of their time together, if that was what it was, had gone. Her mother's fixed gaze indicated the momentary recognition had disappeared into a dark abyss. Hallie held her breath. She longed to reach out and hold her, but she was afraid of what the loving and protective gesture might trigger.

Sadness and confusion clouded her mother's eyes. The blank stare was back. "There was a park." She looked at Hallie. "Do you remember going to the park with me?" Her voice was hushed and edged with trepidation.

Hallie's shoulders slumped. "Yes, Mom. I do."

Her mother closed her eyes and sighed. "Good girl."

****

Her feet aching, her heart heavy, Hallie was thankful for the short elevator ride up to her third-floor apartment in Jackson Heights, Queens. The brief visit with her mother had exhausted her. She hadn't even gotten the chance to tell her about her new job. With the money she'd be making, her mother could have better nursing care and a private room, maybe one overlooking the garden. Sadly, it didn't matter if her mother was living in a palace. She wouldn't have reacted either way.

Sophie met her at the door. "What happened? Where have you been? You didn't text. I've been dying here."

Putting her mother's worsening condition aside, Hallie paid attention to her friend's eager expression. "Shouldn't you be at work slinging something?"

Sophie made a face. "I don't sling. I prepare fancy meals. Besides, I told Jack I'd be in later."

Hallie held her breath and tried to look serious, but she was too excited. "I got it! I got the job!"

Sophie's hug nearly knocked her over. "Congratulations! I knew you'd do it."

"Really? This morning you doubted this job was

for me. You said—"

"I know what I said. Ruthless isn't in your vocabulary. The job might eat you alive." Sophie tilted her head. "Can't a person be wrong once in a while?" She followed Hallie into the apartment. "So what's the great man like?" Sophie flopped down on the red velveteen couch they'd bought at a thrift store.

Hallie kicked off her shoes and collapsed next to her friend. "I thought you already *Googled* him."

"Google isn't the be all and end all to everything. It can't tell you what his kisses are like. He did kiss you, right? Or did you kiss him, you hussy?"

"Sophie, stop." Her frown turned to a giggle. She enjoyed her roommate's banter, but she wasn't going to tell her she'd been dreaming about the same thing.

"Come on—spill. The suspense is killing me."

Hallie glanced at her watch. It was a few minutes after four. She jumped to her feet and grabbed Sophie's hands. "Let's celebrate." She was eager to continue the positive feeling. "We'll go to Mo's Deli for pastrami sandwiches and then later go dancing at the club. Sound like fun?"

"You're avoiding my question."

Hallie made a face. "No, I'm not. I promise I'll tell you all about the great Aaron Knight over a pickle and a cream soda."

Sophie's face twisted in defeat. "Looks like I have no other choice—for now." She grabbed her chef's coat from the overstuffed but sagging upholstered chair in the corner. "I'll put in a few hours at the restaurant, and then it's off to Mo's. But you'd better be ready to tell me everything about your billionaire."

Hallie headed down the narrow hall to her

bedroom. "He's not *my* billionaire."

Sophie snickered.

In her room, Hallie began to strip off her clothing. It felt so good to remove the stiff jacket, blouse, and skirt. She could breathe again.

"Hallie, your phone's ringing!"

"Answer it!" she called back to her roommate.

Sophie appeared in the bedroom doorway holding a cell phone at arm's distance. "This isn't yours."

Hallie, wearing only her bra and panties, crinkled her forehead. "Oh, crap. That's the company phone."

"It's him."

"Him, who?"

Sophie wielded the phone side to side. "Him!" Her voice was strained through gritted teeth.

Hallie's eyes widened as Sophie nodded, vehemently answering her friend's silent inquiry. She grabbed the phone and then shooed Sophie out of the room. Grudgingly, Sophie left.

Hallie took a deep breath and stared at her cell. Aaron Knight's image appeared on the screen, and she was half naked. She kept the phone steady, on her face, and nowhere else. With a shaky finger, she tapped the appropriate icon.

"H-hello." Her squeaky greeting sounded lame, but she was so taken aback she didn't know what else to say or how to say it.

He didn't seem to pick up on her shaky salutation. All business—all the time. "Ms. Cavanagh, pack a bag and be ready to be picked up by my driver in about two hours. Do you think you can manage that?"

Pack a bag? Wait. What now? Was he kidding? "Mr. Knight, I…I don't start my job until Monday. I was going out this evening to celebrate—"

"Ms. Cavanagh, maybe you really didn't understand me this morning. When I say I *need* you to do something, I expect that you'll do it. The days of the week don't matter to me. Neither does the time. Now pack a bag and be ready by six thirty."

Hallie frowned. "All right, but can you tell me why?"

"There's no time for that."

"Then where am I going?" Certainly he would give her a head's-up so she could pack suitable clothing.

His disgruntled expression caused a momentous earthquake within her. A new hire and already pissing off the boss.

"Sea Girt." His response was curt and delivered in a cool, distant tone.

Sea Girt? What the hell? She'd never heard of the place. "What's a sea girt? Where is it?"

A heavy sigh followed his narrowing eyes. "You are full of questions, Ms. Cavanagh." His annoyed tone signaled she might be more of a bother than she was worth. "New Jersey. It's down the shore. I have a house in Sea Girt. You'll be staying there until I say otherwise."

What the hell was that all about? Without a satisfying explanation, Aaron ended the impromptu call. Hallie stared as the phone screen went dark and then back to displaying a few business-related apps. She couldn't believe what he was asking of her. She waited a minute or two, wondering if he'd call back and tell her he was kidding. That it was all a joke. That he just wanted to gauge her reaction.

Calling her back was a crazy thought anyway, but

being ordered to pack a bag and be ready in two hours to head off to another state not knowing why was crazy, too, wasn't it? Moreover, when she arrived at this Sea Girt place, would she be expected to paint on a cheerful and dutiful face and act as though everything was okay? Probably.

His second call, the one where he was supposed to announce his entire directive was a late April Fool's prank, never came. With her comfort zone starting to deplete, Hallie tossed the phone on her bed, grabbed her cotton robe, and wrapped it around her now-trembling body. Weren't there laws against kidnapping?

Sophie appeared at the doorway. "What did he want? Wait, don't tell me. He's whisking you away to some exotic country so you can have your way with him."

"He wants me to go to Sea Girt."

"That doesn't sound exotic. What's a sea girt?"

"That's what I asked. It's a town by the beach in New Jersey. Apparently, he has a house there." The words were coming out of her mouth, and yet she couldn't believe what she was saying. "I'm being picked up by his driver in two hours."

"What?"

"He wants me to stay there." Hallie opened the closet and wheeled out a purple suitcase. It was the only piece of luggage she had saved after…

"But I thought you didn't start the job until Monday." Her brow lifted questioningly. "How long does he want you to stay? Is this some tycoon fetish? Keep the new employee in isolation until further notice?"

"Stop it, Sophie." Hallie stifled a laugh.

"I'm just looking at all the angles. These wealthy, powerful men can get kinky."

"Where do you get your information?"

"You've read *Fifty Shades*."

Hallie rolled her eyes.

"How long does he want you to stay?"

"I'm not sure, but it'll be more than a day. He made that pretty clear."

"Boss or no boss, this guy expects you to rearrange your whole life for a day at the beach? Did you ask him why?"

Hallie shrugged. "I'm sure it involves some kind of business dealing for ARK Enterprises." But what sort of business was she expected to conduct in a New Jersey beach town? Sandcastle initiatives? Snow cone operations? Boardwalk proposals? Was this even about business?

"You guess? Don't you know?"

"I asked him, but he wasn't clear on the reason. In fact, he didn't tell me much of anything except I have two hours to get ready."

"This isn't like you, Hallie. You make lists. Hell, you make lists for your lists. You don't make a move before you know what you're getting into. Why are you so lax about this?"

Sophie's amateur analysis of her complexities was spot on. The girl knew her well. But asking more questions might have aggravated him to the point of cancelling the trip and cancelling her job. She wasn't going to chance that. "Why are you so upset?"

"I'm showing concern. You should be grateful. It's not often I do that. Are you going to be alone with him?"

Hallie's insides squirmed. "There's a housekeeper who lives on the premises."

"Did he tell you that?"

"Before he hung up."

"And you believe him?" Sophie's forehead puckered. "He's got some nerve—"

"There's nothing I can do."

"You can quit."

"Don't be ridiculous. I just got the job." Hallie shook her head. "I guess we'll have to celebrate another day."

"This is too weird."

"Don't worry. It'll be all right."

"I'm texting you every day. And you'd better text back. If you don't, I'm calling nine-one-one."

Hallie's mouth twitched slightly at the corners but drew short of a smile. "This is why I love you."

Chapter Three

He didn't owe her an explanation as to why he was sending her to New Jersey. He didn't owe her a damn thing. What he wanted was her unquestioning loyalty. Just like his other employees. But she was new to this corporate game, and with that novelty came questions. She had every right to ask them. That was why he'd give her some slack. But not too much. He wanted her on her toes, ready for anything. And there would be a lot to be ready for.

Aaron removed his tie and jacket and tossed them on the gray leather couch in the living room of his Upper West Side Manhattan penthouse overlooking Central Park. He never got tired of the stunning view from the outside terrace. Splotches of early afternoon sunlight danced across the dark wood floor, casting bright streaks and shadows simultaneously. Evening would soon toss its gauzy gray over the city, obscuring the majestic skyscrapers until, one by one, they came to life again, their lights punctuating the brick and mortar.

Aaron flipped absentmindedly through a small stack of mail that had been delivered by the doorman. He shrugged. Nothing urgent and no surprises, the way he liked things. Surprises sometimes threw him off his game. Like today.

What was it about this young woman? He'd been in the company of many lovely, unique, and bright women before. All ages. All types. Why was she so different? He hated not knowing the answer.

And now he was sending her to New Jersey. He wasn't much for flying by the seat of his pants. He always had a plan. But this idea had hit him quite out of the blue. Had the impromptu order made her suspicious? Of course it had. Sending his new administrator on a business trip was one thing. Whisking her off without warning to his secluded beach house for the weekend was quite another.

But this *was* a legitimate business trip. He'd learned, quite by accident today, that the owner of an eco-friendly car company he'd had his eye on for years was vacationing on Long Beach Island with his wife. The man's assistant had given up the information on her boss's whereabouts with little effort. He could be charming when he needed to be.

LBI wasn't too far from Sea Girt. What better way to break in the new acquisitions director than by letting her show him what she was made of? True, he hadn't given her any specific details. Was that on purpose? Why was he being so secretive? What did he want from her? His eyes widened, and his mind reeled. What *didn't* he want?

On the practical side, he made a mental note to give Rita, his housekeeper, a call so she could get the place ready. Then he'd get a good night's sleep and leave for Sea Girt in the morning. Was he being manipulative in letting Hallie stay at the house before he got there? Just another way to remind her he was in control. Of course he was. He headed toward the bedroom. "You're a real bastard, Knight," he murmured aloud.

"You certainly are, darling."

Aaron stopped dead in his tracks.

"Surprise!"

He grimaced inwardly. "Miranda, what are you doing here?"

"Waiting." The half-naked woman in his bed purred the words from deep in her throat. "It's about time you came home. I'd almost given up on you."

"Maybe you should have." He tried to remain stoic to her unannounced visit. "Did we have some kind of date?"

Fifty-three-year-old Miranda Tybee frowned. "Am I that forgettable? You called yesterday. Don't you remember?" She let the bedsheet fall away, revealing her red, lacey bra and matching panties. Her ash-blonde hair clustered in short curls around her heart-shaped, almost-line-free face. She was well put together. Her body was toned, thanks to a personal trainer and hours of exercise, and her augmented breasts and tummy tuck, compliments of her second husband, could only be viewed as spectacular. She knew it, too, and flaunted it all whenever she could.

He sighed. She was right. He had called her two days ago to come over. But nothing was set in stone. Nothing had been planned. He'd just needed some female company, and Miranda was always ready and willing.

But that seemed forever ago. Now the idea of her "company" felt cheap and dirty. "So I did." He walked over to his dresser, his back to her, and began to unbutton his crisp white shirt. "Look, Miranda, I'm sorry, but something urgent has come up." Thoughts of Hallie waiting for him at the beach house swirled with conviction in his head.

In a matter of seconds, she left the bed and slithered up behind him. Her arms clasped around his waist, and she snuggled against his back. "Don't go all business on me. You know I hate that."

Though her embrace was inviting, and the brief thought of him inside her made him hard, Aaron grabbed her arms and gently but firmly forced her away. He didn't want to hurt her. He just wanted her gone. He turned to face her. Her eyes held promises she wasn't afraid to deliver. Her expression radiated expectation. But he was having none of it.

"Not now, Miranda. I'd really like you to go." He smelled a hint of his expensive pinot grigio wine on her breath. He caught a whiff of rain and fresh linen.

Her lithe body seemed to deflate a bit. "Not until you show me how much you missed me." She wrapped her arms around his neck, stood on her bare toes, and kissed him hard on his unresponsive mouth.

He pulled away from her. "Miranda, don't." He turned back to the dresser and slipped out of his shirt. The mirror reflected his strained muscles and edgy expression.

It also reflected her suspicious look. "Where are you going, Aaron?"

"It's business. Nothing that concerns you."

"Who is she this time?" Her tone was sharp, accusatory. Her eyes narrowed. Her fingernail pressed lightly into his back and then glided down to the waistband of his pants. "That cute young bartender at Sullivan's?"

"What are you talking about?"

"Don't give me an innocent act. Last week. At that

restaurant. Wasn't she coming on to you?"

He let out a mirthless laugh, amused by her insecurities. "I would have known if she was."

"Don't lie, Aaron. It cheapens you. Was she flirting with you?"

"Well, I am rather charming." He meant it as a joke.

Too bad she didn't take it that way. "Were you coming on to her?" She threw the words at him like stones.

He kept his anger in check. "Stop it, Miranda."

"It never ceases to amaze me how you can be out with one woman and make a date with another. You remind me of Harry, my ex. He used to pull that garbage."

"Harry the cop?"

"Detective."

"Like that changes things. I'll never understand how you two got together."

"What can I say? I love a man in uniform." Her brown eyes grew darker. "Now tell me about the bartender."

He sighed. "Nothing happened, and even if she was flirting, it's none of your business who I spend time with. We're not exactly exclusive. You knew what you were getting into with me."

She grinned with a tight malevolence. "I guess I did."

He shot her a guarded expression. "Get dressed, Miranda. I'll call you a cab."

****

The breeze was warm and seductive on this late spring evening. It was May, close to Memorial Day.

Hallie stood in the shadow of her apartment building. By her side were her suitcase, her tote, and a weekender bag, all bursting at the seams. Not knowing Aaron's expectations, she had almost emptied her entire closet. She'd decided on a business casual look for the trip. Dark jeans, Bohemian-type, off-the-shoulder blouse—though she made sure her shoulders were covered—and red ballerina flats. She glimpsed between the other high-rises across the street. The sky had begun to darken with a purple glaze. Soon it would be evening, and she would be in Sea Girt contemplating Aaron's next move. Would he be there when she arrived? Would he finally explain the reason he'd ordered her to come?

Being in a strange place made her anxious enough, but the thought of being away from her mother, for who knew how long, was nerve-wracking. She'd made a quick call to Joanne and explained her predicament. Joanne reassured her the staff would watch over her mother until she got back. That eased some of her fears but not a whole lot.

Hallie checked her watch: 6:23. Hungry and still puzzled, she chewed worriedly on her bottom lip and considered the implications of this trip. Was catching her off guard one way Aaron showed who was in control? Did he act like this toward all his employees? Maybe. He was the boss, after all, and an intimidating one at that. It was difficult not knowing his plans. She knew nothing about him, only that he didn't believe in love. Why bring that up again? She only hoped this trip would be about the business of ARK Enterprises and not "funny" business.

"Ms. Cavanagh?" The straight-laced voice brought

her back to the present. The shiny black limo at the curb surprised her. A tall stately looking gentleman with kind brown eyes held open the passenger door.

"Yes?"

He nodded. "My name's Nelson, Mr. Knight's driver. It's a pleasure to meet you. Are you ready?"

She nodded. "It's nice meeting you, too." She grabbed for her bags.

"I'll take those." Nelson took her hand and guided her into the limo.

She didn't know why she half-expected Aaron to be waiting inside, but the vehicle was empty. Why was she disappointed?

The soft leather seat molded around her. Inserted on one panel was a bar stocked with bottles of water, glasses, and ice in a covered tray. On the other side were crystal decanters filled with amber liquids. A small metal label marked each one. Bourbon. Whiskey. Scotch. What sort of drinking man was Aaron? She was almost tempted to pour herself something, just to calm her nerves.

Nelson closed the trunk, slid into the driver's seat, and glanced at her in the rearview mirror. "Are you comfortable, Ms. Cavanagh? I could raise the air conditioner."

"I'm fine, thank you. How long is this trip going to take?"

"About ninety minutes."

She nodded and tried to show an interest. But thoughts of being away from home, away from her mother, were making her anxious. That and seeing Aaron again. *He's my boss. And only my boss.*

"This is for you, Ms. Cavanagh. Mr. Knight said

you might enjoy it." Nelson handed her a familiar white and green Starbucks cup. "He sends his apologies. He didn't know how you take your coffee, so everything you need is in the side compartment by the door. Is there anything else I can do for you before we head to Sea Girt?"

She was shocked. Aaron had remembered her fondness for Starbucks. "No, Mr. Nelson."

"It's just Nelson." He looked at her again from the rearview mirror. His eyes held a certain amusement.

As he pulled away from the curb, she sat back dumbfounded. The heat from the coffee seeped through the cup and cardboard sleeve to her fingers. She placed the cup into the holder on the side of the door.

Though the coffee was a thoughtful gesture, she didn't want that to deter her from the reality of the situation. What she wanted was an explanation as to why he was making her travel to this house on a Friday night, and she needed clarification as to why he wanted her to stay there until further notice. But apparently those answers wouldn't come until she saw him face to face. Hopefully, that would be tonight.

****

After much arguing, Aaron had managed to usher Miranda out of his penthouse. She wasn't happy, but Aaron didn't care. She'd get over it. The woman was wealthy and traveled in high-society circles. She'd be just fine with or without him.

He poured himself his favorite expensive scotch. Neat. He downed it quickly without hesitation. It slithered down his throat like a smooth liquid fire. He poured himself another and stared out the window at the city below.

Nelson should have picked Hallie up by now. Would she be surprised he remembered her penchant for Starbucks? Would she view the gesture as innocent and sweet or some prelude to a physical conquest? Was that his motive all along? Why was he wishing she were standing here next to him instead of alone in his limo? Maybe he should have accompanied her to Sea Girt. He took another swig but more measured this time. No, not a good idea. What was wrong with him? He hardly knew the woman. He could control his business, his life, and the people in it. Why couldn't he control these feelings?

Oddly enough, he didn't want to overstep his bounds with her. These fantasies he'd been battling were secondary. His real plan was to groom her for bigger and better things in ARK Enterprises. After all, that was why he'd hired her. This weekend was just the beginning of her career. Her baptism by fire. He had a feeling this ambitious woman had what it took to be successful. Her education alone was enough to transform her into an up-and-coming, high-ranking executive. More importantly, he was sure she'd make ARK more successful than it already was. That was a lot to ask of a person. But for some reason, he knew she would be the one to handle it. And he wanted to be right there by her side as she did.

His thoughts stunned him. He was thinking like a big brother or...a father figure. Shit. Why did he suddenly feel the need to protect her from the big bad world? He knew nothing about her past, present, goals, needs. He smirked. The only thing she might need was protection from him.

Staring out at the darkening sky from the picture

window of his penthouse, Aaron took another healthy swallow of his scotch. Had he been too abrupt, too impersonal when he told her he was sending her to Sea Girt without a feasible explanation? He hadn't meant to be. Truth was, he didn't know how to act any other way. No matter. He was looking forward to knowing her better. Knowing her strengths and weaknesses and what she could handle in the day-to-day workings of the company. Wondering if she had what it took once she plunged headfirst into the corporate world of ARK Enterprises.

How had she responded to his directive? He couldn't tell even though he had FaceTimed her. He guessed she was caught off guard. Who wouldn't be? But afterward…was she angry? Mildly annoyed? Intrigued? She'd said she was going out to celebrate. Celebrate what? Her new job, he assumed. Something else maybe? Who were her friends? What were they like? He didn't even know if she had a boyfriend or maybe a fiancé. Was she married? No, he'd seen no rings on her fingers. He hesitated at those last thoughts and rubbed his forehead. True, he didn't have time for any serious relationship, nor did he want one. Especially not one with an employee. That could get messy. That was against his rules. No, he was doing just fine. Whenever he craved release, he knew what to do, where to go, and who to call.

And Hallie had nothing to do with that.

He drained the last drops of scotch and poured himself a third glass. He was already feeling a buzz, but it still wasn't strong enough to wash away his sins.

****

"We're in Sea Girt, Ms. Cavanagh."

Hallie looked up from her tablet, the backlight of the screen illuminating the space around her. She had been reading some contemporary romance with the predictable happily-ever-after ending that would always make her sigh.

Happily ever after...

That was all she wanted.

She'd thought she was close to her happily ever after three years ago when she met Kyle Weiss at a Harvard mixer. The son of a prominent Connecticut family, he'd been studying law just like his father had. They'd dated, fallen in love, and made plans to marry. They'd bought wedding bands, set a date, and secured a venue. They'd done everything an engaged couple was expected to do. Yes, her happily ever after had once been close enough to hold on to. That was until the day her mother had showed blips of forgetfulness. Then things had changed. If nothing else, she'd learned a valuable lesson. Only she was responsible for her happily ever after.

Putting that part of her past behind her, she busied her mind with the sights outside the window of the limo, which were far more appealing. Nelson maneuvered the sleek vehicle down a street lit with tall, Victorian-type lamps. Electric, not gas, yet still ornate. Though the sky had darkened, it didn't obscure the beautiful, turn-of-the-nineteenth-century houses standing stately along the narrow street. In some houses, tapered electric candles lit the long-paned windows. Soft lighting flooded verandahs. Gingerbread architecture gleamed in the moonlight. The scene swept her away to another time. With a sense of wonder, she slid across the seat to the other window and squinted.

Was that the ocean basking in the silver light of the moon?

At the end of the street, Nelson turned up a hidden driveway and braked. A wrought iron gate blocked their way. Like magic, it swung open slowly, and Nelson steered the car across a brick inlay drive.

"This is Mr. Knight's house?" she asked. The enormity of it made her feel small.

"Indeed."

She grabbed her Starbucks cup and downed the last drop of tepid coffee. Beach house? More like a beach *mansion*. A beach estate. An ocean view plantation. It was difficult to see all of the intricate architecture, but with the many floodlights streaming off corners of the roof, she could make out three stories and a wrap-around porch to die for.

"Wow!" she whispered. She thought she heard Nelson laugh.

The driveway was crescent shaped, and Nelson stopped the limo directly in front of the steps. Hallie gathered her tablet and tote. Nelson opened the door, and she stepped out, thanking him.

"Good evening and welcome, Ms. Cavanagh."

Hallie turned toward the voice. A woman was bathed in the bright light on the front porch. She was middle-aged and average height with a thick waist and full bosom. Her dark hair was pulled back in a loose bun, and her smile lit up the night.

"I'm Rita Donovan, Mr. Knight's housekeeper."

Aaron had been truthful. There *was* a housekeeper. Okay, score one for the man. Nelson was already hauling her bags up the steps, with Rita and Hallie following him.

The foyer was huge. The tile on the floor was the color of driftwood, and painted pictures of beach scenes graced the muted blue walls. Hallie was pretty sure they were originals and not prints. A sweeping staircase was the focal point.

"I've never seen anything like this," she gushed unashamedly.

"It's one of Mr. Knight's favorite places when he wants to be alone and relax." The housekeeper gestured for her to follow. "Of course, he does have parties and get-togethers as well."

"Of course." Hallie nodded. "Who wouldn't want to come here for a party?"

Rita laughed, and Hallie wondered if she was making a fool of herself.

"Nelson, put Ms. Cavanagh's things in the Sandpiper Suite. I made a sandwich for you. It's in the refrigerator."

"Thanks, Rita." Nelson disappeared through an arched entrance.

Hallie's brow rose. The thought of food sounded good. Maybe she could get Mrs. Donovan to make her something as well. Or she could do it herself. She wasn't here to put anyone to work.

The second story boasted an open floor plan. Living in a small New York apartment, she marveled at how this room seemed to go on for miles. The kitchen's dominant colors were white and light blue, with top-of-the-line, stainless-steel appliances. The dining room and living room were combined, creating a great room. The furniture kept the beachy theme using whites and blues and splashes of yellow to emulate the sunshine. But the best part was the double glass doors that opened to another wrap-around deck that faced the ocean.

"I'll show you to your room."

"Is Mr. Knight here?" Hallie asked.

"He's still in the city. He'll be here tomorrow. All he seems to do is work." Her face fell a bit, just like Hallie's heart.

Rita sounded more like a concerned mother than a housekeeper. The effect was surprising and strange. Aaron didn't seem to be the doted-on type.

Rita led the way to another set of stairs that took them to the third floor. "Your suite is down this hall."

Suite? Hallie tried to contain her amazement. This room had everything the second floor had. A set of double atrium doors led to a deck that overlooked the ocean. In another area partitioned by walls were a bedroom with a king-size bed, a lavish bathroom, and an office with state-of-the-art equipment. She'd take pictures and send them to Sophie. Her friend would never believe the sheer extravagance of everything unless she saw it with her own eyes.

Hallie's head was spinning. There was just so much to take in. "This room is bigger than my apartment."

Rite smiled and nodded. "Mr. Knight likes to make sure his guests are comfortable."

"Well, Mr. Knight certainly does that in a big way. Did he leave any instructions for me?" She spied her suitcase and bag already at the side of the bed. Nelson worked fast.

"Yes, in fact he did. There are several reports he wants you to read through. He'd like you to familiarize yourself with some of the newer companies he's acquired, and decide whether they'd be viable for ARK

Enterprises or are better off being sold. You'll find the folders on the desk in the office."

Hallie found it amusing that Rita had turned into Lavelle with her no-nonsense style. She was surprised at the housekeeper's acumen as well. "You sound like a savvy businesswoman, Mrs. Donovan. Have you ever worked in the corporate world?"

She laughed. "No. But working for Mr. Knight these past twenty years, I've picked up things."

"Twenty years?"

"I was the Knight family's housekeeper. Then Mr. Knight asked me to come to work for him."

"You must know him very well."

Rita shrugged. "As well as anyone, I guess."

Hallie nodded. That wasn't saying much. She admired the housekeeper's discretion regarding her boss, but she got the feeling no one really knew Aaron Knight.

So was this why he'd sent her to Sea Girt? To go over reports? Even though the scenery here was better, the air cool and refreshing, she could have just as easily read them in Manhattan. There had to be some other reason he wanted her here. "All right. I'll read through the reports first thing tomorrow morning. By then Mr. Knight will—"

Rita crinkled her nose and shook her head. "No, Ms. Cavanagh. Mr. Knight wants you to start tonight."

Hallie expelled a breath. "But it's—" She glanced at her watch. "—nine thirty."

"Those were his orders. Now can I make you something to eat?"

Her stomach grumbled as if on cue. "That would be great."

"Any allergies?"

"No."

"Vegetarian? Vegan? Gluten-free?"

"Just famished."

Rita chuckled. "I'll be back."

Hallie wanted to tell her not to fuss. A simple peanut butter and jelly sandwich would do just fine. But the woman was already gone before she had the chance.

Alone now, she tossed her suitcase onto the bed, unzipped it, and began to unpack a sundress, skirts, blouses, T-shirts, shorts, slacks, shoes, underwear—everything but a bathing suit. She didn't own one. Maybe she'd buy one in one of the shops she'd seen upon entering Sea Girt. Or maybe she wouldn't be here long enough to enjoy the ocean. And then again…

By the time she was finished unpacking, Mrs. Donovan showed up with a dish of red roasted peppers, portabella mushrooms, and thick slices of mozzarella cheese drizzled with a balsamic vinegar glaze.

"You can start with this." Mrs. Donovan placed the dish on the dining table. The food was plated like expensive artwork.

"Start? This is a meal."

"Nonsense. I hope you like salmon."

The housekeeper left the suite and returned thirty minutes later with the remainder of the meal. The salmon fillet over basmati rice was cooked to perfection. The chocolate mousse for dessert was light and airy.

When Rita came back to clear the dishes, Hallie still had questions. "Any chance Mr. Knight called?"

"No. Sorry."

"I'd better get moving on those reports, then." She

helped Rita put the rest of the dishes on the tray. "Thank you for everything."

Rita smiled and started for the door.

"Mrs. Donavan, wait." Hallie wasn't sure if she should ask, but her curiosity had been building. "What's Mr. Knight like?"

"Miss?"

"What kind of person is he? Working for him for over twenty years must have given you some insight into the man."

Rita's smile was tight. "I don't know if I should—"

"I'm sorry if I put you on the spot, and I don't want to get you in any trouble, but you've been so kind, and I'm just a little confused. I thought I'd be working in the city with him starting Monday, and here I am at the beach on Friday."

Rita's expression softened. She seemed to take pity on her. "I can tell you one thing about the man. Most people in the business world see him as ruthless and controlling, but he's always been nothing but kind to me and my family. He paid for my husband's funeral when I couldn't afford it, and he's financing the tuition for my youngest son's college education. He's a generous man, and I'm lucky to have him in my life." Rita's eyes filled with tears. "Please don't say anything."

Hallie was stunned. "I promise." She held Rita's hands. "Thank you for sharing that."

"Good night, Ms. Cavanagh."

And with that, Hallie was left alone to ponder the unfamiliar tenderness she felt for a man she hardly knew.

Chapter Four

Hallie awoke with a start. After a short bout of confusion, she remembered where she was. New Jersey. Sea Girt. Aaron Knight's house.

A sharp pain hit her hard from her neck to her tailbone. Looking around, she realized she had fallen asleep sitting at the desk in the office. She didn't know how it'd happened. She'd been pouring over the workings of Cooper Electronics one moment and now awakened stiff and sore.

She blinked, stood up, and carefully stretched her back and limbs until she'd worked out enough of the kinks to at least stand straighter. After a quick trip to the bathroom, she stretched, bent over, and dangled her arms, using several yoga moves, to adjust the rest of her body.

Still dressed in skinny jeans and a blouse, she made her way to the mini-kitchen and zeroed in on the coffee maker. Next to it was a small basket filled with every flavor and strength of Starbucks in a pod. She couldn't help but smile.

As the aroma of a morning blend rose from the mug, she wondered if Aaron had arrived at the house. She checked the business cell phone to see if he had called or left a message, but there was nothing. As promised, though, Sophie had texted at least five times and called twice. Afraid her roommate would make good on her promise to call nine-one-one, Hallie quickly shot off a message.

I'm fine. Fell asleep and missed your calls. Love you lots. I'll send pictures.

She finished with a heart emoji.

Her edginess softened when she found a lovely fruit salad in the mini-refrigerator. No doubt the work of Rita Donovan, housekeeper extraordinaire.

She took off her blouse and jeans and tossed them on the bed, still occupied with her unpacked clothes, and reveled in her unfettered freedom. The alarm clock by the bed glowed 6:40 a.m. With mug in hand and a few strawberries on a plate, she opened the atrium doors, confident no one would be on the beach to gawk at her state of undress. As the cool breeze blew back the sheer curtains, Hallie stepped out on the deck in her cotton bra and panties and breathed in the salty sea air. At this moment for her, there was no better scent, except maybe the dark rich fragrance of Aaron's cologne.

Hallie gazed across the narrow street. The ocean was practically at the threshold of this beautiful house. A wooden walkway connected with the sand dunes. Only a few steps and she'd be digging her toes in the pristine white sand. She listened to the pounding of the surf and the early morning cries of the seagulls. So different than the city's wake-up calls of trucks unloading and sirens blasting. Though she loved the vitality of Manhattan, she could get used to this laid-back life. The gray sky faded as she watched the sun's first tinge of yellow push back the gloom. Dawn was breaking, and it put on a damn spectacular show.

She sat on one of the cushioned chaise lounge

chairs, sipped her coffee, and nibbled on a strawberry. Did people really live this way? Having the time to relax like this before she started the day was a gift. Usually about now she'd be fighting Sophie for bathroom privileges.

But even among all this indulgence, she still couldn't figure out why Aaron was insistent on her presence here. Was he still in Manhattan? Maybe he was nursing a Friday night hangover after being out on the town with his latest conquest.

She shrugged and took another bite of the strawberry. No sense in complaining or trying to change it. The man was paying her an obscene salary. He did say travel was part of the job description. Why wasn't it Rome or Paris? Sea Girt, New Jersey, didn't have that international flair. And he did warn her the hours would be long, not to mention her availability all hours of the day…and night. Well, her first night here had been uneventful, and in her opinion, unproductive. Today she'd put that Harvard Business School degree to work by focusing on the reports.

But first, she needed a shower.

The bathroom was a work of art in tones of gray and white. The textiles were marble and stone, with sea grass mats and baskets to give it that warmer feel. Thick white and gray towels were folded neatly on chrome racks. The corner bathtub, complete with massage jets, was sleek and modern. The shower stall could fit a party of twelve. Though she had no idea where it was coming from, the scent of eucalyptus stimulated her senses.

Hallie stripped off the rest of her clothing, reached in the stall, and turned the main handle. Though the large showerhead was as big as a TV satellite dish, it only sputtered, and a trickle of water streamed out. Had she turned the wrong knob? There were so many of them. She twisted the handle back, waited a second, and then turned it again. Same gurgle. Same trickle. She turned some of the other knobs as well. They produced nothing.

Disappointed, she tried the bathtub. No water, not even a dribble, came out of the faucet. Hallie thought a moment. Such a huge house must have other showers she could use. Grabbing the largest towel she could find, she wrapped it around herself and darted out the door of her suite. She tiptoed down the hall until she came to a set of white, double doors. She knocked. No answer. She knocked again, just to be on the safe side. Still nothing. She turned the doorknob slowly and stepped inside the room.

Another suite, similar to hers, met her glance, but the likeness ended there. Where the furnishings in her rooms were light and airy, these were dark and dismal. And quite bare. The walls were painted charcoal gray and empty of pictures. The couch and chairs in the sitting area were a combination of dark and light grays.

She ventured farther inside, her brow crinkling. The bedroom was just as sparsely decorated as the rest of the rooms. The bed was merely a mattress and box spring. No headboard. No fancy bed linens like those on her bed. Only one night table. Even the sheets were gunmetal gray.

Hallie had stepped into a dungeon. At least that was what it looked like to her. All that was missing were the metal bars. Maybe this house was really a prison after all. But whose prison?

A few more steps in and she caught the scent of warm spice and male heat. It was the smell of cologne—dark and rich. His cologne. Hallie inhaled. The fragrance filled the room and bloomed closest to her, making her lightheaded. She remembered it from their face-to-face interview. Could this be Aaron's bedroom?

Common sense told her to leave, but something held her back. The man had certainly been a mystery to her, and now he was even more so. It was almost as if he felt he didn't deserve beautiful things. She fought down the urge to feel sorry for him. He was a billionaire, for God's sake. He could do anything, buy anything, *be* anything. If he wanted to live in an airless, sunless hole in the ground, that was his prerogative.

Without a concern, she made her way into his bathroom. Here his scent was stronger, more alive. So much so she actually turned around to see if he had come into the room. But she was alone, feeling foolish. A crackle of energy passed through her, causing her knees to wobble. What the hell was that?

Hallie eyed the shower stall. It was as big as the one in her suite. If she washed quickly, she'd be out in twenty minutes. Tops. She let go a breath. She'd take the chance.

The powerful pulse of the hot water made her muscles melt like butter, but it was Aaron's body wash that made her senses reel. She lathered herself all over, reveling in its scent. His scent. It was as though he were standing right next to her, holding her...

Eyes closed, she envisioned Aaron's hands caressing her body. The image was so real, so troubling. She whimpered softly, opening her eyes. Her breathing was ragged. What just happened? She didn't know whether to be embarrassed or elated. Truth was, she had never felt so alive. Her entire body flared. What was she doing? She had to stop this. Scent or no scent, image or no image, she shouldn't be thinking about her boss in such a way.

Standing under the showerhead, Hallie let the powerful stream prick her skin. She turned the pressure up to a deep massage, aimed the water between her shoulder blades, and hoped to wash away the disturbing feelings.

Though she was tempted to stay a little longer, she had to get out of there. Any minute she could get caught. Yet the thought of being found out excited her. Quickly, she shut off the shower and squeezed the excess water from her hair. She opened the glass door, grabbed the towel from the rack, wrapped it around her, stepped out, and…screamed!

****

The shock on Hallie's face was worth everything to him. Though the towel covered all her best parts, her wet hair and glistening skin was enough to send him into a mental whirlwind of physical turmoil.

He'd left Manhattan before dawn, before he had the chance to shower, only to find his stall was occupied by the woman who had dominated his dreams last night.

"What are you doing in here?" Her voice was near frantic.

Aaron raised one eyebrow. He couldn't take his eyes off her. "What am *I* doing here? This is my house, my bathroom, and my shower. What are *you* doing in here?"

"The shower in my room wasn't work— How long have you been standing there?"

"Long enough," he teased. In reality, he had just arrived when she stepped out of the shower stall, her sweet body already completely hidden beneath the towel.

"Oh, my God."

Her cheeks turned scarlet as she squirmed under his gaze. Why was he enjoying her uneasiness? Her humiliation? A quick and honest explanation from him about not glimpsing any part of her body would put her at ease. Was he that much of a cad? Did he relish watching her squirm?

The towel slipped a bit, and she grabbed the edges before it fell. But as she tucked in one end, the other loosened. If he was patient, he might get the full show.

Her eyes shone with indignation. "Would you mind giving me some privacy?"

Managing to keep an annoyed demeanor, he reached behind the shower stall. "Try this." He dangled a plush gray terrycloth robe in front of her.

She hesitated and then snatched it from him. "Could you turn around, please?"

He made a face. "Does that matter now?" But he did turn around, if only to hide his amusement and growing erection under the towel wrapped around his waist. He attempted to breathe away the jolt of sexual energy that rocked him to the bone. My God, she was beautiful. He grappled with the vision of her slick body waiting for him in his bed. "Are you decent yet?" He tried his best to at least sound impatient.

"Yes."

The irritation in her voice turned him on as he

faced her. The robe was three times too big, but she looked enticing wearing it. Wrapped up like a present on Christmas Day. How he longed to untie that present and caress her freshly washed skin and run his fingers through her damp hair. What was it about this woman that had him on the edge of exploding?

"So, Ms. Cavanagh, tell me again; why were you taking a shower in my room?"

"Because the water wasn't running in my shower or bathtub. I didn't know I was doing anything wrong."

"Next time, ask Rita to help you. You'll learn that I like to keep to myself. I'm not fond of my private quarters being made public. Even to invited guests."

"I'm sorry, Mr. Knight. It'll never happen again."

He could only anticipate that it might, and the thought nearly drove him crazy.

"Well, at least I hope you left enough hot water for me." He forced a smile. "We'll get together later. Be ready to work. We have a lot to do."

He stepped into the shower, took off his towel, and tossed it outside the stall. Her back was toward him, so she saw nothing. That disappointed him. Still, he couldn't help himself. He poked his head around the glass wall and watched her scurry out of the bathroom.

Chapter Five

Hallie hurried back to her suite, nearly tripping several times on the dragging hem of the robe. She didn't know whether to laugh, cry, or pray that the floor would open up and swallow her. She'd almost seen her boss, Aaron Russell Knight, bare-ass naked.

She closed the door and leaned against it, as the next thought finally sank in. She'd been bare-ass naked. And he had seen her. At least that was what he'd made her believe. But had he? She couldn't tell—and she wasn't about to ask. Shit, shit, shit! She paced. She threw herself onto the bed. A fleeting thought about jumping off the deck to put an end to her embarrassment crossed her mind. Could she pretend it'd never happened?

How could she? It had happened. And being around him would only remind her of what a fool she was. And what about him? Would his opinion of her change? Did he even have an opinion? How would he look at her now? The answer was simple, if not nerve-wracking. He could dial up her naked body any time he wanted. That thought was daunting.

No matter. She had to get dressed and ready herself for the day, but she hesitated in taking off his robe. Instead, she hugged herself, drawing in his warm, spicy scent. The notorious red flag flashed before her eyes. What was she doing?

Maybe she should call Sophie and ask her opinion about the situation. No, that wouldn't work. Her roommate was already skeptical about the man and his ways. That would add fuel to the proverbial fire.

She clenched her fists. *Stupid, stupid, stupid*! Maybe she wasn't right for this position. Maybe she should just give her two weeks' notice for a job she began a day ago. The thought made her smile a little. Maybe she should put on her big-girl panties and stick it out.

With new-found courage, she undid the tie, tossed the robe on the bed, and slipped into a clean bra and panties. She had finished drying her hair when she heard the knock on the door.

"Ms. Cavanagh? Are you there?" It was Aaron, his voice stern and self-important.

Jesus. Did she always have to be near naked to talk with this guy? "Yes, Mr. Knight?" Her voice shook. Would he just barge in? It would be just like him. She hurried to the door, just in case.

"We'll be working by the pool this morning. Wear your bathing suit."

She closed her eyes tightly and crinkled her nose. "But—"

"Twenty minutes."

"Mr. Knight?"

There was no answer.

A bathing suit? She didn't have one. She'd never had a need to buy one. Besides, were they going to work or swim? Was he merely being a good and welcoming host, or did he want to control her in some way? The shower incident made her suspicious. Her reactions were out of whack. Not a good way to start a working relationship. Any relationship.

She grabbed a pair of black linen capris and a white T-shirt and fashioned her hair in a messy bun on top of her head. She looked in the full-length mirror and smirked. At least she wasn't naked.

****

Aaron was surprised to see Hallie already sitting at the white, wrought iron table under a blue-and-white, striped market umbrella by the pool, looking right at home.

But the closer he came, the more he thought about the way he'd seen her earlier this morning. Damp from a shower, wrapped in a towel, and smelling like a spring day. A spike of heat caught him low in the gut.

"Have you been waiting long?" He'd always prided himself on punctuality. He was glad to see that his acquisitions director was more prompt than he was.

Up close, she took his breath away. Her blue eyes rivaled the sky and sparkled like the sun, yet he noticed something weighing on her mind. Tension in the delicate muscles of her face and throat was apparent.

"No." Her eyes flickered warily. "I didn't get to tell you how beautiful your house is."

She was definitely making small talk. Probably trying to divert him from the bathroom scenario. The compliment rolled off his shoulders. He put his phone face down on the table and eyed the manila folders there. "Are those the reports I asked you to go over?"

Hallie nodded. "Interesting projects."

"Then you read them all."

She fidgeted. "Well, not all. I read through two of them last night and then fell asleep."

A burst of laughter escaped his lips, and she

blushed. Was that tension he read in her expression? Embarrassment? "I like your honesty. Eggs Benedict?" he offered.

Laid out on a cart next to the table was a breakfast spread Rita had prepared. He lifted one of the silver cloches to reveal Canadian ham and a poached egg balanced on an English muffin hiding under a thick, traditional hollandaise sauce. A pitcher of mimosas, a French press with steaming coffee, and a bowl of strawberries completed the breakfast fare. He brought over the two dishes.

"Rita?" She eyed the tempting plate.

He nodded. "Rita's indispensable. I'm sure you found that out last night." He poured the champagne-laced orange juice into a fluted glass, handed it to her, and watched as she drank the mimosa much too quickly. "That's not plain orange juice, Ms. Cavanagh."

Her chin trembled ever so slightly. The champagne had hit bottom and was probably seeping up into her brain about now.

"I know."

She'd had no idea. Her body language oozed discomfort. Lips stretched in a thin smile. Legs crossed tightly. When she asked for another glass, he talked her out of it, saying she should eat something first.

"Is your room comfortable?"

She nodded.

"Something wrong?"

"About this morning."

So that was it. The shower. "Let's forget about the whole thing. I should have left when I realized you were in there. I was wrong." *He* was wrong? What the hell made him say that? She was at fault for trespassing.

Well, maybe trespassing was a harsh description, but she was where she shouldn't have been.

"Why didn't you?"

"What?"

"Why didn't you leave?"

He stared at her, not surprised at her question. "Why would I? Men are visual human beings, Ms. Cavanagh, and being a member of the male species, I was intrigued by what I saw. I couldn't help myself."

Her lips twitched slightly at the corners. "And what did you see?"

He pursed his lips. It was time to come clean—so to speak. "Nothing. You already had the towel wrapped around you when I came in the bathroom."

Her eyes widened. "You mean you didn't—"

He smiled and slowly shook his head. "I'll get your shower repaired immediately. In the meantime, if you need to, you can use mine. Just let Rita or me know so there won't be a recurrence of this morning's fiasco." *Maybe someday we can use it together.* A tiny explosion forced him to sit up straighter.

"Is it possible to pretend it never happened? You're my boss. I'm your employee. It'll be awkward if—"

"Say no more. As of right now, we start anew." He could spout all the rhetoric she wanted to hear, but he'd never forget how beautiful she'd looked.

His cell phone rang. He ignored it and took another bite of his breakfast.

She looked at the phone and then at him.

He turned it over, glanced at the screen, and then put it back on the table in its original position. "It can wait." He looked at her with a practiced eye. "Didn't you bring a bathing suit?"

"I don't have one." She took a sip of coffee.

"Everyone has a bathing suit."

"I don't. I just never had a need for one."

He blinked in surprise. "You've been to the beach before, haven't you? Coney Island? Rockaway? Jones?"

"I don't know."

"You don't know?"

She angled her jaw and met his eyes full force, her look serious. "Does it matter?"

"No, but—"

"Mr. Knight, why am I here? I could have looked over those contracts just as easily at ARK." Exasperation filled her voice.

He would never admit it, but he somehow regretted his impulsive decision to control the situation. Still, she had to be ready for such disruptions in the business world. He watched her and listened carefully for certain inflections in her voice. Sure, she acted like a fish out of water, but was she only baiting him? Was she more of a shark? "I thought a change of scenery might get some creative juices flowing. Do you have something against the beach?"

"No, of course not."

"Then why the concern?"

Her mouth twitched. "I thought your plans might include other things besides work."

Though the woman spoke her mind, he somehow knew that wasn't what she was going to say in the first place. "Plans? Like what? Like dinner? Like a walk on the beach at sunset?" He shifted in the chair, leaning toward her. He glared at her through narrowed eyes. "Like watching the sunrise from my bed? Is that the plan you were wondering about? My plan to come on to you?"

He'd hit a nerve. She faltered, her gaze dropping, her cheeks glowing scarlet. "I didn't mean that."

"Of course you did." He lowered his voice, not because he wanted to intimidate but because he wanted her to hear how serious he was. "Ms. Cavanagh, you're an executive employee. I'm your boss. I would *never* take advantage of that relationship." Had he sounded convincing enough? Even though he'd toyed with the idea of having her in his bed, it was a fantasy at best. Those boss/employee affairs could get quite messy. And though he relished being in control, that kind of lording over another wasn't acceptable to him. He had experienced enough of that behavior for a lifetime.

When her gaze once again met his, her prolonged stare sent a rush of desire coiling through him.

A sigh of gratitude escaped her lips. "I apologize."

"No need to." He was good at masking his real thoughts when he wanted to. "I'm flattered, to say the least. Consider this your first 'vacation.' I thought we would just relax and get to know each other. After all, we'll be working closely. I wanted to see if we were a…a good fit away from the office."

"And are we?"

Were they? "Too soon to tell." He forced his focus on the matter at hand. "I will say one thing to put your mind at ease. There is a reason I asked you to come here."

Hallie expelled a breath. She looked more relaxed, more at ease. "What's the reason?"

"I'll get to that later. In the meantime, I want your opinion on those companies you perused last night."

Hallie agreed, and as she turned away from him to grab the folders, he foolishly picked up his cell to look at it. He blew out a breath. Miranda.

****

Looking up from the folders, Hallie saw Aaron studying his phone. His brow was wrinkled, and his mouth was tight with concern. Maybe the call wasn't as unimportant as he wanted her to believe.

She gestured toward the phone. "You can return the call if you want."

"That's not necessary. Now—"

"I'll make myself scarce."

His shoulders seemed to sag a bit. His stony expression revealed nothing of his thoughts. Had she insulted him in some way? His mouth was pressed into a thin line. He'd told her he liked his privacy, so she had offered it to him. He should be grateful for that.

"Thank you. I'd appreciate that."

So the call did hold some significance. She smiled and got to her feet. "Take your time. I'll look around."

The pool was stunning. It was far from the average boring rectangular or oval shape. This one had waterfalls and rocks and secluded niches hidden even more by lush ferns and flowering plants. Wisps of steam rose from a built-in hot tub in an isolated corner. It was as if some tropical island had suddenly appeared in New Jersey, and Hallie was in love with all of it.

She wished her mother were here. Even in her state of confusion, she would have enjoyed the pool and its surroundings. It was difficult trying to come to terms with the fact that her mother was slowly forgetting everything about her life. She'd call the nursing home this evening to check on her.

She kicked off her black slides, lowered herself by the edge of the pool, and dangled her feet in the water. It was heated and luxurious. She stirred the water with her legs, watching the ripples she was making. A strange sense of peacefulness washed over her, and she was calmer than she had been in a while.

She could get used to a place like this. The ocean breeze. The sunshine. Being here with Aaron. That last thought surprised her, yet it seemed right to think such a thing. He wanted to see if they were a good fit. If they could work well together.

Despite what she'd been thinking, she believed him when he said seducing her was the furthest thing from his mind. Should she be flattered he had respect for her, or should she be angry he thought she wasn't worth his time?

That tidbit aside, she'd prove to him he'd hired the right person. She just needed to know the circumstances behind him ordering her to his house. He said he'd tell her.

Still, he was very secretive about the whole thing. Was he messing with her mind?

She glanced toward Aaron. Holding the phone away from his ear, he paced restlessly on the patio like a sleek caged animal. His mouth tight with—was that anger? Whoever was on the other end was causing him a whole lot of misery. Was a client giving him grief? Some corporate bigwig? A woman?

That last thought gave her pause. Though the way Aaron chose to live his life was further than any business she should be privy to, it still made her curious. What *were* his tastes when it came to women? She knew only what the media provided about this self-made man, and even that was suspect. Newspapers, magazines, and the Internet carried stories and photos from time to time about the women who accompanied him to charity banquets and altruistic celebrations that named him "Man of the Year" or some such title. But for the most part, he had never been associated with one particular woman for a lengthy period of time. Maybe commitment to one person wasn't part of his lifestyle.

She looked over at him again. Though she couldn't hear him, Aaron was definitely arguing with the person on the other end of the phone. A muscle flicked in his jaw. His lips drew back in a snarl. Should she take it upon herself as a good and loyal employee to see if he needed help? Or at the very least a distraction that might give him cause to hang up?

I don't believe in love. His words. Why did that suddenly pop into her head? Was it because of the phone call? Was the person on the other end, who was causing him grief, the reason why he didn't believe in love? Her mind was in overdrive, and she had to stop and mind her own business.

Had he ever allowed anyone into his life? His heart? His soul? Yes, love hurt. It certainly wasn't perfect. Nothing was. She knew that firsthand. But love also filled desires, satisfied instincts, and healed the heart. Not to believe in something so basic...so human... She felt sorry for him.

Though the water felt like silk on her skin and the sun warmed her shoulders, she lifted her legs up and out of the pool. She scooped up her shoes and cautiously made her way back toward him.

Something about his expression was making her uncomfortable.

Anger radiated from him the closer she got. A vein pulsed at the base of his throat. His eyes narrowed and his jaw stiffened. She halted mid-stride. It wasn't her place to interrupt him and certainly not a good idea to eavesdrop. Maybe she should just go back inside the house and wait for the call to be over. But something drew her to him, and she got there just in time to catch his last words.

"I told you I had someplace to be. No, I won't be back in New York this evening."

She caught his eye, and his gaze turned glacial. Her heart clinched with an unknown fear, and she shivered a little at his dark expression.

His voice lowered to a menacing tone. "Find someone else…"

Hallie was close enough to Aaron now to hear the other person. A woman's voice. Bitter. Nasty. She bit her bottom lip.

"Don't push me, Mir—" His head snapped up, his eyes impaling hers. "I've got to go. Goodbye."

She flinched when he banged the phone screen side down on the table a little bit harder than he should have.

"What?" he barked, staring at her with cold, hard eyes.

She kept her cool. "Seems you couldn't wait to get rid of whoever was on the other end." She tried to make light of the sour situation with a playful voice.

Without another word, he picked up the cell, got to his feet, and threw it in the pool. His over-the-top reaction made her heart lurch in her throat. She was afraid to move. His body clenched in what she could only interpret as rage, pure and simple. His expression was hard and unyielding.

"I'll need a new phone, Ms. Cavanagh. That one has run its course."

Chapter Six

Damn the phone. Damn Miranda. Damn his temper.

The flash of fear in Hallie's eyes immediately made him regret his foolish actions. It reminded him too much of his mother's expression every time his father went on one of his drinking binges.

The Black and White Ball charity function he was supposed to attend was this evening. When he escorted Miranda from his penthouse yesterday, he'd also made it clear he wasn't going to accompany her. Yes, she was annoyed, but he assumed he'd gotten his point across. Obviously, Miranda hadn't believed him.

"I apologize for my outburst." The words tasted bitter in his mouth. "I acted like a two-year-old."

"You seemed upset at whoever was on the other end." She grimaced slightly. "I know it's none of my business, but if you want to talk about it, I'm here."

"You're right. It's none of your business. Let's look at those reports now, shall we?" Had he hurt her feelings? But like a good employee of ARK Enterprises, she handed him the reports without a word.

With the call from Miranda a distant memory, the morning went by quickly and turned out to be quite productive. Hallie certainly earned her first day of pay, possibly her whole week. Her eyes lit up as she discussed two of the three properties he was thinking of purchasing. She gave him sound advice and showed him where the company could save money as well as make it. Damn, she was good with figures. He listened instead of voicing his opinion, which he wasn't used to doing. He hid his excitement as her excitement grew. They argued a bit, but her arguments were viable and practical. Inside, he was bumping his own fist in a congratulatory gesture. He had hired the right person, and he felt pretty smug about the decision.

Before he knew it, it was lunchtime. Rita had made a huge Cobb salad. The ingredients were all local, sustainable, and fresh, and he grinned uncontrollably as he watched Hallie devour it. He fixated on her mouth as she ate with gusto. He wondered what else that mouth of hers could do.

He focused on her hands and pondered how her fingertips would feel skimming his body and toying with the top button of his shirt—or pants. He stole a quick peek at her curvy body snug in her casual capris and T-shirt. He ached to touch her…

"Mr. Knight?"

He snapped out of the distraction. "Ah, yes, it's in our best interest to—"

"I asked if you wanted another cup of coffee."

"No. No, thank you." He'd been daydreaming about her. "Good work today. I'm impressed." He let go a breath. "Now let's get down to the real business of why you're here."

She sat up straighter, tilted her head, and waited, wearing an expression of intense concentration. Clearly, this information was what she'd been waiting to hear, and she wasn't about to miss a word.

He leaned back and intertwined his fingers as he

always did when giving instructions. "My company is in heated negotiations to acquire Lectra-Pro, this maverick electric-car company. Seems Kevin Carlyle, the owner, is feeling a bit nostalgic and is thinking of pulling out of the deal. He and his wife are vacationing on Long Beach Island, and we'll be having dinner with them this evening. I think together we can convince him to sell."

Her brow lifted. "I've heard of Lectra-Pro. I didn't realize you were interested."

"I've always been interested in things I can't have." Why was he itching to get a rise out of her? He waited for her reaction to what he perceived as clever and somewhat suggestive, but she only smiled. The curve of her full lips had nothing to do with his spark of witticism. A pinch of embarrassment surprised him. He took the bottom folder from under the pile on the chair.

"I've made reservations at The Breakers. Very upscale. Elegant. I expect you to dress appropriately and bring your A game—"

"Mr. Knight?" Her brow crinkled in a frown.

Though annoyed at her interruption, he allowed her to speak. "Yes?"

"You used the word nostalgic. What are Kevin Carlyle's likes and dislikes?"

He looked at her like she had three heads. "What? What's the difference? I want the company. I don't want to be his BFF."

"Humor me."

Though he didn't care for the way this conversation was going, he did like her tenacity.

"He's a bit of a curmudgeon. Eclectic. Older. Late sixties, I'm guessing. Grew up in the sixties. Peace.

Love. All that crap."

"Hmm."

"Hmm? That's it? I was expecting a little more insight from a Harvard graduate."

She didn't seem deterred by his sarcasm. "Can the reservations be cancelled?"

"Why?"

"Good."

"But I didn't—"

She got to her feet but didn't offer any other explanation. "And wear something casual. Really casual." A mischievous twinkle lit her eyes. "We're at the beach, after all."

"Ms. Cavanagh, I can't be intimidating in a T-shirt and shorts."

"Do you own any?"

Was she getting back at him about the bathing-suit remark? "Yes, but—"

"I'll take care of everything else. Do you have the phone number of the restaurant?"

He made a face. "It's at the bottom of the pool."

"Oh. Right." She looked amused. "The restaurant was called The Breakers, right? I'll get back to you with the particulars." She pointed to the folder in his grip. "Is that the company's report?"

He handed it over. Her excitement was making him excited, in more ways than one. "Ms. Cavanagh, what—?"

"By the end of this evening, ARK and Lectra-Pro will be in bed together."

He ran his fingers through his hair. "Interesting choice of words."

"Trust me."

He closed his gaping mouth and watched her hurry back to the house. What the hell just happened? Trust her? His head was spinning. What was she up to? He hated waiting to find out, but he had no choice. Served him right. After all, he had kept her in the dark about bringing her here. Yet the more he thought about her eagerness to close this deal, the more excited he got. He only wondered one thing—how had he lost control so quickly?

****

Hallie went back to her suite to start finalizing the evening. First, she called Golden Living. A nurse assured her that her mother had been quite lucid. "She even participated in our daily Bingo game."

Though the news was positive, Hallie was eager to see for herself. But that wasn't going to happen—at least not yet.

After checking on her mother, she dove headlong back into the business at hand. A quiet panic overshadowed her at once. What had she been thinking? She'd practically guaranteed the sale of Lectra-Pro to Aaron. Sure, she had an idea, maybe even a semi-solid plan to secure the company, but would it work? Could she pull off this deal? More importantly, what was Aaron's take on her newly found chutzpah? Maybe she seemed too aggressive. Maybe he was thinking he'd made a mistake in hiring her. Maybe they wouldn't be a good fit.

She headed to the office to do some research on Sea Girt and its surrounding areas. The windows were wide open, and the sea breeze wafting through invigorated her. She took a deep breath and got started.

God bless the Internet. Her speed-reading course

paid off. In a matter of an hour, she learned the town's history, its cultural features, and of course, places to go for food and fun. She found what she thought would be the perfect venue and made reservations for four. That done, she took a few more minutes to research Kevin Carlyle.

Aaron was spot-on. He was a bit of a curmudgeon and a tree hugger, but all those qualities would hopefully fit into her plan. He was married for the second time, his first wife having died from cancer. He had three adult children, two sons and a daughter. One a doctor, one an engineer, and the other the head of a nonprofit. All professionals.

According to the various articles she scanned, Carlyle had always been concerned with the environment. He'd started the first environmental society when he attended Northwestern. "Our greatest enemy is time," he was quoted. "But if we as a country begin now to preserve clean air, rich forests, and fertile land, future generations will thank us." An interesting and concerned man. She couldn't wait to meet him.

Hallie Googled The Breakers. She found the phone number on the website and cancelled the reservations. She stayed a while longer on the screen and took the virtual tour. Aaron wasn't kidding. It was a beautiful place, elegant and romantic and right on the ocean.

Her thoughts started to race. Was that what he'd had in mind when he made the reservations for this evening as well? Romance? No. This was business, pure and simple. He merely wanted to impress the client. She feigned indifference with a casual shrug. Still, the idea of an amorous evening ruffled her for a moment.

Just like the incident by the pool.

Her thoughts went back to the phone call that had made him so angry. The voice on the other end had definitely been female and just as fuming. Who had he spoken to? What was the argument about? Why did she care?

He'd said, "Mir," and then left it unfinished when he saw her. Well, one thing was obvious. He wanted to keep the caller a secret. And that caller had made him furious enough to throw his phone in the pool. Though he'd been clear the situation was none of her business, she nevertheless tucked the clash away in the back of her mind.

Hallie picked up her own phone. Earlier, she had snapped some pictures of the outside of the house, the pool, and her room and sent them to Sophie. In turn, an amazed Sophie had texted her several times throughout the day.

OMG! Where are you? The Taj Mahal? Holy shit! Can't wait until you're home.

She took a breath. Home. When *would* she be home? She finished off a return text with a line of smiley and heart emojis.

"Ms. Cavanagh?"

She froze for a moment, the sense of dismay returning but for another reason. It was Aaron knocking on her door.

"Yes. Yes, I'm coming." Swallowing the lump in her throat, she opened the door.

There he stood, dressed in a black, fitted polo shirt and khaki cargo shorts. He looked undeniably like the bad boy next door. More like the billionaire bad boy. Whatever the title, she regarded him as positively handsome, dangerous, and lethal. She focused on his face. His mouth slipped into a sexy smile that flashed a desire he was having trouble hiding. She found herself stepping away from him.

"You look..." Her thoughts jumbled in her head. *You look great. You look fantastic. You're a fine specimen of a man. Kiss me now.*

"Yes?"

She swallowed her foolish and untimely feelings. "You look just right."

He cocked an eyebrow and gestured to his clothes. "That's it?"

Her heart hammered against her chest. "Is there something you need, Mr. Knight?"

He boldly stepped closer to her. "You, Ms. Cavanagh. I need you."

****

As soon as he said those words, he guessed she'd blush. But she didn't. She didn't even flinch.

"You need me?"

Was he imagining things, or was her voice that maddeningly sexy? Did she even realize it was? Her tone was gritty as though she'd known he "needed" her all along. She was driving him crazy.

"Yes, I-I need...ah, your honest opinion. Not that I'm 'just right.' " All at once he was tongued-tied. That was a first. Why did he value her judgment? He hardly knew her. The shirt and shorts weren't serious business fare. The entire outfit was wildly inappropriate, even for casual Fridays. Still, he'd listened to her and dressed as she had wished—and he wasn't sure why. He opened his arms at his sides as though to embrace her. It took everything he had inside not to. "Is this casual enough?"

Was that disappointment in her face? Was she hoping he wanted her and not her flair for fashion? What was he thinking? She was his employee, not his stylist. And certainly not a potential lover. *Jesus.* He jerked his mind away from his illicit thoughts.

She studied him up and down with an assessing look. "Perfect."

"I don't believe I've ever been called that before."

She made a face. A cute face. "Perfect for what I have in mind."

"And just what do you have in mind, Ms. Cavanagh?" A tiny spark of what could be whispered in his brain. His imagination ran wild.

A small burst of laughter escaped her sweet mouth, sending sparks of excitement through his body. Was she mocking him? He probably deserved it.

He got hold of himself quickly. "So are you going to let me in on your plan?"

She hesitated. He found that fascinating. An hour ago, by the pool, she was barking orders and taking control. Now she looked positively demure.

"If it's all right with you, I'd rather not."

"It's not all right with me. Do I have to remind you patience is not my strong suit?"

"You'll just have to trust me, Mr. Knight. I'll meet you downstairs in twenty minutes." And with that, she closed the door.

What the…? He stared at the door, part dumbfounded, part excited. Trust *her*? How could he when he couldn't trust himself?

Back to business. Hallie had put on a strong front, though he did detect a little crack in her confidence. He found that endearing. Still, he was concerned. What if this plan of hers went south? What if Lectra-Pro slipped through the company's fingers?

He let go a heavy sigh. As much as he wanted to kick down her door, throw her on the bed, and make love to her, he decided to put away those feelings for another time. Tonight, business would be her lover, her seducer. Tomorrow, who knew? He smiled and walked down the hall.

****

Aaron sat at the kitchen island, his thoughts still muddled from his encounter with Hallie. He had considered pouring a scotch or two while he waited for her, but a clear head was needed for this evening's negotiations. Or whatever Hallie had planned. Not knowing her tactics kept him on edge.

Putting the possibilities out of his mind, he watched Rita empty the dishwasher and concentrated on her calming if not automatic movements. He didn't question when the memories of his mother slipped into his thoughts.

On those good days, she'd sing silly songs as she washed the dinner dishes. While his father, brother, and sister scattered after the family meal, he would help her. He'd never minded the work. He loved being with her—just the two of them. To know she was happy and safe was all he wanted for her. All he wanted for his family.

Kitchen time with his mother was special. They would laugh and talk until his father would yell for them to shut up so he could hear the TV. His memories grew darker. He remembered seeing her tremble at her husband's imposing voice, but then she'd look toward

Aaron and smile.

They would continue their conversation quietly after that. In encouraging tones she would praise him for his intelligence and drive, convincing him he was capable of anything he would set his mind to.

And she'd been right. However, those opportunities had come with heartache. Still, those early years, before it all came to a tragic end, had been the happiest times of his life.

"You're looking thoughtful," Rita said, grabbing the silverware from the basket.

"I was thinking about my mother." He missed her. He missed his family.

"I remember the two of you together."

"You're sounding nostalgic."

"Nothing wrong with that." She paused. "She's very nice, you know."

Aaron regarded the housekeeper with a questioning look. "Who?"

"Ms. Cavanagh."

Hearing Hallie's name brought him back to the present. "What about her?"

"Are you all right?"

Was that a smirk on Rita's face? Aaron couldn't be angry. He couldn't be anything but confused. "Yes. Hallie's very nice."

"Hallie?"

"What?"

"Nothing."

There was that smirk again.

The stretch of silence unnerved him. So did the clanks of plates and pots and pans. What was wrong with him?

"Can I get you anything, Mr. Knight?"

His willpower dwindled. "Scotch. Neat. If you don't mind."

Rita nodded. "Of course."

He thanked her, watched her walk out of the kitchen, and wondered why the wait for Hallie had suddenly become unbearable.

Chapter Seven

The restaurant was called Pete's Fishery, and by all accounts, it was a certified dive. The place was located on the pier on Ortley Island, halfway between Sea Girt and Long Beach. Rustic picnic tables with green umbrellas were lined up on a deck overlooking the water. Inside, the décor was mostly movie and concert posters and paraphernalia from the 1960s. There was a full bar, nightly entertainment, and a small dance floor. Performing tonight was the house band, Stone Cold, whose music was all about the same decade.

Hallie was in love. Aaron's expression was questionable at best.

"So what do you think?" she asked.

He warily eyed the inside of the restaurant. "This is what you came up with?"

"Yes. I think it's wonderful."

"Yes, a wonderfully bad joke."

She shook her head, a bit apprehensive at his critique. "Open your mind, Mr. Knight. You'll see."

The hostess, a young girl dressed in a halter top and tight capris, appeared behind the reservation's podium. "Welcome to Pete's. Can I help you?"

Hallie greeted her back. "Cavanagh. Reservation for four."

The hostess checked off Hallie's name on a page in a book. "Inside or outside?"

"In—"

Hallie put her hand on Aaron's arm and then quickly drew it back. "Outside, please."

He looked at her, his eyes sharp with unease. Maybe it wasn't the smartest thing to do, but she ignored him.

The hostess grabbed four long paper menus. "Follow me."

The picnic table where they sat was close to the railing, where she wanted to be. The sound of the restless waves lapping against the pilings below them added an energizing touch. At least she thought so.

For Aaron, it seemed to be another story.

He looked positively out of his element. Strange. If he couldn't handle the casual "beach bum" life, why did he have a home here? Rita had said he came to the beach to relax. Somehow, Hallie couldn't see it. But never mind that. She had to focus on this meeting. If it didn't go as she had planned, then she was sure there would be some kind of fiscal hell to pay.

The hushed colors of lavender and pink spread across the horizon. Red-orange rays of the setting sun fell across the water. Though the sky was clear, the faint smell of rain permeated the air. Hallie wrapped her flower-printed fringe shawl over her shoulders. She had changed from her T-shirt and capris to a white, sleeveless midi top and a full, knee-length, light-blue skirt sporting tiny flowers. Aaron wore a plain black sweatshirt over his T-shirt. He'd wanted to wear his company jacket, the one with the ARK logo, but she talked him out of it.

"Mr. Carlyle's going to think you're only about the company if you wear that."

"I am about the company. It's *my* company, damn it!"

"Not tonight. Tonight it's just a relaxed evening with some friends."

"I hope you know what you're doing."

So did she.

A waitress appeared at their table, greeted them, flashed an inquisitive look, and then took their drink orders. When she returned with Aaron's scotch and Hallie's white sangria, the waitress once again eyed him in a strange manner.

"Excuse me. I don't mean to pry," the waitress addressed him, "but aren't you—?"

"You see, honey." Hallie jumped in so quickly that he regarded her quizzically when she reached across the table and patted his hand. "I told you that you look like him." She gazed up at the waitress. "We get this all the time."

The young girl seemed embarrassed. Her smile was tight. "I'm sorry. It's just that you look so much like Aaron Knight."

Aaron, now understanding the situation, waggled his finger for the waitress to come closer. "I'll tell you a little secret. I'm better looking than that hack Knight."

Hallie laughed outright at his quick wit. He seemed to put the girl at ease. She smiled and said she'd come back for their dinner order when the other couple arrived.

He displayed a satisfied look. "You're sharp, Ms. Cavanagh, I'll give you that."

She grinned. "Thank you. I didn't want you to be interrupted by gawkers tonight." She took a sip of her sangria. It was yummy. "Do you get recognized a lot?"

He shrugged one shoulder. "It depends. If I attend some charity function, I'm pretty detectible. Here, I'm surprised I was. Not many people know I have a summer home in Sea Girt. Lately, I've been trying to keep a low profile."

"I can guess why."

"Tell me."

"I imagine it's difficult enough running a company like ARK and being in the spotlight, having your every move scrutinized. Even your personal life."

"Are you speaking from experience?"

She smiled. "Not at all. You remember our interview, don't you?"

"How could I forget?"

"I told you I lead a dull life."

His mouth pressed into a smirk. "Then I guess you should be grateful."

Yes, she was grateful. Grateful she still had her mother in her life. Grateful for the job at ARK. Grateful for this time with Aaron.

His chuckle distracted her.

"What's so funny?"

"You called me 'honey.' "

His eyes twinkled with mischief, and she felt the burn of his gaze as it fixed on her. "I did not."

"Yes, you did. You called me 'honey' in front of our waitress."

"Oh."

He was right. She squirmed under his steady stare.

"So now that we've almost seen each other naked and with your term of endearment, I'd say we're pretty much engaged." His straight-laced façade had turned into something she didn't recognize. Was he actually having fun?

"What's this about being engaged?"

Composing herself, Hallie slapped a smile on her face and looked up while Aaron stood.

"Hello, Kevin. How are you?" The men shook hands. "Pamela, how good to see you again."

"Aaron, you look wonderful." She and Aaron embraced. Obviously, they were familiar with one another's company.

Kevin Carlyle looked to Hallie. "Aaron introduced the two of us. I don't know if I should thank him or—"

"Kevin, be nice," Pamela warned.

Kevin burst out with a big belly laugh, even though he didn't have a big belly. In fact, the man was put together well. He was tall with a thick crop of wavy silver hair. Aaron was right about his age. The crinkles in the corners of his eyes and a jowl drop on his face screamed sexagenarian. But those features didn't deter from this quite classy-looking guy.

Pamela sported a silver-haired bob. She was petite and trim and had lovely porcelain skin. She wore very little makeup. The two looked like they were ready for a tennis match.

"So *are* congratulations in order?" Kevin asked.

Hallie glanced over at Aaron. His puzzled look was priceless.

"Is this lovely young lady your fiancée?" Kevin winked at Hallie. "You know, this one's a wild man. I'm surprised a little bit of thing like you tamed him."

Pamela smacked her husband playfully on his shoulder. "Kevin, hush."

"Only speaking the truth, my dear. So when's the wedding? I'll be sure to keep my calendar open."

Aaron's eyes widened, and he laughed nervously. Hallie was amused to see him caught off guard.

"You've got it all wrong, Kevin. This is Hallie Cavanagh, my new director of acquisitions."

Kevin's brow rose. "So are you the one who's going to convince me to sell Lectra-Pro?" His eyes narrowed, but the smile was still there. "I'll tell you, Knight, I might just give it up for this pretty little woman."

Though Kevin's comments were less than PC, Hallie liked the man.

She glanced at Aaron. He looked positively giddy. She wanted him to compose himself. The company was far from theirs. She had more wheeling and dealing to do.

"I said might, and that's a pretty big might." Kevin was steadfast. "Anyway, it's very nice to meet you, Hallie. I knew an engagement was too good to be true. Knight's one hard son of a bitch to pin down when it comes to one woman."

Hallie blushed, her thoughts running wild. Why did she suddenly feel so weird? So out of sorts? Why did the woman comment bother her? "Nice to meet you, too, Mr. and Mrs. Carlyle."

"None of that now. It's Kevin and Pamela."

Pamela took a seat next to Hallie and Kevin next to Aaron. Their waitress scurried over and took the couple's drink orders. Aaron ordered raw oysters, steamed mussels and clams, and a loaf of sourdough bread for appetizers.

"So where'd ya find this place, Knight? A little rustic for your tastes."

His expression was wary. "Actually, Ms. Cavanagh

discovered this little hole-in-the-wall. I'm just along for the ride."

"Well, good job, Hallie. There's nothing like enjoying a beautiful sunset with the people you love." Kevin reached across the table and took Pamela's hands in his. "Isn't that right, sweetie?"

Pamela agreed, her face brightening with what Hallie could only interpret as adoration for the man sitting across from her.

As the drinks and food arrived, Hallie made sure to keep the conversation going. She could tell in Aaron's eyes that he was chomping at the bit to discuss Lectra-Pro, but every time he started to talk business, Hallie interrupted with exchanges that were light, fun, and business-free. As the evening progressed, she discovered that the Carlyles were people who were easy to like.

Dinner came and went. So did dessert. After-dinner drinks soon followed. Hallie excused herself once to use the ladies' room.

"You know, Knight, I don't remember the last time I was this relaxed. How 'bout you, honey?" Kevin rubbed his wife's back.

Pamela nodded. "Kevin, listen, they're playing our song. It's 'Unchained Melody' by the Righteous Brothers."

Kevin listened. "So it is."

Pamela glanced at Hallie and Aaron. "You're way too young to remember this song. Kevin and I had it played at our wedding." She eased herself off the bench. "Let's dance, honey."

"Sure thing. Excuse us, folks. The little lady wants to dance. Be right back." And with that, the Carlyles hit the dance floor as the house band lead singer wailed away on the '60s ballad.

Aaron leaned forward, his jaw clenched. "What are you doing?"

"I'm closing the deal. Be patient."

"I could have closed three deals by now."

"But this is the one you want, isn't it?"

His mouth snapped closed and tightened with a frown.

The song was finished, but the Carlyles remained on the dance floor. Stone Cold began playing "Baby, I Need Your Lovin'."

"Johnny Rivers," she commented.

Aaron took a sip of his cognac. "How do you know?"

"My tastes are eclectic, I guess. There's a lot more out there besides all business all the time."

"Would you like to dance?" He put down his glass.

She stared at him. "What?" The invitation caught her completely off guard. Confused, she could only answer with "You mean you and me?"

He glanced around and then looked back at her. "I don't see anyone else, unless you want me to ask our waitress. Remember, she now thinks I'm better looking than the real me."

The searching in his eyes reflected her surprise—and uncertainty.

He swung his legs over the picnic bench, stood, and offered his hand. Without a word, mostly because she couldn't extract any from the recesses of her stunned mind, she also got to her feet, reached across the table, and grasped his hand.

****

Even though he kept a respectable distance, having Hallie in his arms made him feel complete. It was a foolish thought, of course. How could a veritable stranger make someone whole? Someone second-guessing his mindset? He was Aaron Russell Knight, damn it, a self-made and beyond successful businessman. He didn't need anyone to make him feel important, much less whole. He *was* important.

And yet…

There was something so easy about being with her. She made it so easy. His tightly wound and formal demeanor was vanishing. Was this how folks in the real world relaxed? Holding someone they hardly knew in their arms? Swaying to the rhythm of music and harboring impure but desirous thoughts?

"This is nice." She gazed at him. "You're a good dancer."

"Madame Phyllis's Dance Academy. My grandmother made sure her grandchildren were schooled in etiquettes and cotillions." He shook his head, reliving the insufferable fox trot and cha-cha lessons.

Her laughter rivaled the sweet, slow sounds of the band. "It couldn't have been that bad."

"God, I sound so stiff." He pulled her a little closer, his keen sense of awareness keeping him anxious and alert. She didn't pull away. He liked that. "I feel like I'm at my prom." His words surprised him. He never mentioned his past to anyone.

She threw back her head and laughed. "Wow. Aaron Knight at the prom. I wish I could have seen that."

He flinched. "It's better you didn't."

"What was your theme?"

"What?"

"The theme. Mine was 'Hollywood Nights.' We had this red carpet and fake paparazzi. Old black and white movies playing on screens. Cardboard cutouts of Johnny Depp, Keanu Reeves, and Daniel Radcliffe."

"Sounds…interesting."

She shook her head. "Tacky and unforgettable. What was yours?"

"I don't remember."

"Everybody remembers their prom. Did the color of your bowtie match your date's dress? What kind of flowers did you get her? Corsage or wristlet? What was your date's name?"

"Penelope Winters," he said, surprised he'd recalled such an insignificant part of his life.

"I bet she was tall and blonde and blue-eyed—"

"And I took Miss Winters to the prom because my grandmother made me." He hung his head.

Hallie laughed. "Made you?"

"I'd rather not talk about it."

He spun her around, and she grabbed on to his shoulder. He held her closer. She didn't seem to mind.

"All right, I'll tell you about mine, if you tell me about yours."

She shot him a horrified look.

"It couldn't have been that bad."

"Did Miss Penelope Winters throw up on you?"

His mouth twitched. "Can't say she did."

"My date got drunk on vodka he had smuggled into the cafeteria."

"You hang out with some questionable people, Ms. Cavanagh."

The tilt of her head and the shine in her eyes were driving him crazy. "Does that include you, Mr. Knight?"

A fluttering feeling invaded his body. He shot her a tentative smile, and his breath hitched. "Touché." He paused and then said, "I could do this all night." Did that sound corny? Corny or not, he was surprised he meant it. Because of Hallie, he was truly enjoying himself. He enjoyed holding her close. He enjoyed the way she looked at him. He enjoyed their easy conversation. What the hell was happening to him? Though he wanted her in his arms forever, he forced himself to hold back.

"What? Dance?" she asked.

"Yes. Dance."

Those expressive blue eyes of hers were luminous. He didn't want to read too much into them. Maybe she was just having a good time, no strings, no worries, no complications. The song ended much too soon for him.

She stepped away. "I want you to do something for me."

He wanted to say "anything." Instead, he only asked, "What?"

"Dance with Pamela."

"You're serious?"

"Yes."

There was a quiet strength in her expression. She gave him an easy nod and then lifted her chin a fraction. God, he wanted to kiss those full lips. Luckily for him, the band started to play another ballad, "Yesterday" by Paul McCartney.

They found the couple still dancing. Aaron cut in, and Pamela was more than willing to comply with his invitation. As he guided Pamela around the dance floor, he glanced over his shoulder and watched Hallie stroll back to their table arm in arm with Kevin.

****

"How did you do it?" Aaron turned the wheel of his silver-gray convertible and steered the sleek sports car out of the parking lot of Pete's Fishery and onto the quiet street. It was almost one thirty in the morning. The four of them had closed the place.

The top was down, and the night wind blew through Hallie's hair, whipping it around her face, thrilling her senses. Her heart was beating furiously. She had done what she set out to do, and she was proud of how she'd handled Kevin Carlyle. Thanks to her, ARK had acquired Lectra-Pro.

She shrugged. "I only did some research. The rest fell into place."

"You did more than research."

"I told Kevin I understood how letting things go can be hard sometimes." They had stopped at a light on Avalon and Ocean Avenue. "He told me about losing his first wife, Catherine, to breast cancer. And we just went on from there. It was an insightful talk."

"But you even knew his and Pamela's wedding song."

"That part was easy. Society page archives. There was a big write-up on their wedding and reception, and their first dance was to 'Unchained Melody.' I just asked the band to play it."

"Amazing."

"The sixties music tonight made him remember Catherine in a good way. I merely pointed out that when we lose someone, it's devastating and you feel you can't go on. And then, one day, when you least expect it, someone comes into your life and changes everything. Love changes everything." She waited for a reaction, but he was quiet as he drove toward Route 71. "Oh, I forgot. You don't believe in love." She clamped her lips. Maybe she shouldn't have said that, at least not in that mildly sarcastic way of hers. Still no reply. Maybe he hadn't heard her. He continued to stare straight ahead at the darkened road.

She decided to go on. "When I was at Harvard, there was a student. He was seventy years old, and his name was Marvin Shelguard. We called him Mr. Shelly."

He whistled softly. "Seventy?" At least he was responding again.

"He never finished high school, so he got his GED and applied to the University and was accepted. He was a bright man, and he'd scraped up enough money for tuition."

"What did he do for a living?"

"Maintenance for a local elementary school. Whenever we students complained about how hard we had it with exams and studying, he reminded us how lucky we were to have this time in our lives for a chance at an education. How he had to wait so long for his turn. Mr. Shelly was big on the concept of time."

"It's an inspiring story, but what does it have to do with Kevin Carlyle?"

"Kevin Carlyle is like Mr. Shelly. Like most people, really. He wants to feel like he's contributing something to the world. Kevin was afraid if he let ARK buy him out, he'd have nothing. But I convinced him if he did, he'd have the greatest gift of all. Time. Time with Pamela that he hadn't had with Catherine." Her heart lurched. *Time.* She thought about that word and about the time she had left with her mother. She bit down on her lip and managed to quash a tear that threatened to fall.

"Did Mr. Shelly graduate?"

She shook her head, grateful he wasn't looking at her. "He died of a stroke three months into the first semester." This time, she quickly wiped away a lone tear that she couldn't stop.

"I'm sorry." He sounded sincere.

"We think we have all the time in the world, but it can be taken from us in the matter of a moment."

"Wise words for one so young."

"Now you sound like Mr. Shelly."

He laughed. "I'll take that as a compliment." He looked over at her.

Suddenly, discussing what she considered so sad and so poignant was too much to handle. Her mind was in turmoil, her heart in an uproar. She couldn't stop thinking about her mother and her deteriorating existence. Time wasn't on either of their sides. She wanted to get back home to the city.

"I kept him on, you know."

She was confused. "Who?"

"Carlyle. He's going to consult for us, two, three times a week."

It felt good to smile. "Thank you, Mr. Knight."

"Aaron."

Her muscles stiffened. "I shouldn't." The air around them was charged with tension.

"No harm in trying."

"Aaron," she repeated.

When they arrived at the house, he pulled into the driveway in front of the wrought iron gates. They swung open slowly. He drove the car up to the porch and turned off the motor. The air was dense and quiet. The calm before the storm.

"I don't know how to thank you for tonight."

"Well, that's what I get paid for."

"Yes. Indeed."

Dribs of water hit her bare arms. She looked toward the sky. A lone raindrop hit her squarely on the cheek. "It's starting to rain."

"Yes, it is." He leaned toward her. His scent, spicy and compelling, filled her. Even in the dark, she could feel the weight of his burning gaze on her. Reaching over, he gently swiped the drop away with his thumb.

Hallie's lower lip quivered. This was insane. What was he doing? What was she doing? Whatever was happening here was more inappropriate than calling him by his given name.

"Is something wrong?"

Her mind seesawed back and forth. Everything was wrong.

Uneasy over his next move, she veered her gaze away from him and fumbled with the door handle. "Good night," she whispered. Without so much as a backward glance, she alighted from the car, ran up the porch steps, and hurried inside the house.

Chapter Eight

A soft amber glow from the streetlamps cascaded in through the windows, casting murky shadows throughout the house. Outside, a gentle rain continued to fall.

Alone at the island in the kitchen, Aaron poured himself a glass of single malt scotch, swallowed a generous gulp, and grimaced. Before finishing what remained, he filled the glass again halfway, hoping the expensive booze would make him forget what had just happened. Or at the very least, dull his out-of-control senses. But it didn't take him long to realize that even if he got blindingly drunk, he wouldn't be able to ignore the attraction he felt for his new employee.

Damn! Who knew that wiping away an insignificant raindrop on Hallie's cheek could cause so much havoc inside him? It'd been an instinctive gesture of kindness. A cerebral act. Why then couldn't he stop thinking about it? About her? His thumb throbbed as he massaged it with the side of his index finger.

He suddenly needed to know everything about her. Her likes. Her dislikes. Did she have siblings? Were her parents living? Was there a special someone in her life? That thought bothered him, and he forced it from his mind.

Another bother was that first-name nonsense. It was apparent she didn't want that familiarity between them. Her hesitation and stammering told him as much. Had he forced her to call him Aaron? He had no intention of pushing her. That was the last thing on his mind. It just seemed natural. But when she didn't reciprocate with her own name, he realized he'd acted inappropriately, if not foolishly.

For his own sanity he re-ran the evening in his head in order to understand why this woman affected him in such a way.

Hallie Cavanagh, Harvard graduate, wasn't just a pretty face. She was intelligent, personable, and ambitious. He could clearly see how those qualities might be attractive to someone like him. But the rest of her qualities? The care she'd taken to make sure Kevin Carlyle was comfortable with the deal? The concern she had for the man's feelings?

His throat burned as he gulped the rest of the scotch. He poured another half glass and mulled over the rest of the evening. He'd surprised himself when he asked her to dance. Holding her close had aroused so many conflicting emotions. She'd fit so well in his arms, her body molding to his. He couldn't remember the last time he'd held a woman who made him feel that special.

Hallie had accomplished the nearly impossible. His company had been chasing after Lectra-Pro for years. It had taken a mere neophyte to accomplish what he could not. And she had done it with integrity, grace, and something he thought he had no use for—compassion.

He shook his head as a strange emotion took hold. Compassion. Tonight he had experienced it and truly understood it. She had a genuine compassion for people. He'd heard the caring in her voice when she told the story of Mr. Shelly, the school maintenance man. He'd realized her thoughtfulness when she relayed the talk she'd had with Kevin Carlyle.

If it weren't for her kind heart, he'd have bought Lectra-Pro and tossed Carlyle to the curb. What did he need a consultant for? He had a team of people who would run that business. But watching Hallie tonight had given him pause. He'd never had use for kind people. Kindness meant weakness, and it didn't mix with his personality.

Of course, he was always generous with his wealth. He gave millions to charities, particularly those for children in abusive situations. But he never saw the need to get close enough to really understand the plight of the human condition, especially those less fortunate.

His grandfather would always quote from entrepreneur and motivational speaker Jim Rohn. "If you really want to do something, you'll find a way. If you don't, you'll find an excuse." He could never understand why those who were down and out didn't just dig themselves out of the hole they were in and stop making excuses for everything.

But sometimes it didn't work that way. Sometimes people needed help.

Hallie knew that. She was true…real…everything he wasn't—and that frightened him.

Business aside, he'd almost crossed a line tonight with that damn raindrop. With a flick of his thumb, he had dabbed it away, and though it seemed a trivial thing to do, truth was that tiny gesture stirred up more feelings than he could handle. For tonight, he'd had every intention of kissing her.

He left the glass of scotch and went over to the

double glass doors that made the deck and backyard accessible. After opening the door, he breathed in the damp air and let it swirl around his heated body.

That's what I get paid for...

Those words—her words—had stopped him. Was she gently reminding him of her position in the company and not in his life? Of course she was. She had every right to do that, and he was a fool for thinking otherwise. He'd forget about tonight. Forget about his feelings. There was no room inside him for those dangerous sentiments. It didn't matter how Hallie had gone about procuring the company. Lectra-Pro was his, and that was all that mattered.

The ring of a phone broke into his thoughts. He closed the patio door and frowned. His cell was still at the bottom of the pool. He turned and saw the landline phone on the counter. Who would be calling so early in the morning? More than that—the number was a private one.

"Hello?" His voice was hesitant, if not annoyed.

No answer. No breathing. No one.

"Hello?" he repeated, more firmly this time. "Who is this?"

Click.

He placed the phone back in the cradle and shrugged.

Someone had the wrong number.

****

Hallie turned over in the bed and stared at the ceiling. Her mind raced. For a good hour, she'd been listening to the rain softly falling outside. Worry kept her awake. Inside her, conflicted and confusing emotions clashed. Try as she might, she couldn't stop thinking about Aaron.

Her stomach coiled into a knot. She could have refused. She could have reminded him of her status. There were a hundred excuses she could have made. Instead, she'd said, "Aaron."

At least she hadn't invited him to do the same with her. The corporate wall between them might have a crack in it, but it hadn't toppled over in the debris of unwelcomed intimacy. Or had it?

The night had been magical. She'd enjoyed Aaron's laughter, his determination, and the way he held her as they danced. She even appreciated the fact he'd listened to her when she talked about Kevin and Mr. Shelly without being critical. But it was the gentleness of his touch as he wiped away the raindrop from her cheek that she kept replaying in her mind. Had the gesture merely been a knee-jerk reaction, or did it mean more to him? Startled, she sat up in bed. Did his touch mean more to her?

She shook her head and sighed. The alarm clock on the night table glowed 2:37. She got out of bed, walked over to the atrium doors, and opened them. The rain, now all but a soft mist as light as an angel's breath, moved over the town. Tall grasses around the property rippled gently as the wind whispered through the wispy, fine blades. She took a deep breath. The air was fresh and wild. The ocean's breeze fluttered the sheer curtains, tickling her arms and face. The sound of the restless waves rolling onto the shore reached her ears.

Dressed in cotton pajama bottoms and a tank top, she stepped onto the deck, her eyes adjusting to the night. The streetlights illuminated the wet pavement below, making it shimmer like precious jewels. She looked up. The clouds had parted, leaving behind a partially full moon. Stars crowded the indigo sky. She'd never seen so many of these twinkling little gems before. Where she lived, the city's neon lights obscured them, but here, out in the open, without much artificial lighting, they were brilliant and mesmerizing. She nearly gasped when she witnessed a falling star streaking across the night sky. She'd never seen anything so spectacular. A childhood memory leaped into her head, and she closed her eyes tightly and made a wish.

Please help Aaron believe in love.

She wasn't certain why she made the wish, or even why the thought popped into her head. Maybe it was the way he seemed to flounder tonight, reluctant to expose his true emotions. Her heart grew heavy. She opened her eyes. Her knees went weak, and she grabbed onto the railing in front of her. What was that?

The sound of a door closing and the creaking of the porch stairs echoed in the damp air. Curious at the sound, she peered over the railing. Someone was walking away from the house. Hallie held her breath. It was Aaron.

He was still up and still dressed in the clothes he'd worn tonight. She watched as he followed the cobblestone path to the street and then climbed a set of wooden steps that led to a walkway over the sand dunes and to the ocean. As he moved farther away, the night swallowed him. Maybe he couldn't fall asleep either. Her heart thumped madly. It was none of her business what he did, yet she remained at the railing, her eyes watching for his return.

Ten to fifteen minutes later, he walked back toward

the house. He came to a dead stop at the beginning of the path leading to the porch. The light from a streetlamp encircled him, bathing him in a soft glow. She gasped when he suddenly looked up, his gaze locking on her.

****

Aaron wasn't sure where this mood was coming from, but a rippling tide of joy washed over him when he saw Hallie on the deck above. She was looking out toward the ocean. What had kept her awake? Was she thinking of him? Had she even seen him? Should he forget everything about their work relationship and go to her? If he did that, he knew what would happen. He didn't want to begin something he couldn't—or wouldn't—finish.

He slowed his thoughts and tried to pretend he hadn't seen her. If tomorrow she would ask him about tonight, he could play dumb or disregard her completely. But did he really want to do that to her? Belittle her? Make her feel worthless? Never. Not after tonight. Not after any night.

Gazing up at her obscured face, he wondered if she was reliving those same moments he'd been mulling over. Was she thinking about their time together? How they'd danced? Laughed? Surrounded by others tonight, he'd felt as though they were the only two people left in the world.

An inexplicable emptiness settled in his stomach. He enjoyed seeing his employees react to his orders, relished watching them scramble to please him. So why was he acting so skittish around Hallie?

He thought about her sitting next to him in his car, recalled the story she had told of the old man, evoked the way she had looked, vulnerable yet unshakable. And then came that tiny trifling drop of rain glistening on her cheek. How could a mere touch of her face cause all this friction within him? All he wanted to do at that moment was hold her in his arms and kiss her with long, deep kisses until the two of them couldn't breathe. But he knew in his soul that once he did that, there was no going back. There'd be no way he could stop himself from making love to her.

He believed he was always that man who could have anything or anyone he wanted.

But he had found out tonight it wasn't always that simple.

That tide of joy now turned into something ugly. Something violent. He tried to hold them back, but dark pieces from his past had begun to surface tonight and continued to gnaw at the back of his brain.

When it had come to his family, the outside world had perceived them as the perfect unit. The family that had everything. He almost laughed out loud but swallowed the snicker instead. It tasted bitter. Vindictive. No one knew of the terrible moments, the frightful moments he'd kept hidden for many years. Not until that long-ago night when all hell had broken loose.

He shook his head. Hallie had no idea what demons she'd conjured up in him, and he didn't want her to know. Even now, it made him sick to his stomach to recall what he had done to save his family.

A damp breeze blew across his body. He breathed in the freshly washed air, needing it to calm his whirlwind of emotions. He concentrated on business, on Lectra-Pro, on anything that might make the menacing thoughts go away, but it was no use. The more he fought, the more frustrated he became. What bothered him was that sometimes, he didn't feel sorry for what he'd done. Did that make him a horrible person? A monster? Maybe.

He turned, his gaze on the ocean instead of on her, hoping Hallie would lose interest and venture back inside. The distant-yet-troubling memories became stronger, and he knew they'd never be completely erased from his life. In the eyes of the law, he was still a criminal, plain and simple. Although he'd been careful to keep that part of his life buried all these years, he also knew the sins of the past could surface at any given moment. And a woman like Hallie would never understand. Never.

With a heavy heart, he climbed the porch steps and went back into the house.

****

"Mr. Knight's not here, Ms. Cavanagh."

Rita's words stunned Hallie. "What?"

The atrium doors in the kitchen were wide open, allowing the ocean breeze to blow through. It was a beautiful day, and Hallie had expected to spend some of it with Aaron.

"He left very early this morning." The housekeeper stopped whisking the batter in the large ceramic bowl and looked at Hallie. "He didn't tell you?"

"No." She managed a casual tone, even though she felt like a fool. "Do you expect him back?"

Rita shook her head. "The man comes and goes as he pleases, I'm afraid." She began to carefully spoon the batter into a muffin tin on the kitchen counter. "Blueberry. They'll be ready in about—" She stopped. "Is everything all right?"

"I'm just surprised." *And confused. And angry?* The sentiment crossed her mind. Was it business? Was it just on a whim? Or did Aaron's leaving without telling her have to do with last night?

But last night couldn't have been more successful. He had certainly been pleased she'd secured Lectra-Pro for ARK Enterprises. She conjured up images of the two of them dancing and laughing. Conversation with the Carlyles had been entertaining. Talk between her and Aaron had been light and fun. On the way back to the house, she'd divulged something personal that had touched her life. She'd thought he'd find her story about Mr. Shelly boring. Maybe the story had affected him in some way. But was that a reason to leave Sea Girt?

Of course, there'd been more to the evening. She knew that. When he had gently wiped away the raindrop from her cheek, excitement had rippled through her. She hadn't expected it. The feeling had caught her by surprise. Had Aaron experienced something as well? Was he embarrassed? Pleased? Had he wanted more?

Only hours ago their gazes had met. She on the balcony, him standing below. They'd been like some corporate Romeo and Juliet. Everything around her had seemed to fade away, except for the two of them. Had he sensed the same feelings?

But now, he was gone. And gone alone. He hadn't called. There was no text. No email. Not even an old-fashioned note on her pillow. No. Aaron didn't seem like a note-writing type of man. Still, he could have communicated his sudden absence in some way.

Perhaps putting some distance between them was

his way of managing. Her stomach clenched. Managing what? Managing her? Them? What was he thinking? Did he envision the two of them together in more than just a business relationship?

Her last thought quickly unraveled as she shook the image from her mind. She was making too much of this. No matter what, he was her boss. She was his employee. There would never be—*could* never be—something more between them.

"Did he say where he where he was going?" Hallie asked.

"Back to the city, I assume. He did leave instructions for Nelson to bring you home when you were ready." Rita slipped the filled muffin tin into the oven.

How cordial of him.

"I think I'm ready now." A twinge of disillusionment made her voice quiver.

"You can stay as long as you like, Ms. Cavanagh. It's a beautiful day and the pool—"

Hallie didn't hear much of anything else Rita said. She thanked the housekeeper for everything, sought out Nelson, and set her sights for home.

****

"In here, darling."

Aaron turned the corner and found himself face-to-face with Miranda. She sat deeply on the gray leather sectional, one slender leg crossed over the other. She wore a white, belted raincoat and black stilettos. Even this early in the morning, she looked terrific—and quite dangerous.

His hands curled into fists. "It's nine in the freakin' morning, Miranda. How the hell did you get in here?"

"Good morning to you, too, Aaron. I've been calling you, but you're not answering your phone." Her smile was tight. "You're not avoiding me, are you? Because that wouldn't be very nice."

Avoiding her? What he wanted to do was throttle her.

"Aren't you happy to see me?"

"I asked you a question."

"Darling, the doorman and I are like this." She laughed and crossed her middle finger over her index. Gracefully, she got to her feet and sashayed over to him, her heels clicking on the dark wooden floor. She leaned into him, grabbed his tie, pulled him toward her, and kissed him hard.

He pushed her away immediately and wiped his mouth with the back of his hand. Her citrusy perfume cloyed his senses. "Get out, Miranda. Now."

She only smiled and undid the belt, letting the raincoat fall to the floor, revealing her black lace bra and panties. "Are you sure you want me to leave?"

He picked up the coat and shoved it at her. "Don't embarrass yourself. Put this on and go."

When she refused to take the raincoat, he threw it back on the floor.

"The last time we spoke, you were rather harsh with me, darling. I didn't care for your tone or your attitude."

He gritted his teeth and refrained from physically tossing her out the door. A thought raced through his mind. "Did you call me this morning and then hang up?"

"Where have you been all this time? I had to hire an escort to take me to the Andersons' damn Black and

White Charity Ball last night. Do you know how humiliating that was?" Anger wrinkled her face and thickened her voice.

"I told you I wasn't going. No, I don't owe you an explanation. Whatever this is between us was never meant to be permanent. You know that." He stared into her large brown eyes curtained with heavy, dark lashes. They smoldered without mercy.

"No matter what we agreed upon, you've never been too busy for me, Aaron. For us." Her smile held a hint of smugness. "Who is she?"

Beneath his restraint lay an edge of fury and frustration. "We're done here, Miranda. Now get out before I forget I'm a gentleman."

"There *is* someone else, isn't there?" Her expression seethed with silent rage. "For one so cautious with emotions, you certainly are transparent now. It's almost laughable."

She scooped up her raincoat and held it out to him. Against his better judgment, he helped her into it.

She turned and tied the belt loosely. When she looked at him again, she smiled with a chilling calmness. "I'm sure whoever this little trinket is will bore you in a couple of days." She stroked his chin. "I can wait."

"Get it through your head, Miranda. It's over between us."

But before she reached the front door, she turned. Her eyes sharpened with a powerful glare. "Just don't forget, darling, I know the real you. And once your little friend knows, she'll run as far away from you as she can."

Chapter Nine

It was her first official day at ARK Enterprises. Hallie was anxious to meet her coworkers, settle in her new office, and start earning her paycheck—for real. Not that the Lectra-Pro deal wasn't part of her earnings. She was more than ready to tackle whatever her job entailed. The thought of seeing Aaron again had her head in a tailspin. What would she say to him? What would he say? Would he offer any kind of explanation as to why he'd left Sea Girt without telling her? Had he already forgotten about the intimacy of his touch or the way their gazes locked onto one another Saturday night?

Nursing a twinge of humiliation yesterday, she'd left the house hastily. She hoped she hadn't insulted Rita, but blueberry muffins or not, there was no reason to stay. She was back in Manhattan ninety minutes later. Nelson helped her carry her bags to her apartment.

"Is there anything else I can do for you, miss?" he asked.

She managed a grin. "No, Nelson. You've been very kind."

He left quickly after that, mumbling something about seeing her again. Hallie doubted that. Nothing personal. It was all about ARK Enterprises now.

Sophie was at work. Sunday was a busy day at

Central Parx. Hallie was glad. Sophie would have had a lot of questions as well, and they would all be about Aaron. She wasn't ready to divulge.

Once settled, she called the nursing home. She was told by one of the nurses that her mother had shown signs of agitation during the night, but all was well now. Hallie went to Golden Living later that afternoon. The nurse was right. Her mother, now in a private room, was sleeping soundly.

Hallie kept busy shuffling through some old photographs in a wooden box that she had found while cleaning out her mother's house. On the lid of the box was a stamped painting of a Native American man wearing a colorful headdress. Below the image were the words *The Poconos*. It was one of those cheap souvenirs sold in gift shops in Pennsylvania.

The aged Kodak and Polaroid photographs were mostly of her mother's family and friends. Many Hallie had never known. She had thought it a good idea to use them to help spark her mother's memory. On her visits, Hallie had patiently and painstakingly showed her mother each picture. With brow creased and lips pursed, her mother had studied the photographs, catching them from every angle, scanning the dates or names written on the back in now faded ink. And though Hallie would hope against hope, her mother had never recognized anyone.

"I start a new job tomorrow, Mom," Hallie whispered. "We won't have to worry about money anymore."

Her mother answered with a faint snore and continued to sleep.

"There's this man." She faltered for a moment.

"He's my boss." She had no idea why she had chosen to tell her mother about Aaron. "I've spent some time with him—strictly business, Mom. But there's something between us, and I'm scared. I don't want to be hurt again." She stopped when a nurse appeared at the doorway. A blush heated her face.

"Visiting hours are over," the nurse said.

"Thank you."

The nurse left, and Hallie got to her feet. She leaned over and kissed her mother on her forehead. "I'll try to get here tomorrow, okay?" A twinge of disappointment pinched her heart. She didn't want to leave. Like any daughter, she wanted her mother's advice. She wanted to know if what she was feeling for Aaron was true or if she was just caught up in the hype. A million questions ran through her mind, but her mother wouldn't be able to answer a single one.

This morning Hallie had woken up early and left quickly, but not before checking on her roommate. Snoring reverberated throughout her bedroom. Sophie was a heavy sleeper. Hallie doubted Sophie even knew she'd come home. Tonight would be time enough to explain almost all of what had happened in Sea Girt.

Dressed in a cobalt blue blouse with a black pencil skirt and matching jacket, her hair fashioned into a high, sleek ponytail, Hallie felt confident and ready. She took the number three train from Penn Station. It promptly let her off in the Wall Street District. The Starbucks across the street was calling her name. She made a quick stop and reappeared on the busy New York streets, clutching a soy latte.

ARK Towers was an impressive skyscraper that soared above all the others on the block. Sharp, straight lines and large glass windows made it look like some ultra-sleek rocket about to take off to the moon. Hallie stood on the sidewalk in front of the steps into the building and looked up. Even though the sun was hidden, the windows still shimmered like the stars she'd seen that night at the beach. It was the second time she had seen the tower up close, this time as an employee, but that didn't make it any less intimidating.

She eyed the people entering and exiting the huge glass doors and wondered if some were Aaron's employees. ARK Enterprises occupied about three-quarters of the offices throughout the building. Lavelle Andrews had told her financial companies and other businesses that could afford the rent occupied the rest.

Hallie took a deep breath and a sip of coffee and reminded herself she had already proven her worth with the acquisition of Lectra-Pro.

She squared her shoulders, entered the building, and took the express elevator to the forty-fifth floor. She walked to the reception area, her heels clinking rhythmically on the white and gray marble tile. Around her, people hurried to and from their destinations.

"Good morning," she said to the young woman sitting behind the elongated counter. Behind her on the dark, wood-paneled wall were the words *ARK Enterprises* spelled out in huge stainless-steel letters. "I'm Hallie—"

"Yes, Ms. Cavanagh. Welcome to the team." The woman smiled warmly like they had known each other since kindergarten. "Mr. Knight left these for you. It's this week's schedule." She handed Hallie a black folder embossed with the company's name.

Hallie thanked her. She turned away from the

receptionist when she heard someone call her name. Lavelle Andrews was headed right for her. She looked stunning in a navy-blue jacket and matching skirt. Her light brown hair, fashioned in a topknot the last time Hallie had met her, was now soft and wavy and very chic. Hallie had guessed Lavelle was in her forties, but seeing her now, she might have miscalculated.

"Good morning, Hallie. I hope you're rested. You've quite a busy day today." Lavelle sounded almost menacing. "I've gathered your team in the conference room."

Nerves dancing in her stomach, Hallie followed Lavelle down a hallway. A team? For a moment she'd forgotten her job description. She was executive director of acquisitions. Of course she'd have a team. They stopped at closed double doors.

"Ready?"

Hallie took a breath, and Lavelle swung the door inward.

A large oval table and fifteen or more people filled the room. Some sat in the high-back leather chairs. Some stood around the perimeter of the room. All of their gazes were on her.

"Good morning, everyone," Lavelle started. "I'd like to introduce your new director of acquisitions, Ms. Hallie Cavanagh."

Their applause threw her for a moment. She felt like some movie star who had just walked into a roomful of star-struck fans. It was a little unnerving.

"Don't look so surprised," Lavelle whispered to her. "They've already heard about Lectra-Pro. Good job, by the way."

Hallie blinked. The ink on the contract was barely

dry, and already news of the merger was out. Had someone in the company lit up the social media boards with the announcement? Had Aaron?

Lavelle began the introductions. The two most important members of the acquisitions' team were Martin Rice, her second in charge, and Julian Saunders, her administrative assistant.

Hallie's voice wobbled a bit as she offered some impromptu words to her staff. Reality struck her full force. She couldn't tell if their smiles were authentic or insincere. Were they eager to work under someone new, or were they waiting for her to fail miserably? She'd have to wait and see.

The crowd soon dispersed, and Lavelle ushered Hallie out of the conference room. "I'm sure you'd like to see your office now."

If an office could be compared to what she thought Heaven might be like for the consummate business person, then this was definitely that place. The enormity alone got her attention, not to mention the panoramic view of the city outside her panels of windows. Her desk, consisting of a glass surface atop stainless-steel legs, was sleek and modern. A PC and a laptop took up one half of the desk space. A gray leather chair behind it looked inviting. Empty shelves lined the walls. The floor was mottled with colors of gray, white, and black, and a large area rug, echoing the same colors as the floor, anchored the gray leather sectional couch. Though the decor was purely Aaron's taste, she liked the look. She was eager to bring her own style to the place with maybe a plant or picture of her and her mom.

"What do you think?" Lavelle asked.

"Well, I'm definitely not in Kansas anymore," she

quipped. "It's a lot to take in."

A glint of amusement sparkled in Lavelle's brown eyes. "Here, let me show you how to work a few things." She crossed the room to a thin wooden table behind the couch and lifted a hinged panel set in the top, exposing a line of dials and buttons. "This one's for music. There's a list of stations to choose from." She pressed one of the buttons, and soothing New Age music drifted through a hidden speaker system. "Of course, if you're like me, there's good old-fashioned rock 'n' roll." She turned a dial, and Bruce Springsteen wailed "Born to Run." Lavelle winked at Hallie. "My guilty pleasure." She pressed something, and the music stopped. "Now this dial adjusts the lights, and this one is for the television."

Hallie looked around. "Television?"

Lavelle pushed another button, and the abstract artwork gracing the wall suddenly faded, and in its place was a sixty-inch television screen.

"I thought that was a—"

"Painting? Pretty cool, huh?"

Hallie bit her lip. The last word she expected Lavelle Andrews to use was cool. "Yes, very cool."

Lavelle, now holding what looked like a remote control, pointed it at the TV. The screen came to life with a twenty-four-hour news station. "Just a few channels. All business-related. I'm afraid you can't watch your soaps here."

Was that a dig? Of course not. It was merely friendly girl chatter. "I don't watch soaps. Never had the time."

Lavelle then pointed the remote at the windows. Hallie watched in awe as the gray, silk drapes slid closed, cutting off the view. She opened them again with another touch of a button.

Hallie shook her head. "I never expected all this. It's crazy."

"That's Mr. Knight. Only the best for his top executive team."

She casually scanned the city through the glass, not wanting to appear too anxious. "Is he here?"

"I'm afraid not. He has meetings across town today, and he's not expected back until much later this afternoon."

"Oh." Hallie did her best to hide her disappointment.

"Is that a problem?"

"No, I was just—never mind. I'm sure I'll see him when he returns."

"Well, that's all for now. Julian will be in to brief you about your meetings today. It's going to be a busy day for you." Lavelle smiled and then headed for the door. "If you need anything or have any questions, don't hesitate. I'm only a buzz away."

She regarded the phone on the desk. "Thank you, Lavelle. Your support means everything to me."

"You're most welcome. Good luck to you." And with those kind words, Aaron's highly efficient assistant left the office.

Hallie sighed and checked her watch. It was only 9:55, and she was already exhausted. Her head was spinning, and the thought of diving right into the business at hand was as overwhelming as it was exhilarating.

She sat on the couch, opened the folder, and found her agenda for the day. Mentally, she checked them off one by one.

10:30 a.m. Staff meeting

12:00 p.m. Meeting with reps from Millennium Works

1:20 p.m. Lunch with Board Members in Executive Dining Room

Lavelle was right. It was going to be a busy day. She'd better get her shit together.

Hallie glanced at the agenda again. Strange. The last entry was handwritten. She stared at the message, and a small burst of joy rippled through her as she read...

6:00 p.m. Forgiving the guy who stupidly ran out on you.

****

"It's after six. Shouldn't you be home in your pajamas nursing a glass of wine and sniffling over some romantic movie?"

Blurry-eyed, Hallie glanced up from the remaining contracts strewn across her desk. Composed at the entrance of her office, Aaron looked as handsome as ever, his navy-blue suit jacket hanging open, revealing his blue-and-white striped shirt and red print tie. Even after a full day, he seemed refreshed and invigorated, ready to battle another round of meetings.

She couldn't still her wildly beating heart. His words were lighthearted and flirty, confusing her. She leaned back and eyed him intently. "Can't. Too much work. My boss is a stickler."

He frowned. "Your boss sounds like a real douche." A humorless smile curved the edge of his lips.

She remained indifferent to his attempt at humor and gave him an annoyed look he couldn't miss.

Besides, she agreed with him. Leaving Sea Girt without telling her bordered on douche status. "I have one more thing on my agenda, but I'm not sure it warrants my immediate attention."

He moved closer to her desk. "Really? What's that?"

His fresh scent, clean with sexy undertones, was driving her crazy. "I'm supposed to forgive someone for running out on her."

His demeanor changed. His gaze was now quiet, solemn, and apologetic. Their gazes locked.

"I believe that someone was you."

He hung his head. "I'm...I'm sorry. I should have never left."

Silently, she zeroed in on his contrite look, making her wonder what thoughts were running through his mind. "You don't have to explain." She meant it. "You're the boss."

He took a breath. "But I want to. You deserve that much. Let me make it up to you. Are you free for dinner?"

His question took her by surprise. "Tonight?"

"Tonight."

She blinked. "I...I'm not sure."

"You're not sure if you're free, or not sure you want to go to dinner with me?"

"I..."

"You're not sure it's appropriate."

"Is it? You're my boss."

"So you keep telling me. It's just dinner." He looked thoughtful for a few seconds. "Would you feel better if we called it a business dinner?"

"How so?"

"Well, I never formally congratulated you on the Lectra-Pro merger. We can start there." A silent question lingered in his eyes. "What do you say, Hallie?"

Caught off guard, she blinked in surprise. She had been toying with the idea of telling him how inappropriate it was for her to call him by his name. Now what would she say?

One of his eyebrows rose. "Why are you looking at me like that?"

"You called me by my first name."

"So I did." He gave her a brief, lopsided grin. "Is that okay?"

With a joyous heart, Hallie nodded.

****

He had actually asked permission to call her Hallie. Suddenly, that one tiny change made a huge difference in how he thought about her. Usually people had to earn his respect. But with Hallie, he craved it from her. A strange turn of events, no doubt.

Now, as they headed for the parking garage, he sensed the notion of familiarity. Days ago, she'd been in his arms, the both of them swaying to a retro love song. Later, he'd dabbed that damn raindrop from her face, and a pang of longing had shot through him. It was that longing that disturbed him and made him leave Sea Girt without telling her. With his emotions rough, chafed, and sore, he just couldn't face her the next day. He fought to hold onto his feelings, no matter how strong they seemed to be. He couldn't bear the rejection.

But now his thoughts were blindsided. A barb of heat sliced through his gut. Awareness filled his every pore, even the air he was breathing. Did she feel it, too? True, she was apprehensive about spending the evening with him, even though it was only dinner. He understood that. Boss and employee relationships weren't always the smartest connections in the corporate world. It was a hard, fast rule.

He was getting ahead of himself. Maybe she just saw him as the boss, the guy who had the power to hire and fire and sign the paychecks. Yet she must have sensed something between them on the dance floor, in the car, and as she stood on her bedroom balcony staring down at him.

Might there be a chance for the two of them? His mind was in overdrive, and these strange emotions set his mind reeling. Who was he kidding? She'd never understand the life he'd had before the golden one he was living now.

Before they left the office, Hallie had made reservations at a place called Central Parx.

"You know, the last time you suggested a place to eat, we ended up in a dive." The elevator doors opened, and a hint of gasoline fumes drifted through the garage.

"That dive was integral in getting what you wanted," she said, defending her decision.

He shot her a sideways glance. She was right. He couldn't argue with that. But what did he really want? Lectra-Pro—or her?

He greeted Darrell, the garage attendant. The man hustled to get Aaron's car.

"You'll like this place," Hallie said as he drove the car up the ramp and into the busy city street. "I have an 'in' with the head chef."

"Really. Well, I guess I'll have to trust your

instincts once again."

The lilt of her laughter put him at ease. "I guess you will."

City traffic being what it was, they arrived at the place thirty minutes later. From the outside, Central Parx looked like most city restaurants—brick front, glass windows, low lighting. But once inside, Aaron took in the understated elegance and calming nature of the place.

He followed Hallie into the main dining area. A young woman, dressed in chef's whites, was waiting for them. She and Hallie hugged, and he realized quickly the two knew each other well.

"Sophie Fletcher, this is my boss—"

"I know," Sophie interrupted. Her smile couldn't fit her face. "Hello, Mr. Knight. Welcome to Central Parx."

"It's my pleasure," he said.

"Sophie's my roommate. She owns the place," Hallie continued. "More importantly, she's the executive chef here. Be prepared for something spectacular."

He was impressed.

Sophie ushered them to a table in a private corner. A chilled bottle of white wine, peeking out from a stainless-steel bucket, was waiting for them. She announced a special menu she'd created just for the two of them.

The two of them settled in their seats, and Aaron couldn't pull his gaze away from Hallie. Being with her, watching the candlelight flickering across her beautiful face, made him realize the depth of his desire to get to know her better. Maybe tonight he would. He reached for the bottle of wine and poured them each a glass. "Is everything okay?"

"Yes, why?"

"You seem anxious."

"Just erring on the side of caution."

"Is it being with me?"

She bit her bottom lip.

His body tightened like a bowstring. "If you're worried about the boss-slash-employee thing, I told you this is a business dinner."

"So you said. However, you've yet to back up that claim." Her no-nonsense tone was sending him into a tailspin.

He cleared his throat and raised his glass. "Congratulations on acquiring Lectra-Pro, Miss Cavanagh. Even though your methods were somewhat unorthodox, you really came through for the company. To a long and prosperous working relationship." They clinked glasses, and he took a healthy sip of wine. He leaned back. "Is that 'business' enough for you? Because I can continue."

She parted her lips in silent invitation. "Go on."

"How was your first official day at ARK?"

"Busy, but good."

"The staff?"

"Welcoming."

"Your office?"

"Amazing."

He kept his gaze focused on her. "And that, Miss Cavanagh, concludes the business portion of the night."

****

The first course, warm goat cheese in a caramelized onion tart followed by a roasted baby beet salad, tasted creamy and savory. Their entrée was another winner. Pan-seared salmon served over a sweet rice pilaf with pomegranates. Later, the classic New York cheesecake and French press coffee was the perfect ending to a perfect meal, all thanks to Chef Sophie.

Between courses, Hallie was first to start the conversation. "So tell me about ARK Enterprises."

"I thought we were done with business."

"I'd like to know its history. What makes your company such a success?"

"I'd rather know more about you."

Hallie's face heated as she met his gaze. Her skin prickled, and apprehension rippled down her back. "I asked you first." It was the only thing she could think of to say. She just wasn't comfortable talking about herself.

"All right. You win. This time." He sat back. "What makes ARK such a success? Well, that would be me. Not to brag or anything."

"Of course not." The way he smiled at her was downright sinful.

"You don't really want to know, do you?"

His reluctance to tell the backstory of the company made her curious. She hardly viewed him as shy. Was he holding back for a reason?

"I wouldn't have asked if I didn't."

He relented and spoke of his maternal grandfather's belief in his business acumen and his monetary investment in his grandson's real estate start-up business. Under Malcolm Clark's stern tutelage, he made good decisions that rocketed him up the ladder of success.

"I really don't know how it happened. One minute I'm flipping burgers at McDonalds, and the next minute I'm overlooking the entire city from my executive suite. Truth is, sometimes I feel like a fraud."

Once again, something human emerged from the depths of his corporate existence. She had expected curt and sterile answers to her question. Instead, she got openness and sincerity. Not only did he enjoy talking about his accomplishments, he had a special place in his heart for his grandfather. That was the only family he'd mentioned.

In the course of conversation, Hallie realized the need he had to be accepted for who he was and not what he had. For all his money and success, all the material things he had accumulated, Aaron Knight was a man who was alone.

"Are you bored yet?"

She shook her head. "I find it fascinating." *I find you fascinating.*

He half grinned. "You're probably the only one." He finished the last bite of cheesecake on his plate. "This place was an excellent suggestion. I guess you're redeemed."

"I told you Sophie would do right by us."

"I have to confess something."

The sudden change of subject put her mind in a small panic. *Confessions are good for the soul*, her mother had once said. But this sounded ominous. What did he have to confess?

His smile slipped from his face. "This was more than just a simple business dinner. At least for me. I wanted to be with you tonight."

Her heart started to thump furiously. The awkward

pause between them was brief enough to take another sip of wine. She took a gulp. "What?"

"You seem surprised."

"A little."

"I meant what I said before. I want to get to know you better."

Confusion reigned. "In what way?"

"In every way."

She gripped the napkin that lay across her lap. *In every way*? "I'm not sure—"

"That it's a good idea?" he finished. "Are you hiding any deep dark secrets?"

Her mouth crinkled with a forced laugh. "No." But when she looked at him, his eyes had sharpened with stark concern, as though he were the one who was concealing something.

"Then you have nothing to worry about."

"It's not that. You're—"

"Yeah, I'm your boss, I know. You've mentioned it a few times."

She let go a concerned sigh. "Sorry. I'm just wary over where this is going or worse, where it'll end up. Doesn't ARK Enterprises have some sort of inter-office dating rule?"

"I am ARK Enterprises. I make the rules."

Frustration and curiosity did a dangerous dance inside her. Something clicked in her mind. "Why did you leave without telling me?" She was astonished at the sense of satisfaction she got from asking the question that had been gnawing at her. "Did I do something wrong?"

He drew back ever so slightly. Frown lines marred his brow. "Of course not. The evening was a success because of you."

"Then why?"

The look in his eyes was as turbulent as a summer storm, and the straight line of his jaw clenched. She drew in a disturbing breath.

"It was the way you befriended the Carlyles. How you considered Kevin's feelings when it came to his company. The company I so callously wanted to just pull out from under him."

"I'm good with people. I enjoy them."

"You do have a way about you."

"You should find that a plus."

"I do."

"Then why the quick exit?" Her mind whirled with conflicting thoughts.

"It was the rest of the night. How you felt in my arms when we danced. When I wiped away that raindrop from your cheek. And when I spotted you on the deck outside your room…something inside me, I'm not sure what, grabbed me by the throat and wouldn't let go. I'm cold-hearted and ruthless, Hallie. That's what people call me. Even when it comes to women, my pleasure comes first. Being in control is my MO. It's what keeps me sane. But with you… That's why I left. I felt I was losing that control."

"Because of me?"

He nodded, reached across the table, and covered her hand with his. Her pulse leaped with his touch. She should pull away. She didn't. Once again, she felt the heat of his stare.

"I couldn't face you. You have me confused and off my game." He shook his head. "I told you I was a fraud." His jaw set in a way she was coming to recognize. "Tell me something, Hallie. Do you really believe in love?"

"Yes."

"You make it sound so easy." His voice was strained with a need she didn't understand.

"What about you?"

He tilted his head. "What about me?"

"You don't believe in love."

"We're not talking about me." His gaze met hers with a force that shot through her. "What about forgiveness?"

"What about it?"

"If you forgive someone, isn't that a kind of love?"

His question was curious at best. Who wanted his forgiveness? Was it him? Forgiveness from what? For being cold-hearted and ruthless? Had he hurt people in business? People in his life?

Her heart caught in her throat. "What are you trying to say, Aaron?"

He stared at her, his expression expectant, his eyes filling with awareness. She braced herself. He was about to say something—something important. Something she knew would alter the way she felt about him. But he was silent.

The air in the room changed from expectancy to indifference. He drew back his hand. His expression transformed to a vague, somewhat elusive appearance. It was as though he never spoke the words he just had. She bit her lip, her thoughts spinning.

Aaron signaled for the check. The evening had come to an abrupt close, making Hallie doubt her feelings about the now seemingly uncaring man sitting across from her.

Not long after they were parked in front of her apartment, Aaron leaned back, his gaze focused ahead. "I enjoyed tonight."

Her shoulders slumped slightly. "So did I." *Except for the part when you shut down.*

He got out of the car and came over to her side. Offering his hand, he helped her alight from the car. "I'll walk you to the door." He sounded like a teenager at the end of prom.

"That's not necessary."

"My mother wouldn't have it any other way." His boyish grin set her heart thumping again.

"I'm a big girl. I think I can find my way—"

She looked up. Why was he standing so close? His spicy, masculine scent tickled her senses. His quick mood change threw her off balance. Was he going to kiss her? It sure seemed like he was heading in that direction. Did she want him to kiss her? Her stomach lurched. The wait was intolerable.

"I'll see you tomorrow at the office," Aaron said, once again becoming stiff and business-like.

Hallie stifled her disappointment. With a disturbed heart and a brave smile on her lips, she nodded. "Tomorrow." What else could she say?

Chapter Ten

"He likes you." A mischievous smile played around the corners of Sophie's mouth. Sophie had left Central Parx earlier than usual and was now sprawled out on Hallie's bed.

Even though it was past midnight, Hallie couldn't sleep. Thoughts of Aaron kept her awake. Though grateful for the distraction, she knew Sophie was intent on badgering her about the rest of the evening. Dressed in pajamas and clutching her pillow in front of her, she eyed her friend. "Stop saying that."

"He couldn't take his eyes off you. I watched him. The man has it bad."

"Sophie." Hallie's tone was cautious.

"What's the problem? It looked like you two were having a good time."

"We were."

"What happened?"

"Nothing, really. It's just a feeling I have." She backtracked and told Sophie about Sea Girt and all that had followed.

Sophie made a face. "So he pulled back a little. That doesn't mean he isn't interested. Maybe he does things slowly. That can be a plus, you know." Her exaggerated wink made Hallie smirk.

"I'm not sure if I'm interested."

"How can you not be? He's good looking. Dresses

well. He's mega-wealthy. What's not to like?"

"I don't know if I'm ready to allow someone into my life."

Sophie made a face. "Because of Kyle?"

Hallie shrugged.

"The guy's a loser. You deserve better."

"And you think Aaron is the one to help me forget about my past."

"Why not?"

Hallie buried her face in the pillow and mumbled.

Sophie sighed. "Look, get some sleep. Things will look better tomorrow. They always do." She crawled off the bed and headed for the door.

"Sophie?"

Sophie turned.

"Thanks. You're a good friend."

"Just remember me when you become Mrs. ARK Enterprises Billionaire Boss Man."

Hallie threw the pillow at her roommate, who caught it and threw it back, skimming the top of Hallie's head. Both women laughed and wished each other a good night.

Hallie sank into the mattress. Maybe she was making too much of this. Still, the things he'd said to her. He wanted to get to know her, to be with her, and yet the evening had fallen flat. He'd asked about forgiveness. About love. Conflicting emotions ran rampant through her mind as a pulse throbbed in her temples.

She rubbed her forehead, massaging away her confusion. She wasn't foolish enough to expect anything from Aaron. He had given her a plum job—no, a career. A lucrative career that would allow her to give her mother the care she needed.

Though it had been more than a year now since Kyle had called off their wedding, the sting of a broken heart still lingered. According to Sophie, the guy was a loser, and after all this time, Hallie had to agree.

Sighing, she turned off the light by her bedside and burrowed under the colorful patchwork quilt her mother had sewn. Sophie was right. Tomorrow was another day, and tomorrow always brought new promise.

****

"Did anybody come by to see me tonight, Christopher?"

Christopher, the white-haired doorman at the Beresford, the fourteen-story apartment building that housed Aaron's penthouse, furrowed his brow. "No, Mr. Knight. No one. At least from the time I've been here. I came on duty at five."

Giving the doorman a small nod, Aaron was confident he wouldn't be blindsided by Miranda's presence. He'd been quite adamant about calling things off between them. He could only hope she had taken his warning seriously.

Still, Miranda's ill-conceived threat loomed large in his mind. *I know the real you. And once your little friend knows, she'll run as far away from you as she can.*

He let go a breath. Of course, there was the chance she could go all *Fatal Attraction* on him. The knot in his stomach tightened. It was his fault for trusting her.

He checked his watch. It was a few minutes before midnight. After he dropped Hallie off at her apartment, he'd driven around the city, avoiding the traffic in Times Square and on Broadway. He'd needed to clear his head. Mindless driving sometimes did that for him. But after an hour, his mind was still filled with thoughts of her.

She'd looked beautiful tonight. Confident and approachable. He reflected back to their conversation. He'd been in control when he spoke about ARK Enterprises. Its history. Its meteoric rise in the corporate world. But when she'd brought up that night at the beach house, and how he left without a word, the self-assured, maybe arrogant man he knew so well started to disappear—and sitting there, across from her, he didn't know how to stop his descent into uncontrollability.

As they stood outside her apartment, he had fought the impulse to kiss her. Oh, he'd wanted to. His need had been great to hold her in his arms and brush his lips over her firm sexy ones. But when he didn't, those lips of hers had slipped into a small frown—a confused frown.

All those other women who flitted in and out of his life were no more than casual companions. The women knew it, too. He'd always been upfront with them, probably dashing their dreams of becoming a billionaire's wife. But they accepted his strict policy. No strings attached. Most likely, they thought they could change his mind. It never happened—nor would it. Not with women who only saw dollar signs. Except maybe for Miranda. She had her own wealth. She had always understood his need to control. But now…

He'd handle Miranda if it came to that.

Hallie was different than all these women. He wanted to get closer to her. He wanted her to be part of this ever-changing world of his.

"Is something the matter, Mr. Knight?"

Closing his eyes, Aaron expelled the thoughts battling in his brain. "No, Christopher. Thank you." He headed down the long, marble-tiled hallway toward the private elevators. "Good night."

"Good night, sir." Christopher's voice echoed through the dark green walls.

Aaron pressed the P1 button on the elevator panel. As the doors closed, he leaned back against the wood-paneled wall.

The relief he had conjured up became real when he realized the penthouse was indeed vacant. At last, he could breathe. He shrugged off his suit jacket, tossed it on the couch, and poured himself a scotch.

He gazed upon the untouchable beauty of the city. In the daylight the skyline was daunting with its sharp edges and imposing spires. But at night the buildings seemed to melt into one another, their silhouettes soft and welcoming.

Tonight had been wonderful and strange and disappointing all at the same time. Wonderful because he'd been with Hallie, strange because he never thought he'd talk about himself, and disappointing because he had closed himself off when the night was done. Why? The answer came to him. Trust.

Apprehension wormed its way down his back. He poured the drink down his throat in one gulp and shook away the sting. The imposing darkness of the penthouse weighed heavily upon him as he strode across the hardwood floor in silent frustration toward his bedroom.

He flicked on a switch, and a subtle light illuminated the space. Even with the soft amber glow, the room looked cold and lifeless. If he'd said the right words, would she have been his tonight? Would he have taken her to his bed? Would their bodies have gotten tangled in the cool sheets, their mouths melding and seeking, their minds connecting, their love exploding? The what-ifs had plagued his thoughts as he watched her climb the stairs and disappear behind the ornately carved wooden door of her apartment building. It'd nearly killed him when she didn't look back.

His heart heavy, Aaron went to his office adjacent to his bedroom. Here, in this expansive space, was everything he once considered important. Several "Man of the Year" trophies were displayed on shelves along with numerous plaques and other business awards. Photographs of him surrounded by powerful people in the industry as well as the media rounded out the collection.

The walls, too, were decorated with various snapshots of accomplishments and procurements. One showed him in the Winner's Circle at Belmont next to the racehorse he owned. Hope Is Here, a majestic thoroughbred, had won the Belmont Stakes but petered out in the Preakness Stakes and was eliminated from the Kentucky Derby. The horse was only two years old. There was always next year.

Some framed articles were also hung among the bevy of photos. Magazines and newspapers had been eager to learn about him and his humble beginnings when he first started out as Aaron Russell Knight in the corporate world. They called him "the whiz kid" and "Wall Street's young Donald Trump." He was shrewd, only giving reporters the bare bones of his present and nothing about his past. Because of his evasiveness, his so-called titles were changed to "The Financial Man of

Mystery" and "What is Aaron Knight Hiding?" Now, years later, because of his reluctance to be forthcoming, the interviews weren't always as flattering. Again, to him, criticisms and barbs didn't matter.

What mattered now was Hallie.

What would she do if she knew the truth about him and his dark past? She believed in love—all love, she'd said. She believed in forgiveness. And though he wanted to trust her, those were just words. Words stung. Words most times turned into lies. No matter how the truth was kept hidden, it always had a way of rearing its ugly head. Secrets that had brought him nothing but pain and heartache. Secrets that always had him looking over his shoulder. Always waiting for someone to find out. Always wondering if someone knew and would gladly divulge for a handsome price.

He closed his eyes as an inexplicable sense of emptiness settled in his stomach. If this relationship with Hallie were to go any further, then he would have no choice but to allow her in and hope she saw him for the man he was now and not the boy he'd been then.

Taking a breath, he went over to his cherry wood desk, fished his keys from his pocket, and found the small silver key that looked different from the rest. He sat in the black leather chair and inserted the key into the lock. Was his hand shaking?

Slowly, he opened the drawer and removed a plain manila envelope. He held it in his hand, and for a moment, pretended the envelope held something as benign as contracts or inter-office memos. But those thoughts sputtered to a halt as horrific memories trickled into his consciousness.

He turned on the desk lamp, and with body

hunched, he opened the clasp, pulled out the contents of the envelope, and stared at the small pile of newspaper prints.

Even after all these years, he still blamed himself for what had happened. He was only fifteen, his lawyer had pointed out. It had been an accident. He hadn't meant to do any harm. It had been a matter of self-defense. He'd been trying to protect his mother. On and on and on and the juvenile court had agreed. The records had been sealed, and he was placed on three years' probation.

Aaron unfolded the top paper.

Acquitted Youth Claims Self-Defense

The headline of the article blurred before his eyes. He had been Michael Clark then—a frightened boy who'd tried to be strong for his mother and his family, determined to do the right thing.

But who'd ended up killing his father.

Chapter Eleven

Hallie closed the black leather folder she'd been issued on her first day, almost a week ago. She touched the gold letters of her name embossed on the lower right corner on the front cover. She was grateful every day to have been given the chance to work for ARK Enterprises, not because of the prestige associated with a Fortune 500 company, but because her mother could live out her days in comfort and dignity, without the risk of being asked to leave the facility for lack of funds. Now her salary afforded her mother a private room overlooking the garden and two nurses to look after her. Yes, money did talk, and Hallie was thankful it spoke—no, shouted—loud and clear when it came to her mother's welfare.

Aaron, who sat at the head of the large oval table in one of the many conference rooms ARK provided, now rose to his feet. "Is there any other business?"

"A Mr. Marc Goodwin from CNBS called," Lavelle said. "He'd like you to call him back when you get the chance."

Aaron nodded. "Thank you, Lavelle. Anyone else?" With an inquiring gaze, he regarded his executives quickly, but his gaze boldly locked with Hallie's.

Though excitement sparked within her, she lowered her lids to hide her feelings.

"Very productive meeting today," he continued. "Thank you, everyone. And remember, you and your families are cordially invited to my place in Sea Girt for my annual Fourth of July party. Now go enjoy your long holiday weekend."

Hallie knew he relished discretion, so the announcement of his annual bash had come as a surprise to her. Still, she did remember Rita saying he hosted parties now and again. The department heads of ARK began to talk among themselves. Hallie caught some snippets of conversations, mostly about attending Aaron's party or packing for a long weekend family vacation.

She stole a quick glance at Aaron. He was talking with Thomas Kent, the head of R&D. It had been a month since the two of them had gone to dinner at Central Parx. Their schedules were crazy, to say the least, and trying to find the time for another "business dinner" was futile at best. It made her wonder if she'd ever have time for romance, even if it weren't with Aaron.

But though their working lives were full, he made the time to be attentive and sweet to her, bringing her coffee in the morning and sometimes surprising her with lunch delivered to her office. His gestures, though lovely, left her wanting more.

But with all his small kindnesses, he remained somewhat reserved. Questions gnawed at her. Was he anxious about pursuing something personal with her? Maybe he just enjoyed taking things slowly when it came to relationships. Maybe the boss-slash-employee deal bothered him subconsciously. Aside from that, she felt the bond between them growing tighter in the way he looked at her, his thoughtfulness, the flashes of desire that altered his expression from boss to promising lover.

She pushed back from the table, the wheels of the leather chair rolling over the solid wood floor. Thomas was walking out of the conference room. She and Aaron were alone.

"You throw a Fourth of July party every year?" she asked.

He nodded and squared his shoulders in a defensive pose. "Why? You don't think I'd be a good host?"

"It's not that. Opening your house to people just doesn't seem like something you would do."

"Sure, I like my privacy, but I'm not a recluse. I enjoy a good party every now and then." He winked, and his heated gaze latched onto her.

Hallie's heart pounded like crazy.

"We're going to be there a couple of days before, though."

"We?"

"Yes, you and me. Is that a problem?"

The beach house. Just the two of them. The idea of being alone with him again made her nerves rattle. Still, she played her emotions cautiously. "Aaron—"

"Is that a yes?"

She half smiled. "Do you guarantee fireworks?"

"That depends on what sort of fireworks you're talking about."

She eyed him, curiously.

"Fireworks in the sky or fireworks in other places."

Her pulse hit sonic speed. Did he mean in the bedroom? "Fireworks everywhere."

He exhaled, his lower lip trembling a bit. "Great. I'll pick you up tonight."

She stood as he walked over to her. His expression was gentle, and the gleam of interest in his eyes set her heart thumping. He took her hand, brought it to his lips, and kissed it. A warm glow flowed through her and fired up her desire.

"I promise it'll be different this time." He gave her hand a squeeze, and his mouth curved with tenderness.

She smiled back and left the conference room, her mind reeling with thoughts of a future that might begin tonight.

"Julian, what are you still doing here?" She regarded her assistant, who was at his desk clipping and stapling and stacking important-looking papers. His straight brown hair fell across his forehead, hitting the top of his dark-framed glasses.

He stopped his organizing and looked at her. "Waiting for you. You have a visitor."

She frowned. "Who?"

"I asked, but he wouldn't say."

"He?"

"He wanted it to be a surprise. I could tell him you left for the day, or at least that you're in another meeting."

Why was her stomach suddenly churning with anxiety? "No. That's all right. Go home, Julian. Enjoy your weekend."

"Are you sure you don't want me to stay, Ms. Cavanagh?" He blinked behind his glasses. "It's no bother."

He was looking out for her safety, and she appreciated it, but she didn't see the need. She turned the knob of her office door. "I'll be fine." She caught the worry in her assistant's expression before she slipped into the room.

He was staring out the window, his back to her. Her hunch was right. She knew this mystery man, and her heart sank to her stomach.

"Kyle?" Her voice trembled in her ears.

"Hello, Hallie." He turned and offered her an intimate smile that made her blood boil. "Did you miss me?"

The shock of seeing Kyle Weiss, her ex-fiancé, wore off quickly. Painful memories began to surface. But the pain subsided without much fanfare. In its place came a shimmering wave of pulsing anger, clouding her vision and tightening her jaw.

"What are you doing here?"

"After all this time apart, you can do better than that."

"I could call security and have you thrown out of here. Would that be better?"

She was familiar with the smirk on his face. It always appeared every time she got the better of him. But the smirk only enhanced his arresting good looks, and her heart did a handspring in her chest. His dark wavy hair was combed back from his face that was bronzed by the sun. His intense brown eyes flickered with interest. He was dressed casually in a pink, collared knit shirt, khaki pants, and brown loafers. So Connecticut classy. So Kyle.

"How did you find me? Did Sophie say something?"

He laughed. That same strong, confident laugh she had once found so intoxicating. Now it was annoying.

"Sophie wouldn't give me the time of day. You know that."

"What are you doing here?"

He gazed at her intently. "I wanted to see you."

"Why?"

He shrugged. "I just wanted to know how you were."

Hands planted on her hips, she glared at him. "You could have called, emailed, texted…anything besides show up here." A slow burn was starting to bubble in the pit of her stomach.

"Let's get real, Hallie. You would have ignored any call, email, or text."

"What would you expect me to do?"

"Can't we try to be civil and see where that gets us?"

"We have nothing to say to each other, Kyle."

"I think we do." He surveyed her office. "This is some set up, Hallie. Does Knight know what a prize he has in you?"

She bristled. Why the reference to Aaron? Had he been stalking her? Though the thought was unnerving, the possibility wasn't his style. In all their years together, he'd never been controlling. In fact, it had been just the opposite. He'd always encouraged her to be her own person. Was he now regretting calling off the wedding? Their relationship? Should she even care? It bothered her that her feelings of anger toward him hadn't gone away. Was she still harboring the hurt he'd caused? She had no time for this. She needed to focus on the evening ahead. She needed to focus on Aaron and her.

"I'm going to ask you again, Kyle. How did you

know where to find me?"

His shoulders slumped a bit, and he pressed his lips together. He reached into the back pocket of his khakis and handed her a folded page of a newspaper. She frowned.

"Open it."

She did. Page six of *The City Tribune* was dog-eared. The society page. A picture of her and Aaron stared back at her. "What *is* this?" she murmured.

"You tell me."

She stared at it more closely. She and Aaron were in each other's arms dancing. Though it was black and white and a bit grainy, she could identify the backdrop of Pete's Fishery. It was the night she had closed the Lectra-Pro deal. Her mind tried to make sense of it. Someone must have recognized Aaron, and itching for notoriety or a stipend, took the snapshot to the newspaper. Under the picture was the caption. *Business mogul Knight and mystery lady.*

"My mother found it and sent it to me."

"Your mother?" That revelation was far worse than the photo. She'd always thought Karen Weiss was the one who'd convinced Kyle to call off the wedding.

"I knew Sawyer and Company went under, so you wouldn't be there. Then, when I saw this photo, I put two and two together. Or put you and Knight together. Is it serious?" He tilted his head. "You know the kind of man he is, don't you? Is he stringing you along?" His eyes widened. "Or forcing you? You know that's sexual harass—"

"Kyle, I want you to leave." She gritted her teeth to keep her anger under control.

"All right, I'm overstepping my bounds. I'm sorry.

Can't we just talk?"

"I want you to leave now." Rancor sharpened her voice.

"Hallie, I still care about—"

She put up her hand. "Stop right there. You care about no one but yourself and your precious status."

"Come on, Hallie. I made a mistake. Probably the biggest one in my life. I was so unsure of everything a year ago, and when your mother—"

"Don't say a word about my mother." She looked him dead in the eye. "You couldn't get away from me fast enough when I said she would be living with us. You made me feel ashamed. Embarrassed she was my mother. Who does that?"

"I never meant to. We were planning a life together. I had just been accepted to a prestigious law firm. I needed to prove myself. It was a lot to deal with in a short amount of time."

"Oh, poor you." Her snipe was loud and clear. "You didn't want to be burdened with a mother-in-law who ultimately wouldn't be able to care for herself. You weren't ready to vie for my attention with a crazy old woman who couldn't remember her own name."

"Hallie, you're putting words in my mouth."

"Am I really?"

"All I wanted was for you and me to be together."

"Sorry, Kyle. Life's messy."

He shook his head, his expression quiet and serious.

"She has Alzheimer's. I wasn't going to abandon her."

"Of course not. I wouldn't expect you to."

His sudden turnabout fascinated and appalled her.

Too little, too late, Kyle. She ran an agitated hand through her hair and sucked in a shallow breath. "Why are you really here?"

He met her gaze with eyes darkened with emotion. "Seeing that photo of you and Knight put things in perspective for me. I have to know something, Hallie."

Her bottom lip clenched between her teeth. "Know what?"

He grabbed her hands and squeezed. "Is there still a chance for us?"

****

Yes, this time it will be different. Sitting behind his desk, Aaron rolled the promise he'd made to Hallie around in his mind until it became easy to believe. He'd make sure their weekend together would be special. It wouldn't be difficult. Just being in the same room with her heightened his sense of desire. Every time his gaze met hers, his heart soared and his body tingled. All he wanted to do was touch her, kiss her, and make love to her. There was no logical explanation for the way he felt about her. But then love wasn't logical.

Love.

It hadn't taken him long to appreciate how different she was from the other women he knew. He thought about Miranda and realized it had been weeks since he'd heard from her. At the beginning of their tryst, he'd made it very clear their time together would never become serious. Still, he had enjoyed being with her. She was fun, she knew all the right people, and she traveled in important circles. He, in turn, offered her youth and sex. Truth was, they both used each other for the things they wanted—not the things they needed. But now their time together was over. He didn't want to hurt her, but he was glad she had gotten his message loud and clear. Knowing the woman intimately, Aaron was pretty certain she had found someone new to console her.

He had made up his mind that he would tell Hallie about the other women in his life, but especially about Miranda. He'd stop there, though. The rest of his secrets would remain hidden, not forever, but at least for now.

Hallie believed in love, and he had given up on it a long time ago. Love made people crazy. Made them cruel and callous. Made them hurt others. He had seen this "love" thing control his mother and turn his father into a miserable and dangerous bastard.

But that wasn't love, was it? Not the love that Hallie professed. It wasn't just her beauty he was drawn to—it was her heart. Her view of love included kindness and forgiveness. Was it also a love of desire and temptation? Could she love him? Even with all his emotional scars and weaknesses? Was it possible for him to finally let go of the past and look forward to a future with her?

His new cell phone in hand, he quickly punched in a number and waited.

"Hello?"

"Rita, it's Aaron."

"Hello, Mr. Knight. Is everything all right?"

"Better than all right. I'd like you to make sure the Sandpiper Suite is ready for company. Ms. Cavanagh will be visiting for the weekend."

"Of course."

He noticed the brightness in the housekeeper's voice. "We'll be there this evening."

"You sound happy, Mr. Knight."

He exhaled a long sigh of contentment. Something he hadn't experienced in a long time. "I am happy, Rita. Very happy."

Chapter Twelve

They arrived in Sea Girt about eight thirty in the evening. Hallie was happy to be back. More than happy. She was content. Even her confrontation with Kyle hadn't deterred her feelings. She was with Aaron. She was where she belonged.

After changing into shorts and a flowery blouse, she met him out by the pool. Strings of lights were everywhere, bringing a certain festive atmosphere to the backyard. It was easy to imagine this place filled with people having a good time. She was anxious to be a part of that fun. But for now she had Aaron all to herself.

On one of the chairs was a box wrapped in shiny silver paper. A large gold bow decorated the top. "What's this?" she asked.

"It's for you." An ice-cold bottle of beer in hand, Aaron, stretched out in a chaise lounge chair, flicked her an amused look.

She tossed him a questioning look back, but he wasn't giving anything away. She took the package off the chair, sat down, and examined it from every angle.

"Go on. Open it."

She tore at the wrapping paper, her curiosity mounting. Embossed on the top of the pink box was the name *Cate*. "What is this?"

"Catherine Palmer," he said matter-of-factly.

She waited for more.

"She's a top designer. Why are you laughing?"

"It's just funny that a man like you knows something about women's fashion."

His eyes narrowed. "Open the box."

"Aaron, what did you do?" She pulled off the top of the box, parted the pink tissue paper, and stared. "You bought me a bathing suit?"

He looked pretty pleased with himself. "You said you didn't have one. Now you have three."

Surprised and touched by his gesture, she removed the bathing suits one a time. Each one was different and more beautiful than the other. There was a black, stylish, one-piece halter. The material was soft to the touch. The second one was also a one-piece in a vibrant, shimmering red. The front had a series of ruffles in a lightweight, matching fabric. The third was a white bikini with a key-hole design on the bra and a matching panty with side ties. Maybe he did know something about women's fashion. If nothing else, he had great taste.

"Do you like them?" His expression was eager to hear her remarks.

"They're lovely, Aaron."

"But…?"

"How did you know there was a 'but'?"

"I can see it written on your beautiful face." A lazy smile tipped one side of his mouth upward. "I have an idea. Think of them as a business transaction."

"Pretty expensive business transaction."

"Pretty sexy, too." His face turned upward to the indigo sky. "It's a beautiful night for a swim."

"You're tempting me."

"Maybe we won't need bathing suits. Maybe we

should just go skinny-dipping."

Heat crept up her neck and into her cheeks. He had never talked like this before. A combination of thrills and fright dashed along her nerves.

"Maybe tomorrow." She folded the bathing suits and laid them back in the box. "Thank you, Aaron."

His expression changed from elation to worry. "Is anything wrong? Did I overstep a boundary?"

"No."

"It's just that you were awfully quiet in the car, and now, well, you weren't as excited about the gift as I hoped you'd be." Aaron's gaze remained fixed on her face. "You didn't eat much either. I could ask Rita to bring you something else—"

"I'm not hungry."

The warm breeze stirred the scent of baked patio stones and carried a cloying scent of roses within its balmy caress. The chatter of crickets underscored the mini light show of the fireflies.

Aaron rolled to his side. "Are you sure you want to be here? With me? I can take you home if you're uncomfortable."

The ache in his voice made her heart sink. A twinkle of moonlight caught his gentle and contemplative eyes.

"There's no other place I'd rather be."

"Then what's wrong?"

"Why does something have to be wrong? Can't a girl be distracted once in a while?"

He pushed himself up and sat on the edge of the chaise. "Give me your hand."

She did. His fresh scent mixed with the ocean air, and her body tingled at his touch. He got to his feet and pulled Hallie to hers.

"I need to tell you something. I've never been in a real relationship before." His voice rang with sincerity.

She tilted her head and pondered his words. It wasn't hard to believe that a man like him would prefer to be noncommittal rather than getting tangled up in the web of a romantic involvement. But what did that mean for her?

"The relationships I've had have been strictly for business or profit. When it comes to the heart, I avoid romance at all costs. Too much drama."

"Not something a girl wants to hear."

He laughed and drew her closer. She liked the way his hands now skimmed down her back and rested on her hips. He dropped an unexpected, featherlike kiss on her forehead, light and teasing. She craved more.

"Let me finish. You've changed the way I feel. I want someone real in my life. Someone that makes me know I'm alive. Someone that ties me to someone. Someone that scares the shit out of me." His earnest gaze pulled her in. "I want that someone to be you."

She held on to her heart, though its sharp palpitations were making it impossible. Warmth spread through her body and pooled in her cheeks. She had to tell him, and she had to tell him now before they both went any further. "Something happened today."

He frowned and stepped away from her.

"It was at the office."

"Business?"

"Personal." She hesitated and wondered what telling him would accomplish. But then, for Hallie, honesty was a key factor if they were to take this any further. Her sigh made her entire body shake. "I saw my ex-fiancé today."

"You're ex-fiancé? His face fell the slightest bit. "Wow. Never expected that."

"His name is Kyle Weiss, and he came to see me at the office today."

He cocked his head. "He knew where you worked?"

"He guessed. He saw a picture of us in *The City Tribune*."

"Wow, again."

"Someone snapped it while we were dancing that night at Pete's Fishery."

"Pete's Fishery?" An amused look washed over his face.

"You're laughing?"

"It's funny. I vacation on private islands and in five-star hotels. I eat at restaurants where most people couldn't afford the tip, and of all places, I get caught at a dive like Pete's."

"I guess it is sort of comical. But now everyone…"

"Everyone will suspect something's going on between us. That's what you're afraid of, right?"

She nodded.

"It doesn't matter. What matters is Kyle. Is the operative word 'ex?' "

"We've been apart for over a year."

"Who broke it off?"

"He did."

"What happened?"

She was reluctant to put all the pieces together for him. "It's complicated."

"It always is."

"He wants to get back together."

The animation left his face. "And?"

"And nothing. I told him it's over."

"Good to know."

"That's it? That's all you're going to say?" An odd twinge of disappointment rattled her demeanor.

He surveyed her kindly. "Thanks for being honest. Is that better?"

"A little."

****

All signs had pointed to a night of lovemaking, and she had ruined it. The empty feeling swallowed her. Damn Kyle. Damn her for being honest. Aaron's eyes had widened with surprise—and not the good kind. His expression had stilled and grown serious while she insisted she and Kyle were over. They could never, would never be a couple again. She knew Aaron was curious about the breakup. She could only imagine the questions going through his head. The pain of rejection from someone she had loved and thought loved her still lingered, and she was afraid to open herself up again.

Now, tucked away alone in her suite, Hallie swung open the atrium doors to the balcony and let the ocean air fill the room. The last time she stood here, the air had been saturated with an after-rain mist. Here she had seen Aaron looking up at her, his faint smile holding a touch of sadness.

Though it was nearing ten thirty, she made a quick call to Golden Living to check on her mother. One of the private nurses she'd hired put her mind at ease telling her that, although her mother seemed a bit more forgetful today, she'd taken all her meds, eaten her dinner, and was now sleeping.

Saddened at the news of her mother's continued

absentmindedness but satisfied at the status quo, Hallie sent a quick text to Sophie to make sure her friend knew she was okay. Immediately, a heart and a smiley emoji flashed on the screen.

Her cell rang before she had a chance to slip into bed. She grabbed it off the night table. She thought it might be Sophie, but no name appeared on the screen. But she did recognize the phone number. Kyle. She'd deleted his contact information the day he deleted their engagement.

"Why are you calling me?"

"Where are you? Sophie said you're away for the weekend." He sounded distraught.

"That's none of your business. I'm none of your business anymore, Kyle. Now stop calling me."

"Are you with him?"

"Goodbye, Kyle. I'm blocking your number." She hesitated and then pressed the red circle, cutting off the call. She tossed the phone onto the bed and curled up under the quilt. She never knew Kyle to be so damn persistent. Their relationship was over. Dead over. He'd just have to accept it.

Was that someone knocking? Hallie listened. The knock became louder.

"Hallie? Are you awake?"

Aaron.

She opened the door. His intense gaze jolted her body. "Aaron? Is everything okay?"

"Hallie, I...I was thinking about this ex-fiancé business."

She frowned. "And?"

"And I think the guy's pretty ballsy to track you down you down at work. If I'd been there..."

"Are you...jealous?" Her stomach fluttered. Should she have said such a thing? Too late now.

He didn't seem surprised at her words. "No, I..."

"Do you want to kiss me?" Now she was overstepping. Yet her spur-of-the-moment question felt good. Freeing. Unfortunately, it could also cost her her job. She cringed.

"Do you want me to?" His gaze melted into hers.

For a split second, she wasn't sure if she had heard him correctly.

"I asked you a question. Do you want me to kiss you?"

She didn't hesitate. "Yes." *No take-backs.*

He needed no further prompting. He slid his hand up the nape of her neck, and she responded with a soft murmur that surrounded them and drew him in. He kissed her forehead gently. "Are you sure?"

"Yes."

His lips against her ear, he moved down her throat. Her eyelids fluttered and closed as she savored the sweet feeling. Finally, he sealed his lips over hers, taking possession of her mouth. Her head reeled, and she shuddered in his arms. Invisible threads bound them tighter. The soft sound of his sigh against her lips whispered through her. She wanted more than just his kisses. She wanted him. All of him.

They parted, much to her disappointment.

"I wanted to do that for the longest time," he said, an easy smile playing at the corners of his mouth.

Her gaze met his. "Me, too." She stepped out of his embrace before he could stop her. "I'll see you in the morning, Aaron. Sleep well."

She closed the door, smiled, and imagined all the

good things to come.

****

"I'm all yours." She held out her arms in a gesture that read loud and clear "take me now." Her breath caught as Aaron came toward her with purposeful strides. Surely, he wasn't about to take her up on her suggestion. Not in the kitchen anyway. Not with Rita fussing about.

"First, a walk on the beach. Revs up the old appetite. We'll be back, Rita," he called over his shoulder.

The morning sky was awash with gold, as the sun seemed to rise out of the gray-green ocean. Restless waves pounded the shore, their rhythm intensifying with each clash.

"Beautiful," she whispered, standing at the shoreline. Sandal straps dangling from her fingertips, Hallie let the cold white foam tickle her toes.

"Couldn't agree with you more." Aaron sidled up to her. The warmth of his body made her blush. "I still can't believe you've never been to the beach."

"I lost my dad at a young age. My mother worked two jobs. Going to the beach was last on the list."

"Is your mother—?"

"Alive? Yes." She hesitated. "It's difficult to talk about."

"Family's a complicated matter." He took her hand as they started to walk along the wet sand.

"Yours, too, I take it?"

"Let's talk about something else."

She agreed. She didn't have to know everything in one day. And neither did he. Just being with him was enough. She raised her gaze to his, her heart tripping in her chest. "What would you like to talk about?"

"Last night."

"What about it?"

His smirk made her smile. "Have you already forgotten what went on between us?"

"Oh, you mean the kiss?"

"Yes, the kiss. Our kiss."

She dismissed him with a wave of her hand. "I've already put it out of my mind."

He made a face at her teasing. "Are you demeaning my kissing proficiency, Ms. Cavanagh?"

She tilted her head. "Why, yes, Mr. Knight, I believe I am."

He leaned in, warm and close. "As I recall, you closed the door on me last night."

"I had to get my beauty sleep." She tilted her head. "So are you going to kiss me again?"

"I guess I'll have to if I want to protect my reputation."

"Good answer."

Without another word, Aaron cupped her face with his hands and crushed his mouth to hers. This time his tongue nudged at her sealed lips, coaxing them to part, delving inside to explore. The energy and power behind his kiss took control of her with possessive thoroughness.

Sweetly surrendering, her mind frantically rasped and returned his kiss with eagerness.

His mouth lingered on hers before he pulled himself away. "We'd better get back or Rita will come looking for us."

****

It was Saturday, the height of the summer season,

and Fourth of July weekend. With those three happenings, the boardwalk was bustling with vacationers and townies alike. Hallie reveled in the energy surrounding her. But her savoring the moment was only part of the way she felt. Her mouth still burned from Aaron's mind-blowing kiss. Her senses were keenly aware of its consequences—good or bad. But for now, she would bask in the exhilaration.

The Tenth Avenue Arcade was alive with bells, whistles, and shrills. The air smelled of buttery popcorn and something sweet like cotton candy.

With hands clasped, she and Aaron stepped into the gaudy neon wonderland. Teenagers dominated most of the video games, while eager children dragged their parents to the different coin-op amusements.

"You look shell-shocked. I take it you've never been to an arcade either."

"Can I call a wobbly pinball machine and an archaic game of Frogger in Sal's Pizza Place an arcade?"

He looked like he was weighing the question. "You live a colorful life, Ms. Cavanagh."

She smiled at the faint glint of humor in his eyes.

"Come on. Let's try our luck."

Armed with stacks of quarters, they had a blast flipping metal balls in the pinball machines, driving virtual cars on the Daytona Speedway, and whacking annoying little moles with an oversized rubber mallet. They shared a bucket of popcorn and lots of laughter. She had yards of yellow tickets in her fist.

"Ready for Skee-Ball?"

She tilted her head and gestured to him like a hostess showing patrons to a table in a restaurant. "Lead the way."

He smiled at her, and the smile warmed her heart.

They found an empty machine, and he slipped several quarters into the coin box. Rows of lights on the top, bottom, and sides came on and brought life to the dented, paint-chipped mechanism. Several wooden balls, each big enough to hold in a hand, rolled down the narrow gutter, each one clacking into the other as they came to a halt.

Hallie watched a young boy with his dad a few lanes down from them roll the ball up a short lane toward circular cups—the widest marked with a ten and the smallest marked with a fifty. The boy's ball dropped down into the cup marked with a thirty. He cheered, and his dad ruffled his hair.

"So this game is like bowling without the pins," she said.

"That's one way to look at it, I guess."

"I bowled once. Some friends at school suggested we blow off some steam after a particularly difficult economics exam."

"Did it work?"

"Not sure. I dropped a ten-pound ball on someone's foot and single-handedly ended the evening."

Aaron grimaced. "Ouch."

"Later on, I found out I broke his toe."

"Double ouch. Though please tell me it was your ex-fiancé's toe. It would make my day."

She laughed. "No, it wasn't." She picked up one of the wooden balls and weighed it in her hand. Out of the corner of her eye, she caught him taking a step back. "Don't worry, I'm not going to drop it."

"Just erring on the side of caution."

She shot him a look.

"You're cute when you're annoyed. Now let's see what you've got."

Taking up the challenge, she rolled the ball with a flick of her wrist. The ball missed the rings completely and rolled back into the side gutter.

"Try again," he encouraged.

She did, and again the ball took off, hit the edge of the bottom ring, and dropped into the gutter.

"Not as easy as it looks."

"You try it." She handed him the last ball and stepped aside.

He moved back a bit, sized up the alley, and rolled the ball. It hit the embankment and dropped neatly into the fifty-point ring. He turned to her, bowed from the waist in a princely gesture, and smirked. With a twinkle in his eye, he wiggled his index finger, beckoning her to come to him.

Hallie walked over. He took her by the shoulders, spun her around, and backed her up into him. It all happened so fast she didn't have time react until he circled her wrist with his long fingers. His touch was gentle yet firm, protective yet eager. An acute awareness filled her every pore. Even the air she breathed was alive with expectation. The physical closeness of him made her lightheaded with desire.

Three more balls rolled down the channel. Aaron gave one of them to her, cradling her hand in his.

"Ready?" he whispered in her ear.

She nodded. A crazy little shudder ran up her spine as he pulled back her arm.

"Relax, Hallie. Go with it."

His deep voice was mesmerizing and full of promise. Was he referring to Skee-Ball?

"Now, let it go."

She did and the ball rolled smoothly up the wooden lane, hit the ridge, and landed easily into the fifty-point cup.

Her shout of victory rose over the pings and pongs of the other arcade games. She spun around, her arms up in the air. He scooped her up and lifted her off the floor, his shout just as loud as hers. They embraced, and then he eased her down to the floor. Their gazes locked for what seemed an eternity to her. She leaned into him, and he captured her mouth in a kiss that made her reel with longing.

She didn't want the kiss to end, but when he pulled away, he continued to stare at her, studying her with an intensity that made her forget to breathe.

Without waiting another second, he kissed her again. His mouth was firm and strong, his lips gentle. The kiss spilled through to her soul.

Reluctantly drawing away for the second time, he gently touched her face. "Come on. Let's go."

Without questioning his motives, she handed over her streamers of winning tickets to the little boy who'd been playing Skee-Ball next to them. Wearing a surprised look, the kid barely got out the words "Thank you." Hallie smiled, took Aaron's hand, and the two of them left the arcade.

****

The rest of the day flew by. They played a round of miniature golf, had a slice of pizza for lunch, and watched the sunset from a bench on the boardwalk. Sweet vanilla custard cones from the famous Harrigan's

Ice Cream Shoppe and a spectacular fireworks display illuminating the dark ocean ended an evening Hallie would remember forever.

Aaron, his arm wrapped around her, pulled her into him. "See? I promised you fireworks, didn't I?"

"So you did." Her head rested against his shoulder, her sigh mixing with the warm ocean breeze. "I could get used to this kind of living. I see why you like it here."

"I like the city, too, but this place helps me relax."

"Even with all of these people around?"

"It's not always like this. After Labor Day, the vacationers go home, and the town goes back to normal. Believe it or not, I like it here best in the winter."

It made perfect sense he would say that. She raised her head, but he still held her close. It was a transparent display of possession, inappropriate, and strangely thrilling.

"The ocean you see now is not the same in January. It's darker and more powerful. The electricity in the air makes the body vibrate, and the cold mist pierces the skin like frozen needles."

"It sounds painful."

"It's anything but."

"I guess I'll have to take your word for it."

"Or you can experience it for yourself."

This time she pulled away and looked at him. His eyes, deep, dark, and mysterious, studied her acutely. Heat swept her face. "Is that an invitation?"

His grin was full of hungry anticipation. "What do you think?"

"I think this day's not over yet." With those words,

she knew she'd laid bare her expectations, and she was ready for anything.

Chapter Thirteen

It was Sunday and the Fourth of July. Aaron's open house was that afternoon. Though her sense of expectation continued after they came back from their mini-excursion yesterday, Hallie had kept her want of him at arm's length. They kissed good night, but that was all the physical contact they had.

He seemed okay with it. "Get some sleep. It's going to be crazy tomorrow."

"Crazy good or crazy bad?"

He kissed the tip of her nose. "I guess that depends on you." He winked.

Though she closed the door, both physically and emotionally, she had dreamed of things to come.

Now she watched as Rita feverishly opened cabinet doors and gathered various bowls and dishes from the shelves. Several stops to the refrigerator alerted Hallie that she wasn't just fixing breakfast. "Rita, can I help?"

"I appreciate that, but I'm just getting together the things the caterers might need. They should be here soon."

"Who should be here soon?"

Hallie turned toward the doorway. Aaron, out of breath, his face a bit flushed, zeroed in on her. He must have been jogging. The black and neon green top and shorts molded to his body, showing off every muscle, and those well-developed angles weren't lost on her. He opened the refrigerator, grabbed a bottle of water, and took a generous swig.

The doorbell rang.

"The caterers are here." Rita headed for the front door.

Aaron put the water bottle down on the counter. His gaze held hers in a curious light. "So when are we going to have some alone time?"

Yesterday had been the most fun she could remember having. Playing Skee-Ball at the arcade. Watching the sunset over the ocean. His warm, sweet, powerful kisses. "That's your call."

He was close now, staring at her. "If it wasn't for this party…" His mouth was wet and cold on hers as she drank in his kiss. "I'll cancel it. I can do that, you know."

"But the caterers—" she whispered against his mouth.

"Screw the caterers."

Out of the corner of her eye, she saw a parade of people dressed in white shirts and black pants march into the kitchen carrying silver urns and chafing dishes. They ignored the two of them and went straight to work.

"Guess it's too late to cancel."

"Meet me by the pool. I'll only be a minute."

"Promise?"

"Always."

The serene poolside atmosphere was quickly shattered as tables and chairs were unloaded from the back of a white service truck by another group of workers. Aaron grabbed two beach chairs, and they walked down to the ocean to find some privacy.

"This is nice," she murmured, settling in the chair. They sat at the edge of the water, and the chill from the foam tickled her toes. "So who comes to this party of yours?"

"The usual suspects from work."

"Who wouldn't want the opportunity to kiss up to the boss?"

"Funny. I invite my neighbors, too, if they have nothing better to do." He shifted in the chair. "I have an idea. Why don't you invite Sophie?"

"That's sweet of you, but the restaurant business doesn't take a day off for a holiday. In fact, sometimes it's worse than regular days." She dug her heels into the sand and stared out into the ocean.

"You'd think folks would be home barbequing."

"You'd be surprised." She took a breath, filling the hollow ache in her stomach. "Are you okay with me telling you about Kyle?"

He reached over and grabbed her hand. "I'm glad you did." He squeezed her fingers gently, brought them up to his mouth, and kissed them one by one. "Why so tense?"

He was right. Her shoulders were knotted with stiffness. "What we could have might be too good to be true."

"Could have?"

"I don't know if I'm ready for this. For what's happening between us."

His expression slid into a frown. "I told you how I felt about us. Maybe I'm mistaken, but I thought you felt the same way."

"I do."

"Then what are you afraid of?"

"Nothing." She paused. "Everything. What about the office?"

He laughed. "What about it? We're adults. It's our business. No one has to know."

"You're kidding, right? Everyone's going to know once they see that picture in the *newspaper*. And most of them are going to be here today. What are they going to assume when they see me? That I arrived fashionably early?"

"I think the term is fashionably late."

"Aaron, stop teasing. You know what I mean."

A frown set into his features. "I know you're worried. Did someone at work say something?"

"No. But they're probably too polite."

"Or concerned about their jobs."

Her eyes widened. "You wouldn't…"

"Fire them?"

Was that a wink? "Aaron, please tell me you're kidding."

"I don't care who knows, Hallie." He spoke each word with composure and dignity. "Maybe I'm moving too fast, but all I want to do is be with you. Please tell me it's the same for you."

Her heart thumped. Of course she wanted him. She wanted him to touch her, to kiss her, and to make love to her over and over. She shivered. "Can I ask you something?"

"Anything."

"Do you believe in love now?"

Aaron laid his head back against the chair and pitched a dry laugh. "Maybe a little."

****

"Hallie, it's so good to see you again."

Before she had the chance to say anything, she was pulled into Pamela Carlyle's warm embrace.

"Hey, don't forget about me." Kevin's booming voice transcended the other conversations happening around the pool. Once his wife let go of her, he moved right in with a bear hug that knocked the breath from Hallie's lungs.

Aaron's Fourth of July party was in full swing. Two grill masters from the catering company kept the burgers, steaks, and ribs coming, and three bartenders, set up at various stations around the pool, kept the guests happy with festive drinks sporting maraschino cherries and tiny paper umbrellas. A number of her colleagues from ARK Enterprises had arrived with their families to celebrate. For Hallie, it was nerve-wracking but at the same time fun seeing them away from the office setting and enjoying the pool, beach, and amenities that Aaron had so generously provided. She'd met some of his neighbors, too.

"You two look wonderful," Hallie said. "What's your secret?"

"We just got back from a ten-day cruise to Bermuda," Pamela said.

"First class all the way." Kevin gave his wife a squeeze.

Pamela grabbed Hallie's hand. "I don't know how you did it, but you gave Kevin his life back. He's never been so relaxed and happy."

"Even my doctor says I'm a new man." He patted his stomach. "Lost ten pounds."

Hallie smiled.

Pamela peered over her dark-rimmed sunglasses. "How are you doing, dear?"

"Fine."

"And how are you and Aaron getting along?"

A slight heat stung her cheeks. Did they suspect something? "What do you mean?"

"The last time I saw you, you two were in each other's arms looking quite content." Pamela leaned in. "I saw page six."

Hallie grimaced and tried to keep her composure. Who else had seen the ill-fated photograph? "That was quite the surprise."

"Get used to it, dear. Aaron Knight is media fodder. People thrive on knowing what the wealthy are up to. Why, there could be someone at this party right now gathering the latest gossip about him."

Kevin's brow dipped into a frown. "Stop, Pammy. You're scaring the poor girl."

"I just want her to be prepared, that's all." Her expression softened. "I want you to be happy, Hallie, and if Aaron's the one who makes you happy, then I say go for it and damn the gossip mongers."

Hallie stepped back, not to be rude, but for her own survival. Were her emotions playing out on her face? Her stance? Did everyone already suspect the two of them were a couple? Were they a couple? Her temples began to pound.

Kevin must have sensed Hallie's discomfort, for he winked and steered his wife over to another crowd of people. "Catch up with you later," he called over his shoulder.

The salt air stung her lungs as she took a much-needed breath. She liked Pamela, and she knew the woman meant well, but did she have to be so blatant about her observations?

She scanned the area by the pool. Aaron was conversing with a small crowd from the office. He was engrossed in the conversation, which was just as well. She wanted to be alone for a while.

The house looked like a good bet until she realized just as many guests were milling about inside as they were outside. She turned away and looked beyond the patio.

The beach.

Though some of the partygoers and their families frolicked on the sand or in the water, it was relatively empty. The perks of a private beachfront. The chairs she and Aaron had brought to the water's edge were still there. Relief engulfed her. Even her headache was starting to subside. Yes, a little time away from the festivities and the guests would be just the thing she needed. A waiter circled around her, balancing a tray of stemmed glasses sparkling with white sangria. Without much thought, she took one and headed down the steps of the patio.

Hallie closed her eyes and stretched out on the chaise. It was high tide, and the soft mist from the incoming waves washed over her, cooling her skin. The water ebbed and flowed under the chair, and the sun played hide-and-seek with a few puffy white clouds.

She struggled to relax, gathering her thoughts into some semblance of order. Pamela's conversation had certainly given her pause. If the woman could see something different in her, couldn't others? She took a generous sip of the sangria. The cold fruity wine made her tongue tingle.

I want you to be happy... And if Aaron's the one who makes you happy...

Aaron did make her happy. And didn't she deserve happiness?

"Excuse me?"

Hallie opened her eyes. A woman, her face nearly covered with the wide brim of a black straw hat and oversized sunglasses, stood next to the empty chaise.

The woman gestured to the chair. "May I?"

Bothered at the intrusion but not wanting to be impolite, Hallie nodded.

The woman thanked her and settled onto the navy-blue canvas seat. "It's nice here, isn't it? Away from the party, I mean."

Hallie took another sip of the sangria. "Yes, it is."

She had never seen the woman around ARK Enterprises, but then the company employed so many people it was nearly impossible to know everyone. Maybe she was one of Aaron's neighbors. At any rate, she seemed comfortable with the surroundings.

Trying to be inconspicuous, Hallie's gaze sharpened as she took in the woman's shapely, bronze legs and her bright-red, polished toes dressed in expensive-looking, jeweled flip-flops. She wore a sheer black cover-up that hinted at a black one-piece bathing suit underneath. Her arms were tanned as well, but her hands, with their softened wrinkles, gave her age away. Hallie guessed she was in her mid-fifties.

"I'm Hallie Cavanagh."

It took her a moment, but then the woman turned her head and extended her hand. "Nice to meet you, Hallie." Her voice held a silky tone. "I'm Miranda."

****

"Rita, have you seen Hallie?"

The housekeeper stood by the back door of the

kitchen, nodding her approval as the caterers passed by carrying trays of shrimp and oysters on beds of ice. "No, Mr. Knight, I haven't."

Aaron had finally managed to break away from the boring office conversations with some of his executives. He was glad everyone was having a good time, but he couldn't wait until the party was over. And now the sun was slowly setting. The fireworks he had arranged would be starting soon. He wanted Hallie with him so they could enjoy the celebration together. Where was she?

"If I see her, I'll tell her you're looking for her," Rita told him.

He thanked his housekeeper and left the kitchen.

The last time he'd glimpsed Hallie, she was talking to Kevin and Pamela Carlyle. He'd been distracted by some of the guests, and when he looked for her again, she was gone. Maybe she went to her suite. Maybe he'd join her. The thought of being alone with her for a while in a house full of people excited him. He wasn't acting the good host, but his guests would get over it. He headed for the stairs but was stopped by a voice that made him clench.

"Hello, stranger."

It can't be. He turned sharply. "What are you doing here?"

Miranda frowned. "Well, that's not a very friendly greeting. Would you like to try again?"

Anger began to boil in his veins. "What I'd like is for you to leave."

His dismissive attitude didn't seem to sway her. She removed her hat and fluffed her hair. "I met her. She seems nice enough. Sweet."

He froze, knowing full well her target. "Who?"

"Hallie, is it? I think that's her name. Cute."

With his lips set in a grim line, he grabbed her arm. "What did you say to her?"

She wrenched her arm free, and he stepped back, realizing the intensity of his actions. The lines of her face were hard and unyielding.

For the first time, he recognized her right to some anger, some hurt, and some answers. He blinked. "I'm sorry. I didn't mean to—"

"What are you afraid of, Aaron?"

His palms stung from digging his fingernails into them. "Come with me," he ordered, not touching her again. He led the way to the stairs. Once they were inside his bedroom, out of the way of prying ears and eyes, he closed the door. He knew that being here, alone with her, wasn't the best choice. She could accuse him of anything. He would just have to take that chance.

"What did you say to her?" The acidity in his tone left a bitter taste in his mouth.

Appearing unruffled by the sting of his question, she smiled. "We had a lovely talk—about you, mostly."

Her words kicked him in the gut. "You didn't tell her about…?"

"About us? And break her heart? I'm not that cruel, Aaron. Or that foolish."

"You know what I'm talking about, Miranda. I told you all those things about me in confidence," he hissed, now regretting the decision he'd made so long ago.

Her chin angled up, and she met his defiant gaze. "You mean in a drunken stupor, don't you?"

An old fury rose up inside him. He had been

introduced to Miranda at a charity function. She was older, worldlier, and well-established in wealthy circles that could open doors for a young entrepreneur. Too late now to realize the wrong choice he'd made—it hadn't taken long for them to jump into bed together. She'd taught him how to please a woman. He'd used her contacts and life experiences to further his already lucrative career.

Yet with all his newfound wealth and success, being the cause of his father's death still weighed heavily on him. Years had passed. Years of being estranged from his family. His mother blaming him instead of being grateful he'd saved her life. His sister turning her back on him. His brother turning to drugs.

On the tenth anniversary of his father's death, Aaron had gotten drunk and called Miranda. For some reason, he had trusted her. She had often been a sounding board for him in business affairs, as well as his personal life. She was someone who listened thoughtfully and without judgment. And so he'd poured out his heart that night and told her how he'd murdered his father.

He was surprised at the compassion filling her eyes now. She touched his arm, and he didn't pull away. "I've kept that promise, Aaron. I've never told a soul about what happened that night. Just remember, though, the past has a way of catching up to people."

There was truth in her words. A truth he didn't want to face. Did he believe her? Could he trust her?

"And that's why you have to tell Hallie. If she's your future, then she deserves to know."

Conflicting emotions besieged him. Had Miranda intentionally voiced those words? Was she actually encouraging Hallie and his relationship? A newfound respect for her almost brought him to his knees. "But what if she…?" He hesitated. For the first time since his father's death, Aaron saw his whole life unraveling around him.

"Hates you and leaves you?" She shook her head. "Give the woman some credit."

She was right. Fate had changed his life. Now it was up to him to change the outcome.

"Well, Aaron, I never expected all this when I decided to come here today. I just wanted to see you. I wanted to make sure you were all right. I'm not going to lie. I miss you."

The sincerity in her voice surprised him. "You're a good friend, Miranda." His words sounded hollow, but he really was sincere—and surprised by her loyalty. But was he fooling himself?

"So that's what it's come down to. I'm a good friend." She laughed. "I knew she would be here today. Call me crazy, but I wanted to meet the woman who'd stolen your heart." She smirked. "If that's possible."

She walked up to him and wrapped her arms around his neck. He didn't stop her.

"For old time's sake, my love." She crushed her mouth to his and gently pulled at his lower lip with her teeth.

Without returning the kiss, he let her devour him and drew a ragged breath when she was done. They stared at each other.

A wicked gleam veiled her eyes. "See what you'll be missing?" Her response was curt and delivered in a cool, distant tone. "Well, it's been fun, darling, but my driver's waiting."

He smiled. "Thank you, Miranda." He bent down and kissed her lightly on her cheek.

"If she ever breaks your heart, you know where to find me." She blew him a kiss, opened the door, and left the room.

He jammed his fists into the pockets of his shorts, leaned against the wall, and breathed a sigh of relief. He couldn't believe Miranda had actually been so compliant. No vindictiveness. No jealousy. No bruised ego. The citrus scent of her perfume lingered in the air. He would miss her.

A flash of insight caught him by surprise. Had he just experienced another kind of love? An unselfish and generous kind of love? Why? Miranda could have easily thrown him under the bus by revealing his crime to Hallie.

And yet she hadn't.

It was now up to him to tell Hallie about what had happened to his father. She deserved to know and soon. But would she forgive him? He left his bedroom and started down the stairs.

"Mr. Knight? Mr. Knight!" Rita was calling him.

He met her halfway to the kitchen. "What's wrong, Rita?"

Her expression was strained. "It's Ms. Cavanagh. She's gone."

"Gone?"

"Mr. Carlyle took her to the train station. She was looking for you but couldn't find you. She said to tell you she was sorry—"

His throat went dry.

Rita shook her head. "I'm sure she'll be in touch."

The housekeeper's encouraging words did little to

boost Aaron's mood. Had Miranda been lying? Had she told Hallie his secret after all? He had to know. He had to know why Hallie had left. He shook off his dark train of thought and hurried to find Kevin.

Chapter Fourteen

No one was behind the front desk at Golden Living, so Hallie rushed into the main foyer. It was close to seven and the place was practically empty. Holiday weekends, especially like this one, had the tendency to keep families and friends busy. Vacations. Parties. Sometimes just the idea of a few days of pure relaxation with no interruptions was tempting enough. No one really wanted to be here. Not even the patients.

Turning left, she headed down the hallway. At the double doors, she pressed the buzzer.

"Are you Ms. Cavanagh?" a nurse asked.

Hallie's heart thumped wildly. "I was told my mother is missing." Her voice rose in panic. "What happened?"

"Come with me."

Hallie was adamant. "Please tell me."

"Let's sit." The nurse guided her to a couple of chairs against the wall. She didn't seem too worried about the situation. What the hell was going on?

"I don't want to sit down. I want to know if my mother is all right."

"She is, Ms. Cavanagh. Your mother is fine. She's resting now."

"I want to see her."

"Let's calm down for a minute, and I'll explain." The woman was the epitome of tranquility. It was driving Hallie crazy. "I'm Janet Pearson, the nurse administrator. Your mother had a bit of an episode this afternoon."

"What happened?"

"We're not sure why, but she became extremely agitated. She got away from her caretaker, and we couldn't find her for a short while." Janet emphasized the word short as if that mattered to Hallie.

"Couldn't find her? Where was she? What's wrong with you people?" Anger and frustration whipped through her like a violent storm.

"Getting so upset doesn't do any good. Your mother is fine. She's in her room."

Hallie took a breath, tears clouding her sight. "I'd like to see for myself."

Pillows propped behind her, her mother was sitting up in bed, her head to the side, her eyes closed. At first glance, everything seemed to be normal.

Hallie sat on the edge of the unyielding mattress. She held her mother's hand and noticed bruises on her wrists. "What are these?" Her voice was sharp.

"We had to restrain her, Ms. Cavanagh. As I said, she was quite disturbed and wouldn't calm down."

Hallie's stomach clenched. *It's the disease. This damn disease.*

"It's called 'sundowning.' Patients with Alzheimer's sometimes become confused and aggressive later in the day. We're not sure why it happens. Your mother's nurse left the room to get her medication."

"And?"

"And maybe she took a little longer than usual."

Or stopped to chat with the other nurses. Or went

outside for a smoke. Hallie's frustration was mounting.

"At any rate, there was yelling coming from her room. When some nurses went to check on her, she pushed past them and took off."

"How difficult is it to stop a sixty-seven-year-old woman?"

"You'd be surprised what a person with Alzheimer's can be capable of."

It wasn't the answer Hallie wanted to hear.

"It's a holiday weekend. We're short-staffed. We found her in one of the break rooms huddled in the corner. The positive thing to all this was she had calmed down and went willingly back to her room." Janet's lips thinned. "But as you can see, the place is a little worse for wear."

Hallie looked around and realized that indeed, the room was trashed. The drapes and one of the blinds were torn from the window. The privacy curtain that surrounded her mother's bed was ripped in places. The snack tray was flipped over, and one of the chairs was stuck in the doorway of the bathroom. The family photographs were strewn across the bed. Hallie rescued the souvenir box from the Poconos that was stuck between the mattress and the metal footboard.

As if on cue, the nurse pulled one of the photographs out of the pocket of her white coat. "She was holding this picture when we found her. Do you think it might have set her off?"

Without looking at it, Hallie took the photograph from the nurse. Her mother's eyes started to flutter, and a soft incoherent moan escaped her dry lips.

"Mom? Mom, it's Hallie. I'm here."

Spittle appeared at the corner of her mouth, and

Hallie gently wiped it away with the edge of the sheet.

"Was she given her medication?" Hallie asked the nurse.

"Yes, of course." The nurse sounded offended.

"Rosie?" Her raspy voice caught Hallie's attention.

Rosie? Hallie glanced back at the photo, and her brow lifted with recognition. The colors were faded, but the woman in the Polaroid picture was Rosemary, her mother's younger sister—Hallie's aunt. Before the disease had taken hold, her mother would enjoy looking at the photographs of her family with Hallie. There was Grandma Bev, Grandpa Charlie, cousin Tina, and of course, Aunt Rosemary. She was pretty easy to recognize with her shiny flame-red curls and lively blue eyes. Hallie smiled, remembering her mother telling her that Rosemary used to dye her hair that vibrant color just to get attention.

"My mother, your grandmother, took a stick to the back of your aunt's legs when she came home with that bright red hair. I'll never forget it."

But she had forgotten. She'd forgotten a lot of things.

Hallie studied the picture again. In it, groups of people stood in the background, talking, drinking, or eating. It looked like some party was going on. Hallie looked over at Janet. "You said she was holding this picture when you found her?"

Janet nodded. "I had quite a struggle trying to get it away from her." She looked around. "I'll find someone to clean up the mess." She left the room.

"Rosie?"

Hallie stroked her mother's pale cheek, trying to subdue her restlessness. "I'm Hallie, Mom, and I'm here. I won't let anything bad happen to you."

Her mother pressed her head back into the pillow and remained still.

Hallie regarded the photo again. Aunt Rosemary had looked pretty that day. She wore short shorts and a sleeveless, button-down blouse with the ends tied together to show off her tiny waist.

"Eddie? Ed?" Her mother thrashed her head from side to side. Her eyes were still closed. "Eddie, where are you going?"

Ed was her father. If her mother had been thinking about him, it was no wonder she was distressed. Hallie bit her bottom lip. She had been too young to remember when her father had died. She only knew that every year around his death, her mother would struggle to cope with unresolved feelings. Losing a loved one was never easy.

But her father's image wasn't part of this photograph. Just her aunt Rosemary's. Maybe seeing her sister triggered something else. She couldn't be sure. The disease made her mother unpredictable.

Her mother's jerky movements were cause for alarm. Hallie hated seeing her in such a troubled state. If she herself could take this disease from her mother, she'd do it in a heartbeat.

I believe in love.

And what about Aaron? She had tried to find him but couldn't, and once she got the phone call from the nursing home, she needed to leave quickly. What would she tell him? *Tell him the truth*, she heard her common sense whisper. Would he understand? She'd been down this road before, and it hadn't ended well.

She dug through her tote bag and found her cell

phone. She had to call Aaron. She had to explain.

The sudden shout startled Hallie. Her phone slipped from her grasp and fell to the floor. In an instant, her mother sat up in bed, grabbed hold of Hallie's ears, and smashed their foreheads together. Something exploded in Hallie's brain, a flash of light and then pain. She struggled to pry her mother's fingers from her hair, but she held on with superhuman strength. The last thing Hallie wanted to do was cause harm to her mother, but she had to find some way to escape before something more severe happened. Finally, Janet rushed back into the room, forced her way between the two women, and yelled for help.

"I hate you, Rosie! I hate you!" her mother screeched.

"I'm Hallie, Mom! I'm Hallie."

Two burly male nurses hurried into the room. One of them held her mother firmly by the shoulders, and the other managed to wrench the woman's hands from Hallie's hair.

Hallie staggered to her feet, backed away, and promptly tripped over the fallen snack table. In her fight to remain upright, she slammed against the wall. "Please don't hurt her!" she shouted, still having the wherewithal to go into protection mode.

Janet ran to her aid. "Are you all right?"

"Yes. Yes. Help my mother." Through the haze that was now fogging her brain, Hallie saw one of the male nurses pull out a syringe from the pocket of his scrubs. Before she could blink, he administered the drug in her mother's upper arm, and her mother fell into a deep sleep.

"That won't hurt her, will it?" Hallie winced. The

muscle over her eye was throbbing, not to mention the back of her head.

"It's a mild sedative," Janet explained.

The two male nurses looked shell-shocked and sweaty as they stood back from the bed. They nodded at Hallie and left the room.

"It's best you go home, Ms. Cavanagh," Janet urged. "Your mother will be asleep for a while."

"I want to stay." Hallie took a deep, calming breath. "It's all part of the disease, isn't it? Alzheimer's patients sometimes become violent."

"Yes, some are known to. Can I get you anything? A cold compress for that bruise?" Janet's eyes narrowed as she studied Hallie's forehead. "You're going to have quite a bump there."

Hallie ran her fingers across her brow. The nurse was right. A nasty swelling began to throb under her skin. "She's not getting any better, is she?" Hallie looked at her mother. She looked peaceful as though the last twenty minutes had never happened.

Janet put her hand on Hallie's shoulder. "I wish I could give you some answers."

Hallie felt her heart break. "So do I."

****

Aaron winced when Rita flicked on the light in the kitchen. He sat at the table, nursing a scotch. The party had broken up after the fireworks. The display was spectacular, as always, but without Hallie at his side, he didn't care if they flared with beautiful starbursts or fizzled miserably.

"Why didn't you come find me, Kevin? Why the hell didn't Hallie tell me she was leaving? Why didn't you?" Aaron had been near frantic when he finally tracked down Kevin Carlyle.

"She told me she tried to find you."

"Where was she going?"

"Back to New York."

"Did she say why?"

"Have you called her?" Kevin asked.

Was he hiding something? "Of course I have. Called. Texted." His voice was hoarse with frustration. "She's not answering." Aaron forced himself to calm down. After all, it wasn't Kevin's fault Hallie had taken off. It was his fault for being with Miranda. "Look, Kevin, I'm sorry for getting upset with you. I'm just worried."

"No worries. I get it. You love her."

Aaron had flinched. He hadn't said the words out loud yet, but Kevin's insight made his feelings more real. He was in love with Hallie.

Aaron let go a long, exhausted sigh and downed the rest of the scotch. The more he tried to ignore the truth, the more it persisted. Did Miranda say anything that sparked Hallie's hasty retreat? Maybe Miranda didn't even realize she had. He stared at his phone's dark, blank screen.

"Have you heard anything, Aaron?" Rita asked.

He looked up at the housekeeper and shook his head. She would always refer to him by his first name when they were alone. "No. Nothing."

She pulled out a chair and sat next to him. "Does she have family?"

"A mother. Her father died when she was a baby."

"Anyone else?"

"I don't know. She never said." A troubled inner voice cut into his thoughts. Was this about her ex-fiancé? Had he called her? Did he want to see her again? Did she still have feelings for the guy? Had she only been fooling herself when she told him she and this Kyle were over? Aaron furrowed his brow. Tension tightened his neck tendons. "She has a roommate."

Rita gently covered his arm with her hand. "Do you know the roommate's number?"

He shook his head. "But I know where she works."

"That's a start. Look, I care about you, Aaron, and I know you care about Hallie. I see the way you look at her. The way you look at each other. She cares about you, too."

Doubts filled his brain. "I'm not sure about that, Rita. There are things about me…" He couldn't get out the rest.

Her hold on him was as steady as her voice. "I know, Aaron, but remember this. When you finally learn to forgive yourself, everything else will fall into place."

And with that, his sometimes aggravating but eternally wise housekeeper left the room.

****

Hallie awoke to the clattering of equipment for morning rounds and the smells of breakfast. She'd spent the night in her mother's room in one of those electric hospital lounge chairs that lay flat with a push of a button. She stared at the ceiling tiles, her gaze landing on one with a small dark stain at the corner. She slid her arms out from under the thin, scratchy blanket Janet had given her last night, and adjusted the pillow drenched with her own sweat. The antiquated air-conditioning left little to be desired.

She pushed the button on the side of the chair. The

whirring noise filled the room as the chair halted several times on its way into an upright position. Her mother lay still in bed, eyes closed, the pallid morning light accentuating her frailness. Her forehead throbbed again. She touched the bump. It was still there.

"Good morning."

Hallie looked over at the door. A young, quite-chipper nurse strolled into the room and took a look at Hallie's head. She winced when the nurse brushed her fingers over the bump.

"Can I get you anything? Tylenol?"

"Yes, please. How does it look?"

"Hope you like the color purple." She flashed a smile. "Janet told me what happened before she went off duty this morning."

"Yeah." Hallie threw off the blanket and pushed herself out of the chair. Her legs felt like lead stumps. "Mom got a little feisty yesterday."

"That's what you're calling it?" The nurse scooped up the blanket and pillow. "Would you like an ice pack?"

"No, thank you." Hallie looked back at her mother. "She had a good night."

"Yes, she did. I have to check her vitals now. They're serving breakfast in the dining room. You look like you could use some coffee, at the very least."

That was Hallie's cue to leave. "I'll be back in a bit. I'll be in the dining area. Please come find me if there are any changes."

"Of course. But take your time. Miss Donna has her physical therapy session in about an hour."

The dining room was small but cozy. While the rest of the nursing home could use a much-needed facelift, this place looked out of sorts. Square wood tables, each dressed with a white tablecloth and a small vase of fresh flowers, beckoned her to take a seat. The plates, utensils, and glassware were real—no paper or plastic. On a large TV screen over in the corner, a curvy meteorologist pointed out the weather patterns for the week.

A few patients wrapped in the standard cotton robes, their feet covered in slippers or skid-free socks, ate their breakfasts quietly. From the ceiling speakers, the soft murmur of elevator music drifted through the room. The aroma of coffee instantly awakened her brain, and her body began to crave its dark, comforting flavor. It wouldn't be Starbucks, but it would do.

Hallie found an empty table. On top of the plate was a paper menu listing the breakfast fare and a nominal fee for guests to partake. If she didn't know any better, she'd swear she was in an upscale restaurant.

"Good morning. My name's Patty. Can I get you some coffee?"

Hallie looked up. A woman, probably in her fifties, stood by the table, small pad of paper and pen in her hand. "Coffee would be great. Thank you."

Patty was back moments later with a mug of steaming coffee. "We're serving blueberry pancakes today." She placed the mug in front of Hallie. "And turkey bacon or veggie sausage."

"Pancakes, please."

Patty scribbled on her pad. "If you need anything, I'll be around."

Hallie took a much-needed sip of coffee as soon as the woman left. No, it wasn't Starbucks, but it tasted divine. Hot and rich. Comforting. She reached into her bag, found the small foil packet of Tylenol the nurse had given her, and ripped off the top. She downed the pills with another gulp.

She closed her eyes and took a deep breath. Her muscles were stiff, her face was sore, and her ego was bruised. In her heart, she knew her mother was never going to get better. It was just a matter of time before the damned disease took her away completely from everything she knew.

But what had made her mother so furious? Even in her worst moments, forgetting the simplest things, she'd never been violent. Did her intense feelings have something to do with the photograph of her sister?

A distant memory pushed its way into the forefront. Even though she'd been young, Hallie remembered her aunt Rosemary as vibrant, fun, and flirty. Last night, her mother had frantically called out Rosemary's name followed by her father's.

"Eddie? Ed? Eddie, where are you going?"

Hallie wondered if her father and Rosemary had something to do with her mother's depression when his death anniversary came around. She'd been too young to remember any details, and her mother never offered any. Only that her father had been riding his motorcycle in the rain, skidded, and slammed into a car. He'd been killed instantly. But what if he hadn't died from the accident? What if something else—or *someone* else had a hand in his demise? It was a ridiculous thought, and she knew it. And with that, the idea of foul play was lost and no longer in focus.

Instead, another memory ruffled through her mind like wind on water. It was about Miranda, the woman she'd met on the beach. She thought back to the first time she'd been with Aaron at his house in Sea Girt. The image of him throwing his phone into the pool that day loomed large in her mind. Was Miranda the "Mir" that she had heard Aaron say that morning she'd interrupted his phone call?

She'd seemed like a nice person as they talked yesterday. Known a lot about Aaron. Said she was an old friend. A good friend. Was she more than just a friend?

Had Aaron known she would be at his party? Had he invited her? Had that been the reason she couldn't find him to tell him she had to leave? Had they been together?

She had no proof, and yet the image of Aaron and Miranda in bed kept popping up in her mind. *Stop it. Don't read into things.* Lost in the disturbing thoughts, she didn't hear the waitress ask her to move her arms so she could put the plate of pancakes in front of her.

"Oh, I'm sorry," Hallie said.

"I hope he's worth it."

She looked up at Patty. "What?"

"I hope he's worth all that attention you're giving him. Enjoy. I'll be back to refill your cup."

Yes, he's worth it.

She had to tell Aaron why she had taken off so suddenly. And she had to tell him now.

She dug out her phone from her bag. She had checked her phone before she got to the city and seen that he had texted and called her, but she wanted to take the time to think her story through before she answered him. But it now looked like she'd never get the chance. The screen was shattered after the tumble it had taken when it slipped from her grasp during her scuffle with her mother.

She turned it on. The screen lit up a bright white and pulsated with tiny black lines. No icons were visible. "Crap," she murmured under her breath. The phone, by all accounts, was dead. That was the trouble with technology. She didn't have to memorize anything. Everything, including phone numbers, was readily available at a touch. She'd never learned Aaron's number.

The company phone! Of course. She found it and then nearly dropped it when it came alive with its obnoxious ring. She was even more startled the caller was Aaron.

"Aaron?"

"Where are you?" He didn't sound happy. He didn't sound like anything.

What would she say? How would she explain? "I have to tell you something."

"You certainly do."

His curt tone startled her. "Can we meet—?"

"I'm here."

She slid to the edge of the chair. "Where?"

"Here."

"What? Where?" The bottom of her spine tingled.

"In the lobby."

"Wait—"

But the phone went silent and dark. Her thoughts scattered. She dropped the phone in her bag and left her untouched breakfast behind.

Hallie came to a dead stop when she reached the lobby. Aaron was hunched over in one of the chairs by the picture window.

"Aaron?"

She tried to balance her feelings. What was he doing here? How had he found her? Should she be angry? Embarrassed?

He looked up, his gaze locking with hers. He stood, went over to her, and gathered her into his embrace.

She laid her cheek against his chest, let go a trembling breath, and fought back tears.

He held her at arm's length and studied her face. His mouth slackened. "What happened?" He pointed to the bruise on her forehead.

She shirked away. "It's a long story."

"Are you okay?"

She nodded. "Did you follow me?"

"Contrary to what this seems, I'm not a stalker. When Rita told me you asked Kevin to drive you to the train station, I didn't know what to think." His voice dropped in volume. "I was worried about you."

He was worried about her. Could she argue with that? His lopsided grin warmed her heart. "But how did you—?"

"Sophie told me. Why didn't *you*?"

She took a breath. "Now what?"

"Now, we go see your mother."

****

Hallie walked over to her mother's bed. Aaron remained in the doorway. Donna's hair was damp, and her skin glowed. The bed linens were crisp and blindingly white, and the room smelled faintly of lavender soap.

"Hi, Mom," she greeted a bit warily. "How are you today?"

Donna looked her way. Hallie caught a brief flash

of recognition in her mother's eyes, and then it was gone.

"Who's that?"

Hallie waved Aaron into the room. "This is Aaron, Mom. He's my—"

"Friend. I'm Hallie's friend. It's very nice to meet you."

Donna didn't react. "Could you get me that box?" She pointed to the wooden box on the windowsill.

The photographs. The nurse must have gathered them up. Hallie held her breath.

Donna patted the space next to her. "Sit down, young man."

Hallie caught Aaron's grin as he did what he'd been told.

Donna flipped the lid open and rummaged inside the box. "These are my pictures." She held up a few. "Aren't they nice?"

Aaron nodded, glanced at Hallie, and winked.

His expression took her by surprise. He wasn't being polite. He truly enjoyed being with her mother.

Donna singled out a faded Polaroid photo. "Do you know who this is?" With a shaky finger, she indicated the image of a woman.

He stared and frowned. "I'm not sure. Hallie, maybe you know."

Yes, she did know. "That's you, Mom," she said, recognizing a younger, happier Donna Cavanagh holding a baby. "Is that me?"

Her mother grunted. "Of course not. Why would you be in this picture? That baby is my daughter." She paused. "Her name is…Hallie. Isn't she sweet?"

Hallie glanced at Aaron. Had Sophie told him

everything about her mother? Had he realized the extent of the dreadful disease? He was stone-faced but attentive.

Bringing it closer, Donna stared at the photo. Then those same tired eyes peered into Hallie's. "You're not Hallie. You're very pretty, but I don't know who you are."

Sorrow weighing heavily, Hallie's shoulders sagged. "That's all right."

Donna brightened. "I'm going to the dance tonight, and I must get ready." She grabbed Aaron's hand. "Will you take me? I love to dance. Will you dance with me?"

He didn't miss a beat. "I'd be honored." With his other hand, he covered hers. "But first, I think you should rest. I wouldn't want you to tire out before we had a chance to dance."

Donna's smile was alert and genuine.

He rose from the bed.

"You're such a nice young man. Isn't he a nice young man?"

Hallie agreed, her gaze never leaving him. "Yes, he's a nice young man."

Her mother pulled the bedsheet up to her chin. "I'm tired. Could you leave now?"

"Are you sure?" Hallie asked. "I can stay if you want."

Sadness filled her mother's eyes. "You're so pretty. Who are you again?"

Emptiness entered Hallie's heart, and tears burned the back of her eyes. "I'm Hallie, Mom. I'm your daughter."

"My daughter left me. I have no daughter." Donna's blank stare told Hallie it was no use pushing this any further. Her mother had shut down.

Hallie's heart broke, but what could she do? Berate her mother? Plead with her? It would do no good. "I'll be back," she whispered in her mother's ear.

Donna closed her eyes and sank into the pillows. Aaron crossed at the foot of the bed and reached for Hallie. She hesitated, then slipped her hand into his. Together they left the room.

Looking for privacy, they sat outside in the small garden area. The now-overcast sky held the promise of rain.

Aaron offered her a Styrofoam cup. "It's all they had. Sorry."

The burnt smell of bottom-of-the-pot coffee assailed her nostrils. "Thank you."

He studied her injured forehead. "Are you sure you're okay?" He carefully avoided the bruise as he touched her face, his fingertips sliding over her cheekbone to her lips. "How did it happen?"

His touch was comforting. A lump clogged her throat. The tears came so quickly she couldn't stop them from falling. He held her close. She let go a breath that was half frustration, half disbelief.

"My mother."

"She did this to you?" His voice was measured.

"It was an accident. She couldn't control herself."

"Is she the reason you left the party?"

She closed her eyes and tried to ignore the ache that had settled behind her heart.

"Dementia?" His question made her soul shiver.

"Alzheimer's."

Aaron remained silent. Hallie looked at him and gathered in the quiet strength in his eyes.

"Say something."

"Why didn't you tell me?"

She moved into him, and he held her closer. "I don't know."

"Don't you trust me?"

"I do."

"I'm not Kyle, you know."

She blinked in surprise. "How did you—?" She stopped, and her body shrank a little. "Sophie."

A smile slowly tipped one corner of her mouth. A soft breeze picked up her hair, stirring the strands around her cheeks. Dark gray clouds smeared the sky, and a faint rumble warned of a summer storm on its way.

"Let's get out of here."

He looked at her. "Are you sure?"

She rose and took his hand. "More than I'll ever be."

****

Through the back and forth motion of the windshield wipers on Aaron's car, Hallie was still able to view the magnificent apartment building ahead. With its three distinctive towers and ornate architectural elements, it looked like a castle right out of a fairy tale.

Aaron drove the car into an open garage area beneath the building.

A tall, lanky man appeared and opened his door. "Hello, Mr. Knight."

Aaron nodded. "Harold." He tossed the man his car keys.

The man circled the car, his long legs in full stride, and opened Hallie's door.

"Thank you." She regarded Aaron. "Where are

we?" She had a feeling she knew.

"My place." He took her hand and led her to the elevator.

With the doorman and fourteen floors behind them, the elevator doors opened to a foyer bigger than her apartment. They walked across marble tiled floors. Original artwork hung on recessed walls. A large bouquet of flowers sat upon a round glass table, their fresh scent wafting around her. "Penthouse?"

"Guilty."

"Mmmm."

His grin became lopsided, like the two sides of his face couldn't agree on an expression. They turned a corner.

"There's more," he said.

There certainly was. The tiled foyer led to shiny hardwood floors that graced a large open space furnished as a combination living and dining area, complete with an array of windows overlooking Central Park. She touched the rain-streaked pane. Even in the gray and grime, the city looked majestic.

"Can I get you anything?" he asked.

"I know it's early, but I could use a glass of wine."

"It's five o'clock somewhere. I'll see what I can do."

He disappeared into another room. She sank into the soft leather of the couch. He was going to want an explanation. How much had Sophie told him?

"Found some crackers and cheese, too. It's not much…" He handed her a half-filled glass of pale gold wine.

Just breathing in the fruity scent calmed her.

He sat next to her and clinked his glass against

hers. She didn't respond.

"You're worried, aren't you?"

Unease rolled through her like a dark wave.

"Would you like to talk about it? Despite what you may have heard, I'm a pretty good listener."

She knew that already. "You saw a little bit of what my mother's dealing with. She has her good days and bad days."

"But what about your days with her?"

"It's a horrific feeling knowing that someday she won't know who I am at all. I miss my mother. Bits of her are still there sometimes, and I know she's trying to hold on to those morsels of memory. I also know she's terrified."

"How long has she been this way?"

"About two years. It started slowly. Once she forgot what a pencil was for. She was baking a cake and didn't know why she was holding an egg. She'd always get this blank expression that would turn into fright. Then there was the day she forgot who I was."

"Oh, Hallie. That must have torn out your heart."

"I can't explain what it's like to mourn someone who's still alive." Tears flowed freely from her eyes. She didn't bother to brush them away.

"Those pieces of memories your mother still retains are worth fighting for, Hallie. Never give up."

"I want to believe it, but I know that's not possible. I've lost most of her already, and I will lose her again when…"

He took her wineglass and placed it on the glass and chrome table in front of the couch, then pulled her into his arms. His touch was comforting and disturbing at the same time. Her energy exhausted, she sank into him.

"Just remember for her when she can't remember anymore."

"You sound as if you've gone through something like this. Have you?"

"Not this disease. Not any disease, and not to this extent. But as I said, family is a complicated matter."

She pondered his perceptions. He spoke as if he truly understood. They were both silent, but she'd never felt more connected to another human being as she was with Aaron at this moment.

"I feel like the worst daughter in the world. Especially now. Especially here."

"Why would you say that?"

"I'm here enjoying all this." She looked at him, feeling like her life was unraveling. "Enjoying you, and my mother is back at that nursing home fighting to make sense of what's happening to her."

He held her at arm's length. "Is it possible for your mother to be an outpatient?"

The compassion in his gaze rattled her. "What do you mean?"

"Do you think she'd enjoy spending a few days at the house?"

"Aaron, that's very generous, but—"

"I'd hire a full-time nurse to watch her. Whatever she needed, she'd have." Everything faded away as he kept his gaze on her. "Maybe I should mind my own business." His voice was rough with anxiety.

"I appreciate what you're trying to do. I just don't know why you would want to."

"Because I care about you, Hallie. What bothers you, bothers me. What frightens you, frightens me. And what makes you happy, makes me happy." He tucked her closer to his side, bowed his head, and took her mouth in a soft kiss.

Her heart beat erratically as he eased his lips away.

These are just words, she reminded herself, but as he slid closer to her, her world shifted into his. "I promised I'd take care of her, and I've kept that promise. That's why I'm so grateful I'm working for ARK. The money I make offers me to have round-the-clock care for her."

"And that's why you're worried about us." He wrapped his arm around her shoulder and pulled her close. "About our relationship."

"I can't afford to lose this job, Aaron."

"Sweetheart, you won't. I want to help you anyway I can. Please let me."

It was difficult for her not to notice the hushed tone wedged between his words. His body flinched as though he needed to take an emotional step back.

"Kyle and I were planning our life together. When the doctors diagnosed my mother's Alzheimer's—I wasn't about to abandon her. She was scared, Aaron. What else could I do?"

"You did the right thing. Your mother might not be aware of your love and support, but at least you know you're doing everything you can for her."

A surge of anger swelled inside her. "Then why do I hate her sometimes?" She swallowed her resentment quickly. "I didn't mean to say that. I love her."

"You don't have to quash your feelings, Hallie. I know you love your mother, and I know you're struggling. I can only imagine how overwhelming it can be."

She looked at him. The significance of his words wasn't lost on her. Was he dealing with a similar situation? She knew nothing about his family life. And now wasn't the time to ask. "But she's my mother, Aaron. How can I feel this way about her?"

"Because her disease cost you everything."

And what was your cost? Why was she picking up on his guilt? His regrets? She let go a breath. "I guess our sins do find us. Kyle couldn't handle it. His family is all about image. Having to take care of my ailing mother didn't fit into his plans."

"Asshole."

She paused, trying to make sense of his reaction. "You're taking this personally."

"Why wouldn't I? I told you I care about you, Hallie, and what's part of your life should be part of mine. Actually, I'm amazed by you. Your strength. Your perseverance. Your ability to forgive."

She laid her head on his shoulder. "That's why I know love can change everything. If I hadn't promised to take care of my mother, I would never have met you."

"You really do believe that?"

"I do."

A crackle of energy passed between them as their gazes met. Her whole being was filled with waiting. Aaron's mouth captured hers in a passionate kiss, and Hallie knew that once again her life was about to change.

****

The anticipation to be with Hallie made his body ache with the need for release. Just the thought of her here in his bedroom, in his arms, ready to make love nearly drove him over the edge. He had bared some of his soul and was ready to proclaim his love for her. *You don't believe in love.* But he did believe in Hallie and him together. It was the first step.

He kissed the corners of her mouth. "Are you sure this is what you want?"

Her eyes went a little misty. "Yes."

A smile worked its way up from deep inside him. Hands skimming her sides, he cradled the soft weight of her breasts. He scraped his thumbs over her nipples. They peaked, hard and sturdy, under the thin cotton of her T-shirt.

Her breathing became erratic as he slid his hands under her shirt and bra. She raised her arms, and he slipped the clothing off her. Suddenly shy, she folded her arms across her chest.

He coaxed her arms away, his hands circling her wrists, holding her captive as he gently pushed her down on the bed. Blood pounded in his veins as he removed his shirt and slacks. Reaching for her, he tugged at her shorts and panties and slid them down her legs.

As he drank in the beauty of her naked form, he realized he felt more for her than just wanton desire. He'd gone through the same rituals with other women before—the touching, the kissing, the sex. But this was different. So different that his heart ached and his mind began to take him to places he'd never experienced. Was this really love? True, pure love?

The soft glow in her eyes captivated him, and he covered her with his body, careful not to lose what little control he had left. He crushed his mouth to hers, deepening the pressure, teasing with his tongue.

Every cell in his body erupted with need. His fingers slid over her quivering thighs. "I love the way you feel." Her belly tightened with every roll of his hips. His gaze locked with hers, gauging her response.

She ran her hands over his arms as her breasts rose and fell with each labored breath. He kissed her again, long and hard. She clung to his shoulders while his mouth devoured hers. When she opened her lips to receive his questing tongue, he convulsed with pleasure.

She groaned as he eased off her mouth and left a trail of kisses on the edge of her collarbone. "Are you sure this is what *you* want?" she asked when she finally caught her breath.

Surprised at her comment, he raised himself up on his elbows and stared at her questioning expression. "Are you having second thoughts?"

"I'm thinking about work."

"At a time like this?"

She laughed. "You know what I mean."

"We're adults. We don't have to explain anything to anybody." He smiled at her and stroked the hair from her flushed face. "I won't hurt you, Hallie. And I'm not about to let anyone else hurt you in or outside the office. You trust me, don't you?"

"With all my heart."

"Then that's all I need to hear."

He nipped at her ear and neck, and her moans of pleasure delighted him. A spike of heat hit him low in the gut when she touched him. His reserve of willpower dwindling, he reached across her, opened the drawer of the table next to the bed, and grabbed a condom.

He lifted her slightly off the bed and eased himself

into her. She took him into her and slowly rocked her body against his, rising to meet him in a moment of uncontrolled passion. The fire within him spread to his heart, and he was stunned by the deep peace he felt while inside her. Moments later, they soared to a shuddering surrender.

Breathless, he fell against her. "You know that love thing?" he whispered in her ear. "I think I'm believing in it, Hallie, and I believe I love you."

****

The rain stopped and the clouds had parted, allowing the silver light of the full moon to pour through the bedroom windows.

I believe I love you.

His surprising yet sincere words had made her heart soar. The subtle scent of him enticed her to move closer. She rubbed her cheek against his warm bare chest and listened to the rhythm of his heartbeat.

"Are you okay?" His breathy voice sent a shiver through her.

"Better. I feel at peace. Content." She dropped soft kisses on his face and throat. "I feel like I'm…home."

Chapter Fifteen

"Don't forget your lunch meeting with Shoe-Luv, Ms. Cavanagh." Julian stood in front of her desk, a stack of ARK-embossed manila folders in his hands. He handed her the one on top.

Hallie looked at him, her mind not on work. "What?"

"It's almost twelve. The restaurant's across town. I've already called the company car service." He stopped. "Are you all right? You seem distracted."

Her smile was a tight grin. Distracted? That was an understatement. A week had passed since she and Aaron had first made love. She couldn't help feeling a bit uneasy when she'd gone back to the office. Her coworkers had been curious about the bruise on her forehead, and even Lavelle, who made it a point to stay out of the employees' personal business, made mention several times of Hallie's preoccupation. Hallie wasn't sure why, but Lavelle's questions seemed to border on intrusive.

In the weeks following her employment, Hallie and Lavelle had become close. Hallie was grateful for Lavelle's wise advice about office activities when she needed it. Working so close with Aaron made her very protective, and she would subtly, yet often, remind Hallie of the importance of her position. Hallie took the singing her praises in stride. She wondered what advice the woman would give if Hallie told her what had happened at the penthouse.

Sophie had offered no apology for telling Aaron about Hallie's mother. "I know he cares about you, Hallie. He needed to know."

Hallie wasn't angry. She let her roommate know how kind Aaron had been to her mother, how interested—maybe even invested now that they'd become intimate. She told that to Sophie, too.

"See?" Sophie had said. "He *is* your billionaire."

"Ms. Cavanagh?" Julian's impatient voice now made Hallie focus.

She got to her feet. "Yes, thank you, Julian. I'm on my way."

The car service dropped her off at Breo, an indoor/outdoor bistro in Greenwich Village.

"Can I help you?" The hostess greeted her by the door.

"I'm meeting someone," Hallie said. "She might already be here."

The hostess nodded, and Hallie followed her through the maze of mahogany tables and a smattering of patrons. At the back of the restaurant, against an exposed, red brick wall, sat a lone woman, her spiky hair dyed pink, her focus on her phone.

"Clarissa Burns?"

The woman looked up and smiled. "Hallie Cavanagh?"

Hallie thanked the hostess, who promised a server would be right with them.

The women shook hands, and Clarissa invited Hallie to sit. "It's nice to have a face to go with a voice." Her brow rose. "A very insistent voice."

Hallie tilted her chin. "Once ARK Enterprises is interested in a company, it's hard for us to give up."

"Us? You mean Aaron Knight, don't you? His reputation of gobbling up companies precedes him."

Hallie placed her briefcase on the chair next to her. "Actually, Mr. Knight wasn't briefed on Shoe-Luv. I've done the research, and I'm very impressed with the growth of your company. But I'm even more impressed with your principles."

Clarissa looked puzzled. "How do you mean?"

"Well, for every pair of shoes sold, you give another to a child in need. I find that admirable."

"Does Mr. Knight? I've heard he's not exactly philanthropic."

At first, Hallie wasn't sure how to respond. Did Clarissa know Aaron personally, or was she just lumping him in with other self-made men whose only altruistic ways concerned their bottom line?

Hallie chose to ignore Clarissa's snide comment. She wanted the company, not the woman's personal position on greed. "As I pointed out when we talked, under the ARK umbrella, your business will grow faster—"

"There it is—money."

"But needy children benefit, too, don't they? The more your company grows, the more your charitable contributions expand."

Clarissa didn't argue that point. She drew her lips into a tight smile.

Though there was something about the woman she liked, Hallie couldn't help the bad vibe she was getting. "A week ago, you were much more agreeable with the terms I offered you. But now you seem a bit put off.

What's changed?"

"Look, Hallie, I like you. I think we can work together. In fact, I'm sure we can." Clarissa took a sip of water from the tall glass in front of her. The clinking of the ice cubes unnerved Hallie for some reason. "But my lawyer said ARK Enterprises might not be a good fit."

The mention of a lawyer didn't surprise Hallie. Having representation was the norm in business.

Clarissa glanced at her watch. "He should be here soon."

Hallie grinned, her lips a thin line. Now she would have to convince two people that ARK would do right by Shoe-Love. She squared her shoulders. She was up for the challenge.

"Sorry, I'm late, ladies." The husky male voice drew Hallie's attention immediately.

Her jaw dropped as she stared at the man standing by their table. "Kyle, what are you doing here?"

****

Aaron had decided to work from his home office. Hallie had a meeting today with some company she seemed excited about. He didn't want to distract her. She had enough on her mind.

Like her mother.

He was glad to have found out about Donna Cavanagh. He guessed Hallie would have eventually told him about her mother's condition, but now that it was out in the open, he felt even closer to her.

Her disclosure about Kyle dumping her because of Donna's condition had his ire up. The guy was an idiot. Heartless. Insensitive. And Aaron couldn't thank him enough. If it wasn't for Kyle's unwillingness to accept

Hallie's mother, the two of them would have never met, let alone become intimate. A thoughtful smile turned up the corners of his mouth. He remembered Hallie's words. "That's why I know love can change everything. If I hadn't promised to take care of my mother, I would never have met you."

But what about him?

She had willingly revealed important parts of her private life. It was brave of her, and he admired that.

He wanted intimacy. Not just physically, but in every way. When they were apart, something was missing inside him. They made more sense together. When he was with her, he was a whole person. An unbroken man. Was that love?

He pushed himself away from the desk and went into the kitchen to make a cup of coffee. Thoughts of calling her entered his mind, but he presumed her meeting was still going on. He smirked. And the meeting would continue until she signed the client. In the weeks Hallie had been working for ARK, she'd proven herself an excellent negotiator. The businesses she'd acquired had added nicely to the company's bottom line.

At work, they managed to keep their relationship a secret. But for how long was anybody's guess. Not that it mattered to him whether his employees knew about them or not. He was only protecting Hallie and her feelings.

Mug in hand, he wandered over to the window to watch the traffic—both vehicle and foot—on the city street below. Students hauling backpacks, food truck vendors securing prime space, and motivated joggers punctuated the cityscape along with quick-stepping corporate employees and swerving yellow taxis. One of those touristy horse and carriages clomped and rolled down the street. Would Hallie enjoy a ride in one of those carriages? The lofty thought melted away like an ice cube on a summer sidewalk.

Was he doing the right thing protecting her from his past? What was he afraid of? Losing her respect? Losing her altogether? His thoughts turned to Miranda and how easily she could have told Hallie about what he had done. And yet she'd kept quiet. Why? He had no idea but was grateful for her discretion. But as much as he didn't want to agree with her, she'd spoken the truth. Hallie had a right to know. The thought put his mind into a tailspin and tightened his stomach. He had to share his dark past with her—and soon. Though his juvenile record was sealed, nothing was kept secret for long.

His cell phone on the desk suddenly buzzed. Hallie? He turned it over and was disappointed. It was Lavelle. He hit the speaker icon.

"Yes, Lavelle?"

"Sorry to bother you at home, Mr. Knight, but I have Marc Goodwin from CNBS on the phone. You were supposed to call him. He seems a little impatient."

"Marc Goodwin?" He searched his memory. "Oh, yes, you're right. What does he want?"

"He'd like to talk to you about a television proposal."

He was surprised. Television proposal? His company owned several smaller TV news stations, but CNBS was the big time, one of the first stations to broadcast the news twenty-four seven back in the late '80s.

He shrugged, his mind running through possible scenarios of selling or buying. "Okay, Lavelle. Put him through."

****

"What were you trying to do, Kyle?"

Kyle leaned back, a damaging look plastered on his face. "Just protecting my client."

"You almost cost me a lucrative deal."

"Clarissa signed, didn't she?"

"Barely."

Even though she had acquired Shoe-Luv from Clarissa Burns, it'd taken a lot of convincing that ARK Enterprises was going to do right by her company. And it hadn't helped that Kyle shot down every proposal Hallie made. Thank goodness Clarissa was a savvy businesswoman. The final deal Hallie had offered her was an excellent one, and Clarissa would have been a fool if she rejected it. Even Kyle had seemed impressed, though Hallie suspected he was furious on the inside. But by the end of the meeting, Clarissa had signed with ARK, and although Hallie had offered much more for Shoe-Love than she first proposed, she knew the acquisition would be profitable. Aaron might balk at first, but she'd convince him Shoe-Luv would be an asset for ARK.

But aside from her success, she was still annoyed at Kyle. Just her luck he was Clarissa's lawyer, but it was more than that. His smug expression was annoying the hell out of her.

Clarissa had left the restaurant about a half hour ago, leaving Kyle and her alone. Though she should get back to the office, Hallie needed to confront him on his excessive intrusion.

"Come on, Hallie. Did you really think I'd ruin this deal for you?"

"You came close."

"I just wanted what was best for Clarissa. You can't fault me for that. I was being conscientious."

"You were being an ass."

His brow rose. "Wow. Tell me what you really think."

She took a sip of water from her glass. "I just wonder if you would've been here protecting your client if I wasn't the one trying to acquire her company."

"Can we stop talking about business?"

"There's nothing else we have to talk about. I have to go."

She began to get up, but he grabbed her hand. She yanked it back.

"A few minutes, Hallie. Give me a few minutes."

"For what?"

"To talk. I just want to talk."

It was against her better judgment, but she remained. "I've said everything I needed to."

A pained look crossed his face, followed by a shadow that made her cringe. "Then there's no chance for us?"

"Things haven't changed, Kyle. My mother needs me. She's going to be part of my life."

"I know that. You have a big heart, Hallie. That's why I fell in love with you." He glanced at the table. "Why I'm still in love with you."

"Kyle, please don't."

His gaze once again locked on hers. The darkness there sent a tingle down her spine.

"Does he love you?"

She paused. *I believe I love you...* She heard the words in her head as clearly as he'd said them to her days ago. "Yes, he does."

"And you? Do you love him?"

"Yes. I love him." The words surprised her. She hadn't even told Aaron yet. But yes, she did love the man.

"Have you told him?"

How dare he interrogate her. "That's none of your business."

"Then you haven't told him." He slugged back the rest of the tequila he'd ordered during lunch.

Anger churned in her chest. "You have no idea what the two of us have. Respect. Closeness—"

"But not love. At least not on your part."

She stood and grabbed her briefcase. He had forced her to face her fear, and she hated him for it. "Goodbye, Kyle. Have a nice life."

"You need to be careful, Hallie. Knight is not who you think he is."

His words stopped her cold. His features carried a startling amount of information, and his arrogant smile revealed an air of conquest.

She did her best not to get drawn into his machinations, even though his warning had her wondering. "Kyle—"

"I'm only looking out for you. I don't want you to get hurt."

"Aaron's not going to hurt me."

"I don't mean that kind of hurt."

She stared at him and blinked with bafflement, her mind whirling with a stir of emotions. What the hell did he think he knew?

He pushed himself away from the table and stood. "The man has secrets, Hallie."

"Everyone has secrets. What are you talking about?"

"Not like this. Just be careful."

And with those ominous words, Kyle exited the restaurant and left Hallie trying to quell the chaotic images racing through her mind.

****

Hallie lay next to Aaron, the damp sheets pulled up to their waists. He cradled her body next to his. She felt small, vulnerable, and soft in his arms. His heartbeat strong and steady under her ear, she delighted in their passionate lovemaking. She pressed a kiss against the hollow of his throat, making him moan.

"Don't, unless you're ready to go again," he teased.

"Whenever you are, Mr. Knight."

He grabbed her and pulled her on top of him. Their laughter blended together in a full, rich, and contagious sound. She gave him a light playful kiss, just enough to still his resistance.

"Oh, Ms. Cavanagh, what you do to me."

She rolled off him and stretched out on her side of the bed. Though their lovemaking had once again left his heated imprint on her skin, she couldn't turn off Kyle's warning. *The man has secrets. Just be careful.*

It had to be jealousy. Kyle was lashing out with anything he could—maybe even with lies.

"So how did your meeting go?" Aaron propped himself up on his elbow, his hand under his head.

"You are now the owner of Shoe-Luv."

He eyed her with a strange look. "Shoe-Luv? Is

that really the name?"

"Yes."

"Never heard of it."

"Trust me. You will." She tapped his nose. "And your day?"

"Interesting. Have you ever watched the TV show *Product Pitch*?"

"The one where small upstarts present proposals to big companies in hopes that they'll give them money to further their businesses?"

"That's the one. Marc Goodwin, president of CNBS, called me today. Seems Richard Edwards, the CEO of Edwards Initiatives, is leaving the show."

Excitement tingled her skin. "And they want you to take his place?"

He nodded, though apprehensively.

"You're going to do this, aren't you?"

"Obviously you think I should."

"You don't?"

"I haven't made up my mind. I wanted to tell you first."

She smiled.

"Then you think I should take Goodwin up on his offer?"

"Of course. Think what the exposure would do for ARK."

"The taping will take some of my time away from you."

She tapped his nose. "I'll survive. Besides, now I can tell people my boyfriend is a television star."

"Boyfriend? I don't think I've ever been called that before."

"Never?"

He shook his head.

"What about Miranda? She never called you her boyfriend?" Though she knew next to nothing about his and Miranda's relationship, Hallie had the distinct impression they were more than old friends. Should she tell him about Kyle?

"Hallie." The tone was sharp.

"Tell me about her."

His eyes widened. "Now? We just made love, and you want me to tell you about another woman."

"Yes."

He sank into the pillow. "You met her. What was your impression?"

"Confident. Beautiful. In love with you."

"It's not love. It was never love." He was quite adamant about that detail.

"You were talking to her that day you threw your phone in the pool, weren't you?"

"You knew?"

"I had a feeling. I'd call that passion."

"I call it over."

"Is it?"

"For months."

"Why did you invite her to the Fourth of July party?"

"I didn't. I suspect she showed up because she wanted to meet you."

"You told her about me?"

"I was just getting to know you. I knew I wanted you in my life. There wouldn't be room for her."

"Thank you."

"For what?"

"For trusting me."

"I love you. Of course I trust you. You've changed my life." He kissed her gently, sweetly. "You've changed me. What makes you happy?"

The question was so surprising she frowned but didn't hesitate. "You. You make me happy."

"I love you, Hallie."

Her frown turned to a smile. Distorted images of Kyle and Miranda scattered her true thoughts, while conflicting emotions swirled in her head. *I love you, too, Aaron.* The words were loud, clear, and tender in her mind. Why couldn't she voice them? A slow throb pulsed through her. She clung to him, and his body leaped in response, his tender touch a reminder of the passion they'd shared moments before. A small moan of pleasure escaped her, along with a good measure of apprehension.

Love does change everything. Her body molded into his. Maybe that was why she was careful in keeping her true feelings hidden.

Chapter Sixteen

Park Studio, one of many workspaces on the downtown waterfront, was bustling with creative energy by the time Aaron and Hallie arrived. Camera crews, directors, and stage managers whisked through the semi-lit terminals, barking or taking orders. Aaron had signed a tentative contract with CNBS two weeks ago, and now *Product Pitch* was ready to start taping a new season with a new CEO on the panel.

The show introduced budding entrepreneurs, who hoped to get a chance to bring their dreams to fruition by having someone on the panel invest in their product and thereby turning their ideas into lucrative empires.

"So what do you think? Am I ready to be a star?"

Hallie turned to see a smiling Aaron behind her. Encircling his neck was a disc of paper preventing makeup from scattering onto his clothing. A woman flitted past, checked his face, and plucked the paper from him.

Hallie straightened his tie. He looked so handsome, so confident that she couldn't help herself. She kissed him quickly on the cheek. "That's for luck."

"I can't believe you talked me into this."

"You're going to be great."

He made a face.

"We're ready for you, Mr. Knight." Another woman holding a clipboard and sporting a headset sidled up next to him and grabbed his upper arm. Her name was Cathy Mayes. She had introduced herself earlier as the director's assistant.

"I guess this is it," he said.

"Can I stay to watch the taping?" Hallie asked before the woman whisked him away.

Cathy shrugged. "Sure, if you want to be here for about eight hours. We're going to tape several episodes."

Hallie looked at Aaron. "Do you want me to stay?"

"Truthfully, you're making me a little nervous."

"Okay. I'll see you back at the office." In her mind, she was already making plans to celebrate his television debut tonight. She waved as Cathy guided him to the tastefully decorated set, readied with four chairs and long glass tables in front.

She wanted so much to tell him she loved him. And she did. Why couldn't she say the words? What was standing in her way? Miranda? No. She believed Aaron when he said the two of them were over.

Kyle? *The man has secrets. Just be careful.*

We all have secrets. She sloughed off his unwarranted warning. No matter what Kyle thought he knew, she wasn't going to allow him to dissuade her feelings for Aaron. She was learning to trust again, thanks to him, and the scope of possibilities for the two of them seemed endless.

Hallie stayed for a while, watching Aaron and the other panelists being fitted for lapel mikes and getting last-minute directions from Cathy. The same makeup artist from before was putting last-minute touches on the only female in the group.

When a booming voice came over the sound

system warning that taping was about to take place, Hallie headed for the exit doors, being careful not to trip over the heavy cables along the floor.

Past the danger of the cables, she looked up. Something caught her attention, making her stop dead in her tracks. Someone was standing in the far corner of the studio. The shadowy figure should have meant nothing to her. The studio was bustling with people. But this was different. Though the person was too far away for her to identify the man or woman, a strange feeling came over her. She was being watched.

"Be careful, miss," a worker warned as he passed by her.

Distracted, she looked straight ahead. She was about to slam into a pole that blocked her way. "Thanks," she called out. When she looked back, the person was gone.

****

Hallie found her mother in the common room where she was engaged in another card game, this time with several other patients. The serene scene looked so ordinary. A foursome of white-haired, pink-cheeked ladies playing cards, bonding over the latest gossip in the neighborhood. But Hallie knew the truth. Her mother's life could never go back to that kind of normalcy.

"Hi, Mom." She lightly touched her mother's shoulder.

Her mother turned and looked up, a frown on her face. She shrugged Hallie's touch away. "What are you doing here?"

"I came to see you."

"You're sticking your nose in where it doesn't

belong, Rosie. Like you always do."

Rosie. Once again, her mother was somewhere in the past, thinking Hallie was her younger sister. Hallie ignored her harsh words.

The other ladies seemed too engrossed in their cards to care about the exchange between mother and daughter.

"How are you today?"

"What do you care?" Her eyes clouded with suspicion. "Who are you again?"

Tears rose behind Hallie's eyes. The other women now regarded her, each smiling but not connecting with her disappointment.

"Well, I'm busy now, so you need to go." Her mother shooed her away with a flip of her gnarled hand.

Hallie remained steadfast and determined to make her mother recognize her. "I think I'll stay for a little while."

Her mother's face turned to stone. "Then sit over there, whoever you are." She pointed to an empty table on the opposite side.

Gathering her composure, Hallie nodded, excused herself, and made her way to the table. Settled, she sent a text to Aaron to see how the taping was going. She didn't expect an answer, but it felt good to connect to someone.

She watched her mother return to the card game. Once again, she seemed vibrant and happy with her friends. It saddened Hallie. There was still so much she wanted to tell her mother. So much she wanted to hear from her. She wondered if she'd ever get the chance.

She especially wanted to understand more about her aunt Rosemary. The last time her aunt's name was brought up, Hallie had been caught in the middle of her mother's reality and had paid dearly for it. She rubbed her forehead. The bruise was gone, but her head still pulsed with a phantom pain once in a while.

Why was her mother channeling that particular part of her past? What was going on in that disorderly mind of hers? Had Rosemary done something long ago to make her mother lash out? Being an only child, Hallie wasn't familiar with the dynamics between siblings, especially sisters. But she knew there had to be some bad blood between the sisters.

The *ding* on her new phone signaled a text message. It was from Aaron.

Hi, sweetheart. Taping going well. I was told the camera loves me. I think I can get used to this. See you soon.

She bit down on her bottom lip, not to stop herself from laughing out loud but to stop a ragged sigh of disappointment in herself. Even the camera loved him. Why couldn't she express her true feelings? What was she afraid of?

I'll be sure to put a gold star on your office door at work. Don't turn into a diva.

With a tentative smile, she sent the text.

She mulled over the invitation Aaron had extended to her mother to come to Sea Girt. The nursing home, no matter how accommodating, was confining. A change of scenery might do her mother some good. She'd have to seriously think about it.

"Hello, Hallie. It's good to see you again."

Hallie put her phone back in her bag and got to her feet. "Joanne, how are you?"

The administrator smiled. "I'm fine. Better than

fine really." She pulled out one of the chairs. "Sit, please."

Hallie noticed the controlled excitement on Joanne's face. It was obvious the woman had important, if not wonderful, news. Maybe the news was about her mother's prognosis. Perhaps it was a new drug to stop or at least slow down her mother's disease. Was she grasping at straws?

"How is she?"

Joanne pulled her mouth in at the corners, her elated expression now serious. "Good days and bad days."

"But more bad than good."

Joanne nodded. "I'm sorry for that."

Hallie shrugged, knowing she was fighting a losing battle.

"She sometimes calls out the name Rosie. Do you have any idea who that is?"

"My mother's sister. I never knew her."

"She thought I was Rosie one day."

"Be careful. That's what set her off." She tried to make light of the situation but wasn't succeeding. The image of her mother's tussle with confusion surfaced, and she felt a faint throb along her forehead.

Joanne's face brightened once again. "I do have some good news. It affects your mother and others with Alzheimer's. A generous contribution was made—"

The sudden scream coming from her mother was raw and guttural. "You cheated! You cheated!"

Anticipatory adrenaline arising in her, Hallie rushed to the table. One of the women was crying, and the other two sat there in a semi-catatonic state.

"Mom, it's all right." Hallie grasped her mother's

shoulders.

Surprisingly, she calmed down immediately at Hallie's touch. Realization flashed in her tired eyes.

"I'll get help," Joanne said.

Hallie put up her hand to stop Joanne from leaving. "No, wait."

"Hallie?"

"Yes, Mom. It's me."

A smile broke out on her mother's face. "Oh, yes. Now that you're here, I can't wait to tell you about my day." Her mother looped her arm through Hallie's.

"Is she okay?" Joanne asked, looking a bit doubtful.

Hallie nodded. "We'll be fine."

Arm in arm, they walked out of the common room, and though the reversal was dazing, Hallie was just happy her mother had recognized her.

****

"I don't think I've been this exhausted after working a fifteen-hour day," Aaron said to his colleagues on the panel. They laughed and agreed.

Though only three episodes of *The Pitch* were taped, it was the stopping and starting and the fixing of lights and sound that took up much of the day. Two of the three small businesses took the offers made to them by two different CEOs. The third was embroiled in a bidding war between Aaron and Barbara Yeager, the president of Yeager Works. The savvy entrepreneurs finally and happily accepted Barbara's proposal. Though disappointed, Aaron yielded to her winning bid.

"Good work today," Marc Goodwin said, joining the group. "The episodes should air next week. We'll be taping more in a few days. Keep your schedules open." The other three executives dispersed, offering their goodbyes to Marc and Aaron.

"Thanks for the opportunity, Marc. I really enjoyed it."

"I'm glad. Listen, Aaron, this envelope's for you, but we were already taping."

Aaron frowned. "Do you know who it's from?"

"No. It was left on my desk." Marc handed over the large, interoffice-type envelope.

Aaron pushed his bottom lip forward in thought. There were no markings, no identification as to who gave it to Marc or what was inside.

"See you next week." Marc left.

"Yeah. Thanks, Marc." He took one more look at the envelope. Probably business. What else could it be? He'd open it once he got to the office.

****

"How did everything go?" Lavelle, her arms laden with binders and folders, strolled into Aaron's office. She carefully arranged them on a long side table.

"I want to make it clear you're in the presence of a megastar."

She managed a smirk, and he knew she was having none of his good-humored bragging. "Well, Mr. Megastar"—she pointed to the piles of files and folders—"I'm afraid these demand your immediate attention, so don't get any lofty ideas. You still have a company to run."

He growled. Leave it to no-nonsense Lavelle to bring him back to reality. "You really know how to put a damper on my dreams." He looked at her. "You look nice today, Lavelle. Your hair's different. And your clothes." He eyed the formfitting red dress and taupe heels she wore. "It looks good on you."

Her brow rose in surprise. "Thanks, Aaron. You know I do it all for you."

He laughed at her sarcasm. "And I'm grateful."

"I'm sure you are." Still sporting that same smirk, she made a *humph* sort of sound and left the office.

Aaron eyed the stack of work ahead of him and exhaled. He'd rather be doing anything but signing papers and making decisions. He'd rather be with Hallie.

She had texted him earlier that she was with her mother, that everything was okay, and that she'd be at the office later. He had thought about going to the nursing home for support but decided against it.

The contribution he'd made to Golden Living was earmarked for a new wing that would treat men and women exclusively with Alzheimer's. He wanted to remain anonymous, and although the very grateful Joanne Allen had promised she'd keep his identity a secret, she might gush over his generosity if she saw him. And with Hallie there…

He would tell Hallie when the time was right and in his own way.

He got up from behind his desk silently, swearing at all the work he had to finish before day's end. As he got to his feet, he unintentionally swept some papers off his desk. They fluttered to the floor, revealing the large envelope Marc had given him at the studio. He'd almost forgotten about it.

He unwound the red string on the flap and pulled out the contents. At first glance, he thought it was a contract of some kind. It wasn't.

The New York State seal at the top left-hand corner jumped out at him, but it was the bold heading underneath that drew him in.

Office of the Courts
August 15, 2003
Case 1127C

His breathing became shallow, and his entire body tightened. Fighting a lethal mix of disbelief, rage, and frustration, he scanned the rest of the text, zeroing in on the name Michael Clark interspersed throughout the document. His given name. His real name. He read further.

Let it be known that Michael Clark's conviction of voluntary manslaughter, dated August 15, 2003, was expunged in reference to the Juvenile Criminal Procedure Act. Because of said offender's age, records will be sealed accordingly to ensure that no reference is made to the specific conviction.

He read and reread the words. He flipped through the rest of the document, reading portions of the paragraphs. Was this some kind of joke? His criminal record was supposed to be sealed fifteen years ago. Who had gotten hold of this?

He checked the envelope again. No other papers. No other information. Fear knotted and writhed in his stomach. Was someone blackmailing him? Was this just the beginning? He grabbed his phone and punched in Marc's number. Trying to remain calm, he asked him if he was sure he hadn't seen the person who dropped off the envelope. Marc's answer was the same as his earlier one.

"Is there something wrong?" Marc asked.

Aaron took a breath. "No. Thanks, Marc." He hung

up without saying goodbye.

His blood slid through his veins like cold needles.

I guess our sins do find us.

The past has a way of catching up to people.

Hallie's and Miranda's forewarnings rumbled through his head.

One by one, he stuffed the papers into the shredder under his desk. The whirring sound offered little comfort. With the last piece of paper destroyed, Aaron could no longer deny what he was up against. But even though old fears and uncertainties found their way to the surface, he vowed no one was going to extort his past—no matter who it was.

****

With a quick greeting, Hallie hurried past Lavelle's desk, eager to tell Aaron that her mother had recognized her.

"He's not here, Hallie."

She backtracked to Lavelle's desk. "Where is he?"

"I don't know. He left about twenty minutes ago in a big rush."

"Did he have a meeting?"

"Nothing was on his agenda for today."

Was something wrong?

"Why don't you call him?" Lavelle suggested. "Maybe he went home."

The tone of Lavelle's voice drew Hallie's attention. It was different. Expectant. As though Hallie's next words would reveal a secret. "Lavelle, is everything okay?"

Lavelle's face showed a delicate dimension of femininity. Suddenly, she wasn't the ramrod-straight, no-nonsense woman Hallie saw her as most times.

There was something different about her. She pushed herself away from her desk. "Come. We'll have some privacy in Aaron's office."

"What is it, Lavelle? Is something wrong?" Hallie sat next to her on Aaron's couch.

Concern lurked in the depths of her eyes. "If you call dating the boss wrong."

Hallie's face started to heat up. She knew. How many others knew as well? "You know about us?"

"Whenever you two are in the same room, it's written all over your faces."

"Oh, God," Hallie moaned. "Does everyone suspect?"

Lavelle shrugged. "I can't speak for anybody else. I only know what I see."

"Oh, God," she repeated.

"So what if all of ARK Enterprises knows about the two of you? What are they going to do? Complain? Aaron would fire them in a minute. Do you think they want to lose their jobs?" Lavelle placed her hand on top of Hallie's. "Honey, you're trembling. There's no call for that. I'm happy for the two of you."

Hallie let go the breath she'd been holding. "You are?"

"Anything that can make Aaron smile like he does when you're around is a good thing. He's not the same Aaron Knight we're used to around here."

"What do you mean?"

"In case you haven't noticed, he channels his emotions into business. You annoy him enough, and he'll buy your company. You offend him, and he'll send you into bankruptcy. You insult him, and he's going to make another acquisition to show everyone he's the boss."

"You make him sound callous."

"He is—was." Lavelle paused, her expression thoughtful. "You've changed all that."

Hallie swallowed. She didn't want to be given credit for something so personal, even if she did care for Aaron.

"His life hasn't been that easy. Oh, he'll be the first one to disagree, but I know he struggles with things."

"What things?" The warmth in Hallie's cheeks had turned to a slight chill up her spine.

"He's never told you? I'm surprised. But then he's a private person. It's difficult to get him to talk."

"About what, Lavelle?"

"That's his story, Hallie. He needs to tell you. Give him time."

Time for what?

"He's attracted to your kindness, you know. He's impressed by the way you care about others. He's told me that much."

Lavelle changed the subject, which didn't please Hallie.

"Really?" She wasn't surprised that Aaron confided in his administrative assistant. She'd been with him a long time. He trusted her like any good boss would.

"Don't get me wrong. He likes that you're ambitious, but he likes how you balance that ambition with care and concern more."

Hallie faltered with Lavelle's explanation. "Are you warning me for some reason?"

"I guess what I'm trying to say is keep a grasp on your heart. Like I told you, the Aaron Knight you see is different than the one we've seen at ARK over the years. His reckless ambition, the callous decisions he sometimes makes, his dark temperament. Those destructive qualities can come back in a matter of a deal gone wrong." She paused, her expression tightening. "Oh, and then there's the constant array of women he's had in his life." She looked away. "None of them serious contenders, though."

Lavelle's unexpected declaration caught Hallie by surprise. It wasn't the fact that Aaron had been with different women; it was that Lavelle was aware of his dating prowess. Maybe she had even seen them coming and going. Then, with a long sigh, she got to her feet. "Don't let what I've said here scare you. I'm on your side, Hallie. You two belong together. Trust me."

Hallie managed an uncertain smile. "Thank you, Lavelle. You're a good friend."

The ringing of her phone ended their conversation. Hallie glanced at the screen. "It's Aaron."

"Well, at least we know he's alive. Go on and take it. I'll leave you alone." Lavelle closed the door behind her.

"Aaron?" Her voice was stiff and unnatural. "Where are—?"

"Meet me at the penthouse as soon as you can." The order was clear and impatient.

"But—"

"The penthouse, Hallie," he repeated.

She watched the screen turn to black. The call was over.

****

Who else should he call?
The police?

No. Law enforcement could access such records. Could a wayward cop be the culprit? His lawyer? That was a viable possibility. George knew all about the accident. Lawyer-client confidentiality and all that. And it had been an accident, Aaron repeated to himself. He'd never meant for his father to die. He'd had to protect his mother. That was why he'd done what he had. That was why he'd wrestled his father off her, punched him hard in the head, and sent him flying across the room. The sharp corner of his parents' bedroom dresser drawer had finished the job.

"What did you do, Michael?" He could hear his mother's screams, see her bent over the monster she called her husband. Images of her battered and bloodied face and body were now as clear as they had been fifteen years ago. "He's not breathing, Michael. What did you do?"

"He was killing you. I had to do something." The small, shaky voice of a young, confused, furious boy rang in his ears. His voice. His fear. His fault.

He'd been driving aimlessly on Route 87 North for about an hour. Being away from the city might give him some perspective on handling the explosive situation of his criminal record. But even though the scenery had changed from skyscrapers to grass and blue skies, Aaron feared nothing would stop the person behind this threat—if that was what it was. What else could it be?

He got off at the next exit and pulled into a rest stop on the side of the highway. He had to call Hallie. He had to tell her before she found out some other way. He'd tell her to meet him at the penthouse. Once again Miranda's wisdom was spot-on.

That's why you have to tell Hallie. If she's your future, then she deserves to know.

Hallie was his future. And with that future came trust. She was a forgiving person. A person of strength and integrity. But most of all, she believed in love. And even though she hadn't yet said those three magic words to him, in his heart he knew she would. She needed time.

He pulled back his thoughts. Would revealing his past to her make her rethink their relationship? He heard Miranda again. *Give the woman some credit.*

His anxiety at bay, he waited for Hallie to arrive.

Chapter Seventeen

Nelson dropped her off at Aaron's building. The doorman recognized her, escorted her to the elevator, and told her Aaron had not yet arrived at the penthouse. He brought the mail with him. Hallie took it, thanked him, and placed it on the glass table in the dining room.

A restless feeling surged through her. Aaron had sounded so intense and so demanding. Though dozens of dire questions swirled through her mind, his reasoning for her to be here had to be important.

She went into the kitchen and took a bottle of water from the refrigerator. What she really wanted was a drink, but she would wait until Aaron arrived.

She mulled over her earlier conversation with Lavelle. Once the shock of Lavelle, and perhaps some employees, knowing about her and Aaron's romantic relationship had settled in, Hallie felt more at ease. The woman had been more than forthcoming in her observations of her boss. She'd been downright helpful. Lavelle insisted that no one was spreading hurtful gossip nor would they start. If Aaron learned of such talk, he wouldn't hesitate to rid ARK of the offender.

That behavior bothered Hallie. Could Aaron really do such a callous thing? She recalled the first time she'd come in contact with him. Her interview. He'd been all business then, threatening to oust her should she falter in a sale, break confidentiality, or make the smallest mistake that would cost ARK money.

But that was then. She knew a different Aaron. A kinder, gentler man. She had seen that with her own eyes when he was with her mother. He'd treated her with respect and dignity, even if she didn't reciprocate. He understood what she was going through. What Hallie was going through.

Was this new Aaron just a façade? Did he bed every new female executive and then rid himself of their romantic designs by firing them? She hated second-guessing herself. She hated that her mind was drifting to places that might not exist. She trusted Aaron. Whether in business or in bed, she trusted him.

She passed a three-paneled mirror in the dining room and caught her reflection. "I trust you, Aaron," she said aloud, noticing how her smile broadened and how a satisfied light came into her eyes. "I trust you." A flash of heat shot through her body. "I love you, Aaron." This time her eyes glowed with a savage inner fire, and her heart sang with delight. "I love you." Blissfully happy and fully alive, Hallie made up her mind. She'd express her feelings of love to him tonight.

When she turned away from the mirror, Hallie's eyes went directly to the mail the doorman had placed on the table. She focused on a plain white envelope balancing on top of advertisements and magazines. She picked it up. The address was correct, but it was her name written above it.

Ms. Hallie Cavanagh
Beresford Penthouse
211 Central Park West
New York, NY 10024

There was no return address. It had to be some

mistake. Why would mail for her come here? She was uncertain if she should open it, but then it was addressed to her. Who else knew she'd be here? Anyone at the office. That thought made her bristle. Sophie? Between Aaron, her mother, and work, she could hardly carve out time for her roommate. Was this Sophie's way of getting her attention? She shook her head and grinned. Classic Sophie. Probably filled with confetti and a note that said, *Remember Me?*

She carefully tore opened the flap and pulled out what looked like a photocopy of an article cut out of a newspaper. A tremor came from somewhere, making the hairs on her arm stand up straight. What was she nervous about? Well, the last time she'd had an encounter with a newspaper was when Kyle showed her the page six photograph of Aaron and her dancing.

She unfolded the paper and read the boldly printed headline: *Acquitted Youth Claims Self-Defense in Killing Father.*

A muscle quivering at her jaw, Hallie stared at the words. She read the heading again, trying to make some sense of its meaning and why it was addressed to her. The message was disturbing to say the least. Heartbreaking.

Hallie moved toward the couch, as if under water. The date at the top right-hand corner of the paper read August 16, 2003. She did a quick calculation. Fifteen years. Then she focused on the article itself. The piece reported on a fifteen-year-old male—name withheld because of age—who allegedly caused the fatality of his father, William M. Clark, age thirty-seven. It went on to say that the son was trying to stop his father from physically abusing his mother, Bianca "BiBi" Clark, age thirty-five, when the supposed casualty occurred. The son grabbed Clark and pushed him away, which led to him hitting the back his head on the corner of a dresser. The paramedics were called and pronounced Clark dead at the scene. His skull had been fractured.

Her mind seesawed back and forth. Though the story was indeed a sad one, it certainly had nothing to do with her. She knew no one by those names. She scanned the article again, but nowhere was there mention of a city or state.

And who was Michael Clark?

The only thing she could do was wait for Aaron. Maybe he had some answers.

****

"Aaron?" Miranda's shocked expression said it all. "What are you doing here?" Her eyes narrowed. "Did Hallie finally have the good sense to leave you?"

He made a face. "I don't have time for your sarcasm. I have to ask you something. Can I come in?"

She stepped aside. Though it was nowhere close to his penthouse, her apartment was luxurious in its own right. As the only child of an entrepreneurial father and a mother who came from money, she'd inherited their fortune, which was tucked away nicely in nontaxable foreign countries and tropical islands. Having married and divorced two prominent and wealthy men, Miranda had everything she needed to live beyond her means. Her big mistake had been her third marriage to a New York City cop.

"You look miserable," she commented as he passed by her.

"Scotch."

"What?"

"Do you have any Scotch?"

"No, I'm a tequila girl. But even if I did, I wouldn't offer you any. Not the way you're acting." She followed him into the living room. "What's got you on edge?"

The stark white furnishings nearly blinded him. "I have to talk to you, Miranda, and I need you to be honest with me."

She stroked his arm. "Darling, you're scaring me. Sit down before you fall down."

He pulled himself away from her touch but didn't take her up on her offer. "Can your ex—the cop—get his hands on court records?"

Her brow flickered a bit. "I don't know for sure, but I imagine he could. Why? Do you need a favor?"

"Someone, I don't know who, got a hold of my criminal record."

"How do you know?"

He quickly told her about the taping of *The Pitch* and the delivery of the document.

"You mean you physically have it?"

"Had," he corrected. "I shredded it. I think I'm being blackmailed."

Her face paled. "That's a nasty word."

"Those records are supposed to be sealed."

A questioning expression took over her face, and then her lips puckered in annoyance. "You think Harry did this, don't you?"

"I didn't say that."

"But you're thinking it. You came here to see if I was protecting him." She paused, and the silence was deafening. "You don't believe *I* had something to do with this, do you?"

He didn't answer. It hadn't crossed his mind that Miranda could have asked her ex about his records until she mentioned it. Was she trying to get back at him for leaving her? Did her goodbye really mean goodbye to him and everything in his life?

"Get out," she ordered. "Get out of my house. How dare you think I'd stoop that low?"

He tried to dissipate her unleashed fury. "I'm sorry, Miranda. I just don't know what to think anymore."

"I promised I wouldn't say a word, and I've kept that promise."

Something cautioned him not to ask the next set of questions. He ignored the warning. "I know you have, but what about Harry? Would he be vindictive enough to pull a stunt like this?"

Again, she shot him a hostile glare. "Get out, Aaron. I never want to see you again." She headed for the door and opened it wide.

With a heavy heart and questions still unanswered, he did what he was told. He turned. "I'm truly sorry, Miranda."

She slammed the door in his face.

****

Aaron tossed his extra car key to Harold. The parking attendant greeted him, but Aaron hurried away without answering. His mind was preoccupied. It was a wonder he'd found his way home.

Guilt over badgering Miranda weighed heavily on his conscience. But what else could he think? She knew about his past, and though she'd insisted repeatedly that his secret was safe with her, he waned in his confidence of her. Then there was the matter of her ex-husband. As far as Aaron knew, the guy was a deputy chief on the force, climbing the ladder to assistant commissioner. The high ranking alone could open doors for him.

Miranda liked her tequila. Maybe one night she had carelessly blabbed to Harry what she knew, without realizing she'd blurted out the sensitive info. He might have seen this as an opportunity for blackmail.

"Afternoon, Mr. Knight." The doorman tipped his hat. "How are you holding up in this heat?"

Aaron blinked. "What? Oh, yes, Christopher. The weather. Yes. As well as can be expected. Did Ms. Cavanagh arrive?"

"Yes, sir. About forty-five minutes ago."

"Thank you." Aaron hurried to the penthouse elevator. He pushed the button, and once again, his attention was elsewhere.

Kyle, Hallie's ex-fiancé, was a lawyer. It wasn't unheard of for his kind to manipulate a judge or anyone involved in the justice system of New York. Could he have gotten ahold of Aaron's records? Maybe Kyle hoped that once Hallie found out, she'd leave and go back to him. But then how would he have found out about his criminal records in the first place? He was driving himself crazy.

"Hallie?" he called.

She was already walking toward him.

His arms enveloped her, and his lips covered hers. He savored the taste of her, her intoxicating fragrance, the way she kissed him back. Parting from her mouth, he nipped at her neck while unbuttoning her pink silk blouse. Her gasps made his senses come alive.

All he wanted to do was to forget this day and all its unpleasantness. And being with Hallie was all he needed to do just that.

****

A bolt of want and fire laced through her. They moved clumsily to the couch, and he lowered her gently upon the leather cushions. Hallie watched as he fumbled with his clothing, tossing everything to the floor. He came to her naked and swiftly, full of desire and virility. He was beautiful.

She shimmied out of her skirt and panties, and a throb sprang up between her legs. He eased onto her, and she altered her curves to the hard, flat planes of him. He made love to her mouth, letting her know how he would make love to her body. His hand slid up her leg, and her body rocked against his.

She moaned and arched, her thighs opening almost of their own volition. She bucked against him, and he grabbed her hips, holding her still.

His eyes, full of passion and want, locked with hers. There was an unspoken challenge in the depths of those midnight blue eyes of his.

"Make love to me, Aaron."

She didn't have to tell him twice. He rushed to grab a condom and groaned as he slid into her. Her body stiffened, her breath coming fast and harsh. She dug her fingers into his hair and wrapped her legs around him. She convulsed with pleasure from every thrust. Her body flamed, the heat moving from her thighs, up her stomach, and to her breasts and face. Thrill after thrill shot through her, as his possession of her grew stronger. Finally, with three hard, furious thrusts of his hips, pleasure like she'd never known splintered inside her. Together they had found the tempo that joined their bodies together.

As he fell against her, she tightened her hold, her

own arousal reaching its peak. He kissed her again, and the kiss sang through her veins. A deep feeling of peace entered her being.

"I love you, Hallie."

Tears welled in her eyes, and Hallie knew she had no desire to be anywhere except here in his arms. "I love you, too, Aaron."

The smile in his eyes contained a sensuous spark. With his mouth opened against hers, he silently asked permission to take more.

****

A night of lovemaking with Aaron had affected her deeply. He protected her from the world outside. In his arms, she was safe. Expressing her love for him filled her with happiness and an intimacy that she was powerless to resist. Her gaze riveted on his face, Hallie watched him sleep, drinking in the comfort of his nearness, his rhythmic breathing, and the strong beat of his heart.

She assessed his qualities: intelligent, ambitious, dynamic, and thoughtful with a hint of maddening arrogance. All that aside, something in his manner last night had soothed her. Still, her enlightening conversation with Lavelle had her questioning herself. *The constant array of women he's had in his life.* How did she compare to his other conquests?

Aaron's eyelids began to flutter. "Say it again." His voice had that sexy morning huskiness that made her insides jangle with excitement.

"What?"

His eyes opened now, he slipped his fingers into her hair and brushed the loose strands away from her face. His expression was as soft as a caress. "Say you love me."

Her smile broadened. "I love you." The words were so new, so pulse-pounding.

"How much?" His hand took her face and held it gently. "How much do you love me?"

In one forward motion, she was in his arms. She buried her face against the corded muscles of his chest, and he clasped her body tightly to his. She raised her head and kissed him with a hunger that belied her outward calm.

"You're playing a dangerous game, Ms. Cavanagh."

"Yes, and I intend on winning, Mr. Knight." Hallie lifted herself onto his body and rocked against him. He was on fire—hot, hard, and ready. The hysteria of delight rose inside her. With her passion mounting, she saw her future so clearly it terrified her.

****

"What are you doing?" Hallie came into the kitchen, her hair wrapped in a towel. Draped around her was Aaron's robe, his earthy scent still clinging to the expensive silk fabric.

He expressed his approval of her with a grin. "Making breakfast. How do you like your eggs?"

Hallie eyed him with curiosity. "The great Aaron Knight cooks, too? How lucky can I get?"

"Come here and I'll show you."

"You, sir, are insatiable."

"It's one of my many qualities." He held up the egg carton. "Well?"

"Surprise me."

An hour or so later, her scrambled eggs, toast, and coffee finished, she pushed away from the table and brought her dish and mug to the sink. "We're going to be late for work."

He leaned back. "No, *you're* going to be late. I'm the boss. I don't have to go into the office if I don't want to." His grin was positively evil.

"Oh, really?"

"You've got a lot to learn about this relationship."

Grumbling, she walked past him. He grabbed her hand and pulled her onto his lap, making her yelp with delight.

"Aaron, I've got to get dressed."

He nuzzled her neck and nipped at the earlobe. "I'd rather have you undressed."

His teasing tone excited her, despite her protest.

Her breath came in spurts, and her pulse skittered alarmingly. "Are you trying to get me fired?"

"Being nice to the boss might get you a raise."

She broke free of his hold and stood. "What a guy," she said, her sarcasm showing.

"Come on, Hallie. Let's ditch work and spend the day the bed."

"Don't tempt me."

He got up from the chair and made a grab for her. "No one will miss us."

Scooting away from his grasp, she smiled at his wanton suggestion, but then her mind clicked. Lavelle again. *So what if all of ARK Enterprises knows about the two of you? What are they going to do?* If the both of them were out, would gossip run wildly throughout the office? Did it matter? Her musings were interrupted.

"So you're getting mail here now?" Aaron had left the table and was standing by the couch. In his hand was the envelope that had been addressed to her. In the throes of their spontaneous passion, she had forgotten to show him the curious correspondence.

The elation running through her veins now turned to an uneasy feeling. Searching for a plausible explanation, she urged him to look inside. "I have no idea who would have sent this to me. Or why."

Frowning, he removed what was in the envelope and unfolded the paper.

"It's such a sad story." She unwrapped the towel around her head and ran her fingers through her damp hair. "Do you have any idea who those people are?"

He didn't answer. When she looked at him, a nagging in the back of her mind refused to be stilled. He stared back at her, his expression worrisome, almost fearful.

Her breath caught in her throat as her heart pounded furiously against her chest. "You do know who they are, don't you?"

****

Aaron's desperation was a steel weight pushing him down into a dark abyss. Yet it didn't suppress the anger seething within him. Who could have sent Hallie this? Who could have known she'd be here? Miranda? Harry? Kyle? His throat ached, his head bowed, and his shoulders slumped in despair. Someone was out to destroy him, and this someone was using Hallie now.

Her hands caressed his face. He made no move to touch her or look at her.

"Aaron, what's wrong?" Her desperate plea fell on his deaf ears.

Finally, he stepped back. A raw, primitive grief overwhelmed him as he stared into her eyes. Eyes darkened with questions he had to answer. Darkened with a lightless future he had to reverse. He took a tormented breath. "I should have told you about this, Hallie."

"About what?" A glazed look of anguish began to spread over her face. "Tell me what?"

His jaw tightening, his legs heavy, he picked up his suit pants he had thrown on the back of the couch last night and found his keys in the pocket. Taking her hand, he pulled her along behind him. In his office now, he guided her to the couch and told her to sit down.

"Aaron, you're scaring me."

"I'm scared, too, Hallie. I don't know how you're going to react to what I have to tell you." His voice grated harshly as he choked out the words. "I don't want to lose you."

Her gaze flew to his in surprise. "You're not going to lose me. Now please tell me what's upsetting you."

The keys jingled in his hand as he separated the small silver key from the others. Opening the desk drawer, he pulled out a large manila envelope, stared at it for a moment, and then turned to face Hallie. "Here." Hands shaking, he gave her the envelope and then took a step back.

"What is this?"

"It's about me. My life before ARK." He took a breath. "My life before you." He took a seat in the high-back chair by his desk.

She opened the envelope and took out its contents. He watched her with a guarded eye as she read the court documents that were on top. She flipped through the pages and scanned the information. When finished, she looked at him, her eyes probing, obscured with a multitude of emotions.

"There's more," he murmured.

She shuffled through the small stack of articles cut out of newspapers and stopped when one of them caught her attention. He could read the headline from where he sat.

"Acquitted Youth Claims Self-Defense in Killing Father."

"This is…" She hesitated.

He nodded. "A copy of the same article someone sent you."

"I don't understand. Why do you have these things?" She waved the stack of papers in the air. Was that confusion or anger in her eyes? "Who is this family, Aaron? Who's Michael Clark?"

He sat silently and watched the questions on her face fade into disbelief.

"You?" Her voice trembled with dread.

Strength drained from him as the secret he'd kept hidden for so long became part of his reality once again—and now part of Hallie's as well. "Yes," he said warily, "I'm Michael Clark."

Chapter Eighteen

"Say something, Hallie." Aaron leaned forward, hands grasping the tops of his knees. He could see how uneasy she was under his scrutiny, but he needed to know what she was thinking. "Please, say something."

She placed the rest of the papers at her side. Her sharp gaze bore into him, revealing everything she felt. Would she feel differently about him now? Would she hate him for his crime? Would she leave him?

"Tell me what happened."

He blinked. He hadn't expected that. *Give the woman some credit.* He heard Miranda's sage advice loud and clear. He rubbed his face with his hands, his stubble scratching his palms. "It's not something I talk about."

"But you remember it?"

"Every blessed day."

"Then tell me. I want to know."

He took a deep breath, the painful memories crowding for dominance in his mind. Fifteen years had passed, and his mental scars were still fresh, still haunting him. Though tormented by the images, he knew it was time to make Hallie understand. She was the woman he wanted to be part of his future, part of his life. He owed her the truth.

"My father was William Clark, and for as long as I can remember, he had a temper. I'm not talking about the kind where a father gets annoyed because his kids don't always obey him, or his car gets a flat tire. My father was an abuser. Any glitch, any problem—anything that would be insignificant to most people, was cause for him to be cruel. If dinner wasn't ready when he got home from work. If my brother or sister or I brought home mediocre report cards from school." He shook his head. "If it rained and he wanted sunshine.

"He lost jobs because of his temper and blamed his failures on us. Especially my mother. She always got the brunt of his anger, and that anger eventually led to his drinking." He stopped and took a breath. He had to continue, even though his body ached with exhaustion. He had to do this for Hallie and for himself.

"Then the beatings started. He slapped us around at first, calling us names, telling us we were worthless, that we'd never amount to anything. We never knew when he was going to fly into a rage."

"What about your grandfather?"

Her question surprised him. She remembered their talk about Malcolm Clark. "What about him?"

"Didn't he realize what was going on? Couldn't he have stopped the abuse or gotten some help for your father?"

"As brilliant as my grandfather was in business, he was clueless about our family matters." He shrugged. "Either he truly wasn't aware of his son's behavior, or he ignored it, hoping it would run its course."

A look of disbelief played along her face.

"My mother always made excuses for the bruises that appeared on her arms or legs. She was clumsy. She fell. She didn't look where she was going. When he'd had enough of using my mother as a punching bag, he tried to make it up to her. Telling her he loved her. Promising he'd never do it again."

"It's a pattern."

He waited for a moment, his mind staggering with the images of what was to come.

"One day my mother and I were the only ones in the house. My father came home drunk as usual. He had lost another job, and he was ready to explode. My parents' bedroom was next to mine, and when I heard him accusing my mother for his failure, I rushed to their room. He had her by the hair and was slamming her head against the closet door. All she could do was whimper and beg for him to stop. But he wasn't going to stop, not until he killed her this time. At least that's what I thought."

A momentary look of sorrow crossed Hallie's face. What was it about that look that made his fear vanish?

"I had to do something. I had to protect her. I had to make him stop." His words were pouring out of him. "I figured if I could just get him off her, it would be over. I grabbed him by the shoulders and yanked him off her. The surprise on his face turned into the evilest look I'd ever seen. He seized me by the throat and squeezed, mocking me, cursing me. To this day, I don't know where my strength came from. I managed somehow to pry him off me, and I pushed him away with such force that he flew backward, and his head hit the edge of the dresser against the wall. He was dead before he hit the floor." He choked on the bitter words.

Hallie covered her mouth with her hand, her eyes wide and probing. "Oh, Aaron. How awful for you."

"The real shock came when I ordered my mother to call nine-one-one, and she didn't. Instead, she went to my father and cried over him. I fought that monster to save her, and she picked him over me."

"Where is she now?"

Were those tears in her eyes? "Somewhere in Pennsylvania last time I heard. We don't talk anymore."

"And your brother and sister?"

He shook his head. "Like my mother, Selena and I are estranged. Bradley is in and out of rehab."

"I'm so sorry, Aaron. You went through so much."

He watched her wipe away a tear and remembered that rainy night in Sea Girt.

"How old were you?"

"Fifteen. And that's why those court records are supposed to be sealed."

"What do you mean?"

"Someone sent me a copy of them."

"When?"

"Yesterday. Someone wants me to be reminded of what I did. Someone might be blackmailing me."

"Did this someone demand something?"

"Like money?" He shook his head. "Not yet. I thought it might be Miranda."

"She knows?"

"I was drunk one night when I was with her, and I told her the story."

"But how could she—?"

"Get her hands on the documents? Her latest ex-husband is a high-ranking cop. Maybe he managed to get them. I even thought your ex might have done it."

"Kyle?"

"He's a lawyer. He could have swayed some judge. Remember, someone sent you that article. Maybe he's trying to break us up."

"Kyle's a jerk, but he wouldn't jeopardize his career. It means too much to him."

He closed his eyes. "Then who, Hallie? Who wants the world to know about my past?"

When he opened them, she was standing in front of him. She took his hands and pulled him to his feet. Instinctively, he wrapped his arms around her.

"I really thought you'd leave if I told you," he whispered in her hair. "Why would you want to be with someone who did such a terrible thing?"

"You didn't mean to do it. You were trying to save your mother. You were trying to save yourself. No one should blame you."

"I blame me. If only I had done things differently that day. If only *I* had called nine-one-one right from the start. The police would have come—"

"And your mother might have been dead before they got there. Maybe your father would have killed you as well. No, Aaron, this isn't your fault, and people will understand that if this news gets out."

He held her tighter. "What would I do without you?"

"You won't have to worry about that." She looked at him. "But I want you to do something for me."

"What's that?"

"Forgive yourself, Aaron. You have to forgive yourself."

****

Hallie perused the top of her desk, shrugged in mock resignation, and shelved the papers and folders that waited on her attention at the moment. She leaned back, closed her eyes, and thought of Aaron. Stunned and sickened by what he had told her about his past, she had decided not to go into work yesterday. He needed her support. He'd been so brave in telling her that she couldn't dismiss his grief.

She could only imagine how horrible it was to live with an abuser. Even more horrible to know that the abuser was his father. His own flesh and blood. And to have to live with accidentally causing his father's death, not to mention having his family members desert him—the guilt and grief would eat away at his heart and soul.

Forgive yourself, Aaron. You have to forgive yourself. Her words to him were heartfelt and true, and she vowed to support him, no matter who or what was behind this threat to expose his past.

She'd made sure they spent the day together doing normal things. Shopping. Lunch. A leisurely stroll through Central Park. She took him to MOMA, one of her favorite haunts. There, while admiring the classic artists and their work, they also managed to blend in with the other museum patrons.

By the end of their day, Aaron seemed a bit more at ease. She admired the way he had fought hard to allow their excursions to revitalize him, taking charge with quiet assurance.

They had dinner at Le Coucou, a restaurant known for its rustic but chic French cuisine. The staff there greeted Aaron like an old friend, and the head chef took care to serve only his best. Hallie quickly came to realize, with all the attention given him, Aaron frequented this restaurant, and though it was silly, she wondered what other women he'd brought here.

Lavelle's observations about his other female companions had struck an uneasy chord with Hallie. She had always been confident, her self-esteem rising with each life accomplishment. Valedictorian in high school. Getting into Harvard. Graduating second in her field.

But her confidence had been shattered when Kyle had called off their engagement. She'd thought he loved her and would vow to spend the rest of his life with her. But her insistence on caring for her mother had turned him off. He had said he didn't want to be burdened, but was there a deeper fear? Was he afraid she would develop Alzheimer's as she aged? What about their future children? He was a coward, and she was better off without him.

When Lavelle told her about Aaron's dating preferences, she'd felt a shift in her confidence once again. She was no innocent when it came to sex, but the women in Aaron's life were wealthy and sophisticated. *He's chosen me. Aaron's chosen me.*

As night fell, they took in an off-Broadway play. It was a drama about a has-been musician trying to get back to his music roots. Aaron liked it; she had mixed feelings.

After the play, they headed for Central Parx, had dessert and a late-night drink, and saw Sophie.

"So what's going on?" she asked. "Hallie tells me nothing."

"I tell you things," Hallie replied.

"I haven't seen you in a week."

Though Sophie said it good-humoredly, Hallie suspected her roommate was a bit ticked off at her. She'd make it up to her soon.

Their night ended at the penthouse—her telling him she loved him and him kissing her passionately.

"Thank you, Hallie."

"For what?"

"For making me feel normal again."

Normal. Hallie opened her eyes and sat up in her chair. Wasn't that what everyone wanted? To live their own kind of normalcy?

Those projects and proposals were screaming her name. Aaron had meetings with clients across town. An upcoming trip to California was in the works as well. He'd already asked her to join him.

They had even discussed the strong possibility of bringing her mother to Sea Girt for the Labor Day weekend. Aaron had promised he'd hire a full-time nurse, and of course, Rita would be there to help out as well. The idea sounded wonderful, and even though her mother might not remember it, at least she would live the experience of seeing the ocean in present time. Hallie would call the nursing home and make them aware of the plan.

Her daydreaming squashed by work she had to get done, Hallie opened the folder on top. She was expecting a stack of contracts. They were there, but they were preceded by a piece of plain paper with a single sentence written boldly in a black magic marker.

He's not who you think he is.

She held her breath. It was happening again. Someone was warning her about Aaron. Someone was trying to scare her, or at the very least, turn her against him. But she already knew about his past, and it was obvious that whoever the culprit was didn't have that information.

Should she tell Aaron? Should she just ignore the threat? Should she investigate further?

Deciding not to let this go, she made her way to

Aaron's office with the reasoning that Lavelle might be of some help. Maybe she had seen something or someone acting strangely.

Hallie wasn't dismissing Aaron's privacy. Though he'd never made her promise to keep the information secret, she'd never reveal anything about his past with his father. She just thought Lavelle might have a hint as to how the message had wound up on her desk.

Rivaling a fortress, Lavelle's desk was situated outside the door. "He's not here, Hallie." She didn't look up from her computer screen. "He has meetings all day. I'm not sure if he'll be back at the office at all."

Hallie already knew his agenda. "I'm not here about Aaron." She regarded Lavelle's disregard of her, all the while noticing how different the woman looked today. Her hair was sleek and smooth, and her makeup was impeccable. The first three buttons on her white blouse were unfastened and hinted at a bit of cleavage. The glasses she usually wore were gone as well.

"You look pretty today, Lavelle."

Hallie's compliment wasn't lost on the woman. She looked away from the monitor and smiled, but the smile didn't reach her eyes. "Thank you, Hallie. What can I do for you?"

Hallie showed her the paper. "Do you have any idea what it means?"

Lavelle frowned and zeroed in on the writing. "Where did you get this?"

"It was lying on top of some contracts. Did you put the proposals on my desk this morning? Did you notice anything out of the ordinary?"

A quick shrug usurped her nod. "They arrived via the acquisitions department yesterday." She lifted one finely arched eyebrow. " 'He's not who you think he is.' " Lavelle read the message aloud this time.

"Clearly it's directed at me. Could it have been one of my staff?"

"Anything's possible, though it's hard to believe." Lavelle gave a quick jerk of her head. "Do you think it concerns Aaron?"

"If it is about Aaron, why would someone want to warn me about him? What has he done?" She felt a wee bit empowered at knowing his past already.

"I don't know, but it's obvious someone's aware of your relationship with him."

Something, some force hiding behind her unreadable expression, made Hallie sense she was treading on shaky ground. "What does this person hope to gain?"

"I wish I had an answer for you. Whatever it is, I don't like it." Her words had an angry bite.

"Maybe it's just a practical joke. Someone pulling prank."

"Are you going to show Aaron?"

"Of course. Don't you think I should?"

"Like you said, it's probably a prank. Aaron Knight is a powerful man, and he's made a lot of enemies. Adversaries who would give anything to bring him down." Lavelle held the up the paper. "And they have more formidable methods to destroy him than this. They'd find it laughable."

She was acting like a lioness protecting her cub. Hallie found it endearing, indiscreet, and maybe a bit annoying.

"I don't know, Lavelle. Don't you think he should be told? Especially since it might be directed at him?"

"Well, that's your choice, Hallie. After all, you're the one who seems to know him so well. Unlike the rest of us, I mean."

"Excuse me?"

"I told you, Aaron's a private person."

"I know that."

"Do you? If it's not a joke, whoever sent this message knows something about him."

Hallie bristled. "Am I hearing you right? Are you accusing me of something?"

Pain gleamed in her eyes. "Of course not." She leaned forward. "I thought we were friends."

Hallie instantly regretted her question. "We are, Lavelle. I'm sorry."

"I can see you're troubled by this. Take a deep breath. It'll all be okay. You'll see."

Hallie nodded and acquiesced to Lavelle's advice.

"Now I think we should both get back to our jobs."

"You're right. Thanks, Lavelle." As Hallie turned and started back down the hall, a noise caught her ear. Already a few feet away from Lavelle's desk, she glanced over her shoulder and watched the woman tear the paper in two, four, and then eight pieces. Her hand over the silver mesh wastebasket, she released the torn fragments. They fluttered into the bin like butterflies mourning the end of summer.

But it wasn't so much her actions that bothered Hallie. It was her expression, clearly marked with loathing, which sent a chill down her spine.

Chapter Nineteen

"Have you given any more thought about your mother coming out to the house? Labor Day is only two weeks away."

"I have to talk to Joanne first, but I'm sure it'll be all right." Hallie put her glass of Merlot down on the kitchen island. She had met Aaron at the penthouse, where he had dinner catered by the Mandarin Oriental Hotel, one of the most expensive restaurants in the city. But as lovely as the evening was turning out to be, Hallie had other things on her mind.

Aaron's expression was troubled. "You've been distracted all evening. What's the matter? Is it your mother?"

"No. Lavelle."

"Lavelle? What about her?"

"I don't know. I'm getting this strange vibe."

"Has she done anything to make you feel that way?"

"No…"

"Then what?"

Without much fanfare, she told him about the piece of paper and the spiteful warning.

His face grew hard and cold, but his anger wasn't directed at the incriminating message. "Are you insinuating Lavelle is responsible? That's ridiculous."

It didn't surprise her that he defended Lavelle. She

was a loyal and indispensable employee from the beginnings of ARK Enterprises. "I know it sounds crazy. Even I think I'm crazy for assuming she could be involved. But there was something weird between us yesterday." She shrugged. "Like I said, it was this vibe."

He patted the couch cushion, signaling her to come sit by him. He wrapped her in his arms and kissed the top of her head. "I'm sorry. I didn't mean to discount your feelings."

"You trust her. I know that." She snuggled into his chest, the scent of his cologne traveling along her nerve endings.

"And there aren't many people I do trust."

Though her troubled spirits quieted, her mind still wavered. There was something about Lavelle's demeanor that Hallie couldn't dismiss. Still, belaboring her beliefs would be a wasted effort. Aaron wasn't about to agree with her bashing his assistant.

"Let's forget what I said and try to figure out who would want to—"

He put his finger on her lips, the conversation over. "Not tonight. Tonight I only want to concentrate on us." His mouth came down on hers, firm and strong, his kiss gentle.

She met his lips eagerly, the slow burn of desire curling through her. His hands plunged into her hair, pulling her head closer, and his mouth opened against hers, demanding more. She opened her lips, and his tongue boldly swept in. His first swipe took her breath away. Now greedy, hot, and hungry, he possessed her mouth with heat and unspoken promises.

He grabbed her shoulders and lowered her onto the

length of the couch. She groaned, savoring the taste of him. His hands coaxed and caressed the rest of her, while she brazenly unzipped his jeans. His groin jerked in insatiable expectation. Heat consumed her as she slid her hand inside his underwear to cup his warm, hard, silky flesh. His moans sent incredible sensations of desire along her pulses.

Energy abounding, she pushed him off her and forced him to his back. Her hands moved quickly. She tugged at his jeans and underwear and slid them down his legs. He was thick, erect, and ready for her.

"Jesus, you're killing me." His voice was hoarse with a distinct excitement.

She grinned, slipped out of her panties, and climbed on top of him. She lowered herself slowly and accepted the fullness of him, hearing, smelling, seeing, tasting, and feeling him within her. He grabbed her hips and drove himself into her. She readily took all he was giving as the rhythm of her moves seized their bodies.

She took his hand, guided it to her swollen bud, and arched her back when he fondled her there. Her breathing labored, she unbuttoned his shirt and slid the palms of her hands up his chest. Small spasms ran through her when his muscles shuddered under her fingers.

His raw sensuousness carried her to greater heights. The bright flare of his near completeness was evident on his face. She responded, driving her passion to that moment of ecstasy, the hysteria of climax rising within her. Her body tightened and pulsed around him, and pleasure tore her apart as her orgasm seemed never ending.

She fell against him, out of breath, out of strength,

and out of control. He held her close, his own breathing labored. In his arms, she felt protected and satisfied.

He stroked her hair. "I love you, Hallie. I need you. Say you'll stay with me."

"Where else would I be?" she whispered. She climbed off him and stretched out at his side. She could feel his uneven breathing on her cheek as he held her close.

A sudden knock on the door shattered the mood. Their gazes locked.

"Who the hell is that?" Anger edged his voice.

They jumped up from the couch and hastily arranged their clothing. He went to the door.

On the other side was Christopher, the doorman. "Sorry to bother you, Mr. Knight. This was left for you." He handed Aaron a large envelope with his name scrawled on the front.

Hallie joined Aaron and greeted the doorman.

Christopher tipped his hat. "Evening, Ms. Cavanagh."

She smiled, but when she saw the envelope, her body stiffened, and she entwined her arm around Aaron's. His forehead creased with worry, and the strain in his voice prickled her skin.

"Wait, Christopher. Who gave this to you?" Aaron asked.

"It was already on the desk when I arrived tonight. I assumed it might be important."

"Then you didn't see anyone?"

"No, sir. I'm sorry." The doorman tipped his hat once again, said good night, and walked back into the waiting elevator.

Aaron closed the door and stood there for a

moment. Hallie figured he was upset.

She reached for the envelope, and he willingly let her take it. "Should I open it?"

"I'd like you to burn it."

She walked back into the kitchen and ran her fingers under the flap. He followed her.

She drew out the single paper. Just like before, the words were written with a black marker. But the anonymous note had a different message now.

Aaron Knight is a murderer.

Her spine jerked. "This can't continue, Aaron. You have to go to the police."

"What can they do?"

"They'll investigate."

"They'll have questions."

"And you'll answer them. And I'll be right by your side."

The anger in his expression subsided somewhat. "I love you for that, but I can't go to the police."

She didn't ask why. She didn't want to push him. Yet she knew this warning, like the previous one, was meant for her.

"Get rid of it," he ordered. "I'm going to take a shower."

She was aware of the strain in his voice. She wished she could ease his dread. She had reminded him that the incident happened fifteen years ago, and when people found out the truth about his father, they would be sure to understand. But he had shot down her views. She couldn't convince him, so she let it go…for now.

Besides, there seemed to be no bodily threat connected to these items. No demands for money or whatever else blackmailers wanted. No, this was different. She started for the living room, still mulling over the message. As she passed the dining room, the light from the chandelier caught the paper.

Hallie stopped, her breath seizing. She held the sheet up to the light. Her eyes widened, and her heart beat faster. There, revealed in all its glory, was ARK's watermark embedded in the corner. Realization came slowly, destroying her world. The warning was written on company paper.

He looked relaxed when he emerged from his shower. Hallie breathed in his scent, aware that telling him the news about discovering the watermark might ruin his Zen mood.

"Let me see," he said.

She handed the paper over. He held it up, and the light from the chandelier revealed the telling sign. He shot her a troubled glance. "Someone who works for me is behind this? I don't believe it."

She gave him a look.

"I know what you're thinking. Who you're thinking of."

"It could be anyone. You have offices all around the world."

"But you think it's Lavelle."

She repeated her feelings about the woman. "She practically accused me of sending you those threats."

"You never told me about that."

"Because we were otherwise engaged." She smiled slyly.

"Oh, yeah."

"What if it is Lavelle?"

He shook his head. "It can't be. Where would she get this information? Why would she want to do this to me?"

"I have a theory, but you're not going to like it."

"Try me."

"I think she's in love with you."

****

"How would you like to spend a few days at the beach, Mom?" Hallie asked as they strolled arm in arm down the hallway toward the common room. Today, her mother was a bit weak, but at least she recognized Hallie as her daughter. "We could sit by the ocean. Get some sun."

Her mother's face brightened. "Can we really go?"

She smiled at her mother's childlike enthusiasm. "Yes, Mom. We can really go."

It had already been a year since the doctor had referred to the disease as moderate stage four Alzheimer's. Now, according to the specialists, she was in the throes of a moderately severe decline, or stage six. Her major personality changes, confusion, and wandering justified the diagnosis. Her behavior problems, such as random outbursts, were becoming more frequent. The medication she took might be slowing the dreadful process a bit, but Hallie knew, in her heart, her mother would never recover. Every now and then, though, she rallied, like today. At the very least, that gave Hallie hope, no matter how false a feeling.

"When can you take me?"

"In a few days. We're going to spend a weekend at a beautiful house with people you'll like. Remember that man you met? The one who wanted to take you dancing?"

Her mother clapped her hands. "Oh, yes. He was so

handsome. He'll be there?"

It was a little miracle she had remembered Aaron. Hallie smiled. Hope. "Yes, he'll be there, too."

And then again, maybe not.

Though he tried not to show it, Aaron had been annoyed with her. He disagreed with her accusation of Lavelle, and when she'd voiced her hunch about the woman's feelings for him, he refused to believe it. Their lovemaking was quick and robotic, and Hallie knew he was just going through the motions. She wanted to talk about his moodiness. He wanted to sleep.

"This thing with Lavelle is only my opinion," she tried to explain as they lay in bed. "I don't have any proof."

"You seem pretty sure."

"Are you angry?"

His expression softened. "I could never be angry at you. I just have a lot on my mind."

"Tell me. Let me help with whatever's bothering you."

"Not now, Hallie. Go to sleep." He had kissed her on the forehead and turned on his side, his back toward her, signaling the abrupt end of their conversation.

The television in the common room was tuned to some afternoon talk show. A few patients had chairs lined up in front of the screen, but only one was watching. The others, some in wheelchairs, their heads bowed, were asleep. A faint odor of disinfectant assailed her nostrils.

Hallie guided her mother to one of the couches along the back wall.

"He was so nice to me." She paused, frowned, and then looked at Hallie. "What was his name again?" Her cheeks turned a dark pink as though she was embarrassed she'd forgotten.

"Aaron." At the mention of his name, Hallie's face heated with excitement.

"Aaron." Her mother nodded. "Such a strong name."

Hallie agreed. Seeing her mother like this, communicative, coherent, and eager, she looked forward to the trip to New Jersey. It would do her good to get out of this dreary place, even if it was for only a few days.

"Should I get ready now?"

"No, not yet." Hallie had become used to repeating her words.

"But I want to go now." Her mother sat up straighter, her face distorting with annoyance.

Hallie braced herself for the storm. "I know you do. But you won't have to wait long. I promise."

Surprisingly, her mother didn't balk this time. Instead, she stared past Hallie, suddenly lost in her own reveries. "I had a promise made to me once. But he broke it. He broke the promise."

He? Hallie was curious. She held her mother's hands. "Who broke a promise to you?"

Her mother appeared frightened and fragile, as though she'd said something wrong. "Can you take me back to my room?" The sharp tone of her voice caused Hallie to grimace. "I don't like it here."

Not wanting to upset her, Hallie quickly obliged her mother's directive. She helped her to her feet and then to her room.

Settled in one of the chairs by the window, her mother pointed to the box of photographs on the bed.

"Can you give me those?"

"Here you go." Hallie wondered why she wanted them.

Would the photos trigger something unpredictable, like last time? Her mother's hands shook as she struggled with the stacks.

"Can I help you?" Hallie asked, reaching for the box.

Her mother pulled it back from Hallie's grasp. "I can do it. Ah, here it is." She looked at Hallie and crooked her finger. "Come here and see."

Hallie obeyed and crouched down by the chair. "What is it, Mom?"

She pointed at the man in the picture. "This is your father."

Hallie already knew that. Though there weren't many, her mother had shown her pictures of her dad.

"He's very handsome, isn't he?" Her mother sighed and then stared at nothing in particular. Hallie guessed she was desperately grasping for an elusive memory. "He broke the promise. He was the one."

"Do you mean Dad's accident?" Hallie figured her father might have vowed to always be there for her, as many people in love did. Sadly, that wasn't the case for her dad. Life was cruel. There was pain in her mother's eyes.

Her mother's delicate features hardened like stone. "What accident? There was no accident. What are you talking about?" A frantic pitch crept along her words.

"Dad was killed in a motorcycle accident."

"No, no, no. There was no accident."

As insistent as her mother was, Hallie figured her memories were collapsing again. She had always been told there was an accident. A motorcycle accident. Her father died in a motorcycle accident. "Mom—"

"There was no accident." Her mother threw the photograph into the box and slammed down the lid.

Voices in Hallie's head screamed beware. She was afraid of this happening. Her mother was headed for another one of her episodes. "Okay, Mom. There was no accident." Better to appease the woman than to argue.

"There certainly was not." Her mother's tone was irate now. She closed her eyes and leaned back. "I'm tired. I have to rest. You need to leave."

Hallie wanted—needed—to know more. Was she telling the truth? Did she remember something, or was the disease consuming her even more? If she did recall something, which was unlikely, then what had caused her father's death? Was he even gone at all? The last thought gave her pause. With her heart pounding, Hallie couldn't help herself. "Mom, what happened to my father?"

Her mother rubbed her eyes with her fists like a child. When her eyelids fluttered open, Hallie realized the pain there. Pain that for some reason could not be expressed.

"Hallie?"

"Yes, Mom?"

The pain was replaced by an expression of confusion and then sheer happiness with a grin as wide as her face. "Hallie, what are you doing here? Have you been here long?"

The moment of making her mother explain herself about her father had passed. "No, Mom. I just got here."

****

During the two weeks leading up to Labor Day, Aaron received nothing detrimental in the mail or otherwise. Still, he refused to let down his guard. If someone at ARK was behind the damaging messages, it was unlikely they would stop.

He had been in a few situations like this before. After a few hostile takeovers or buying family-run businesses and then selling them off, he'd had his share of enemies. What influential and powerful person didn't? Yet this was different. Someone was out to expose him. Maybe to destroy him. He couldn't help but worry that if the story got out, the media would have a field day.

Usually he depended on Hallie to be the voice of reason. She had insisted if the circumstances of his father's death were known, people would be forgiving. After all, the incident had happened a long time ago when he was barely a teenager. But no matter how unrelenting she was about his past, he'd been adamant about how wrong she was about Lavelle.

He'd been at Park Studio from early in the morning until four p.m., taping four more installments of *The Pitch*. Though he'd made some solid business deals, he was bleary-eyed and exhausted. How did actors do this?

His first time in the studio had ended badly for him. The anonymous delivery of his criminal record documents had thrown him for a loop that day. The one good thing that had come out of all this chaos was that he'd been forced to tell Hallie about his past. Her sympathy and support were unexpected. Why had he assumed she'd be disgusted by his actions and leave him? Miranda had been right. He had to give the woman he loved more credit.

Until Hallie had come into his life, the only women he trusted were Rita and Lavelle.

As his family's housekeeper for over twenty years, Rita had cared for the Clark children as a mother would. Aaron remembered his sister, Selena, had called her Mom once. BiBi Clark never found out. Sibling code and all that.

Now that Rita worked for him, she'd become a significant presence, and he was more than happy to have her in his life. He was most grateful, however, that she had not been at the Clark house when his father died. When she learned what had happened, what he had done, Rita had taken him into her arms and cradled the distraught young boy, who had only been trying to save his mother from harm.

When he first met Lavelle Andrews, she'd been a secretary working in a cosmetics business he'd bought. No matter what the flailing company tried—promotions, commercials, celebrity endorsements—it failed to produce a substantial income for ARK. Aaron sold it off, making a lot of workers lose their jobs. But not Lavelle. Somehow, she convinced him to keep her on.

She first impressed him by her knowledge of ARK. Her extensive résumé was another swaying factor. She brazenly advocated her business savvy and organizational skills to the hilt. Aaron was fascinated by her moxie and hired her—first as a department associate and then, after watching and reviewing her work, promoted her to his administrative assistant. That was more than ten years ago. He'd made the right choice. Lavelle was loyal, a keeper of company secrets, and a friend. Hallie had to be wrong in thinking Lavelle was behind his possible ruination.

His wager was on Kyle.

"I didn't expect you back at the office." Lavelle looked over her computer screen, surprised at Aaron's presence.

"I have some work to finish."

"How was the taping today?"

"Good, but it eats up a lot of time. I did pay out two hundred fifty thousand dollars for a twenty percent stake in a start-up company called LawnBot."

"Sounds interesting."

"It's a robot lawn mower. If my instincts are correct, it'll make a fortune for ARK."

"Always a good thing." She smiled. "What are you doing for Labor Day?"

He was surprised by her question. She wasn't one to get personal. "Going to the house."

"Are you taking Hallie?"

That was a little too personal. One of his eyebrows rose a fraction. "Why do you ask?"

Elbow on the desk, she cupped her chin in her palm. Her deliberate expression was suddenly annoying to him.

"What do you think you know, Lavelle? Tell me."

"What we all know around here. You and Ms. Cavanagh are an item."

"Jesus, Lavelle. Everyone knows?"

She nodded. "Well, most of your executives, anyway. You two aren't hiding it very well."

He found that amusing.

"What happened to your 'never get involved with an employee' dictum?"

Something intense flared in her face.

Unaccustomed to her encroachment, he felt a certain tension building. Mentally, he shook the feeling away. He had to be mistaken.

"Yes, Hallie will be there."

Her triumphant grin bothered him. "Don't get mad. We're looking out for you. *I'm* looking out for you. Isn't that what a trustworthy assistant does for her boss?" She rose from her chair and made her way over to him. She clutched his hand. Her other hand found its way to his shoulder and then down his back. "We just don't want you to get hurt."

He froze. This wasn't the Lavelle he was used to. Her unbelievably blatant gestures made him cringe inwardly. He pulled away from her. "Lavelle, what are you doing?"

A flush of scarlet colored her cheeks. "Can't I care about you?" She tilted her head. "Don't you care about me?"

"Of course I do, but—"

"Uh-uh." She put her finger on his mouth. He promptly pushed it away. " 'But' negates everything you said before." She threw the words at him like stones.

Her odd behavior caused him to change his plans about staying. "I'm going home now, Lavelle. I think you should do the same. We'll forget this"—he waved his hand between the two of them—"ever happened, okay?"

Her face contorted with disdain. "If you say so." She went back to her desk.

"Good night, Lavelle." He walked past her. "Enjoy your time off."

"Aaron?"

He reluctantly stopped and turned. "Yes?"

"I just hope this"—she mimicked his hand wave from before—"doesn't find its way to a public forum."

His breath caught in his throat. "Excuse me?"

"Sometimes what we fight so hard to keep hidden rears its ugly head when we least expect it." She flashed him a smile that sent a chill down his spine. "Have a good evening, Aaron." Her head bowed, Lavelle concentrated once again on her computer screen.

Chapter Twenty

What the hell was that all about?

His mind reeling, Aaron drove through city traffic for a half hour and tried to make sense of Lavelle's bizarre behavior. Though he knew nothing of her life outside of ARK, he wondered if she was dealing with something traumatic. What else could have flipped such an outrageous switch? Her last words, though, were telling.

Sometimes what we fight so hard to keep hidden rears its ugly head when we least expect it.

What did she know?

"Hallie, are you here?" he called out, finally arriving at the penthouse. After the long day of taping *The Pitch* and dealing with Lavelle and all her craziness, he deserved a peaceful evening with the woman he loved. There was no answer. He'd send her a text. Better yet he'd call.

"Call Hallie," he said into his phone.

"Calling Hallie," was the robotic-sounding answer. The phone began to ring…and ring. She wasn't picking up. He left a message.

"Hey, honey, it's me. Just wondering where you are. I'm at home. Call me. Miss you. Love you." He hung up, satisfied she'd answer soon. She always did.

Someone was knocking. That was quick. "Hallie?" He opened the door and froze. "Lavelle? What are you doing here?"

He noticed her hair first. Usually pulled back, it was now straight and shining. Wisps of bangs covered her forehead. Her glasses were gone. Her white blouse was nearly transparent. Her tight black skirt was short, revealing shapely legs and thighs. *What the hell?* Had she been wearing these clothes when he saw her at the office earlier? He couldn't remember, nor did he want to. An unsettling feeling skittered across his nerve endings. Red flags were popping up all around him. Something was wrong with this picture. Very wrong.

"I brought you the work you left behind." Her arms were loaded with folders and binders.

He took them from her. He hesitated at first, ignored the warning signs, and invited her inside. He caught the subtle smell of her scent, part woman, part something else. "I appreciate it, but you didn't have to go out of your way."

She perched herself on one of the island stools in the kitchen. "I don't mind." She smiled. "Time is money. Isn't that what you always say? Besides, I have an ulterior motive. I wanted to see you."

His gut feeling stirred uneasily. Was she flirting with him? He swallowed an unexpected knot in his throat.

"I came to apologize. I don't know what came over me back at the office. I wouldn't blame you if you fired me."

Her usual no-nonsense attitude was now sultry, almost predatory, and she was making him uncomfortable. "I'm not going to fire you, Lavelle. It's just that you weren't yourself. You do understand how inappropriate your behavior was, don't you?"

She glanced around, completely ignored his cautionary advice. "Is Hallie here?"

"No—"

"Good, then we can talk honestly." She slid off the stool, moved close to him, and fiddled with his tie. "She's not the woman for you."

What the hell is she saying? He held up a hand in restraint, as if warning her off. "Lavelle, we shouldn't be—"

"I've known women like her, and they're all the same. Only looking out for what they can get from powerful, unsuspecting men like you. Hallie's no different, Aaron. Yes, she's young and pretty, and I'm sure great in bed—"

"Lavelle, stop. We're not going to talk about this. It's wrong." He ran an agitated hand through his hair.

"What's wrong is your infatuation with her. In the ten years I've been at ARK, I've seen the women you've dated come and go without so much as a hello or goodbye from you. Why is Hallie so different, Aaron?"

"Lavelle—"

"Does she know something about you? Is that why you're keeping her around?"

Lavelle's suggestion interested him. It also stunned his senses. Was Hallie right about her all along? "Why would you say that?"

"We all have something in our lives we're ashamed of, Aaron." She moved nearer to him. "Something we wouldn't want the world to know."

"What do you think you know about me, Lavelle?"

She laid her hands on his chest. "Frankly, I don't understand why she hasn't left you yet. I certainly wouldn't want to be associated with a...a murderer."

He stiffened. A small vein throbbed over one eyebrow.

"What's the matter, Aaron? Did I shock you?"

"I'm not a murderer."

"Really? The court says otherwise."

The rage inside him was building quickly. "It's you, isn't it? You're the one sending the threats. You're the one who somehow got ahold of my records. How did you do it? Why did you do it?"

"Because you belong with me, Aaron. Not with Hallie. I've given you ten years of my life. I've been your confidante, your stronghold. The keeper of your secrets." She gave him a wry grin. "Until now."

"What do you want, Lavelle?"

"You, Aaron. I want you."

****

Hallie looked at her phone. Three missed calls and one voice mail—all from Aaron. He was at the penthouse waiting for her. Hopefully, he was in a better mood than yesterday.

She used ARK's car service and asked the driver to take her to her apartment first. She needed to get a few things, and she wanted to see Sophie. Harboring a healthy dose of guilt about not connecting these last couple of days with her roommate, Hallie was determined to make it up to her with an invitation she couldn't refuse.

"Well, well. The prodigal friend returns." Sophie, her eyes wide and accusatory, was sprawled out on the couch, her biting sarcasm coming through loud and clear. As if amused with Sophie's comment, laughter from a sitcom audience she'd been watching burst through the television.

Hallie struck her heart three times with a closed fist. "*Mea culpa.*" She remembered her high school Latin. "Forgive me?"

Sophie shut off the TV via the remote and got to her feet. Breaking the playful tension between them, she embraced her friend.

"How come that billionaire gets to be with you all the time?" Sophie cocked an eyebrow. "Is he funnier than me? More thoughtful? Does he cook? Oh, wait, he's cuter than me, right?"

"Oh, I missed this. I miss you." Hallie hugged her again.

Sophie dragged her to the couch. "So tell me. Has he proposed yet?"

"Sophie, we've been together less than five months."

"But the wait is killing me."

Hallie took her friend's hands. "What are you doing Labor Day weekend?"

"What else? Working."

"You can't take some time off?"

"Why?"

"Because I want you to come with me and my mom to Sea Girt."

"Aaron's house?"

"Of course."

"Really?"

"Yes."

Sophie, the palms of her hands turned upward now, moved them up and down, weighing the options. "Let's see. Stifling kitchen or the beach? Insufferable customers or relaxing by the pool?" She raised one of her hands up high. "Sea Girt wins."

"Yay!" Hallie threw up her hands. "We'll leave tomorrow. About one o'clock, okay?"

"Your mom's coming?"

"Aaron thinks it'll be good for her. So do I." Hallie told her about the kindness and patience Aaron showed toward her mother's condition.

"So unlike Kyle, huh?"

Hallie made a face at the mention of her ex. "I'm about to revoke your invite, my friend."

Sophie cringed. "All right, all right. I take it back."

****

"I'm sending Nelson to pick up you, your mother, and Sophie. The nurse is already at the house."

Aaron's change of plans had Hallie confused. Phone to her ear, she moved about her apartment as though under water. "I thought you were coming with us."

"I have a few things I have to take care of at the office, and then I'll be there. This way you can get your mother accustomed to the house without me being in your way."

"You could never be in my way."

Was he smiling on the other end of the phone?

"Nelson will be at the nursing home around eleven. This way you'll get an earlier start. I'm glad you asked Sophie to come."

"But, Aaron—"

"Don't worry, honey, I'll be there."

"Promise?"

"Yes. Don't you believe me?"

"Of course I do."

"Have a safe trip. I'll see you soon." Aaron hung

up, leaving Hallie with a dull ache in her heart. Dropping her phone onto the couch, she hugged herself, her mind a jumble of unasked, unanswered questions.

As Aaron had promised, a prompt Nelson was at Hallie's apartment to pick up Sophie and her. Golden Living was next. With Joanne's blessing, Donna Cavanagh, complete with a floppy straw hat the nurses had bought, was ready for her adventure. Her eyes lit up when she saw Hallie.

"You look beautiful," Hallie said.

Her mother giggled, raised one hand, and twirled around. "Don't I, though?"

Hallie guided her mother to the limo and carefully helped her inside.

"Where are we going again?"

Hallie grimaced but answered with patience. "To the beach, Mom."

Her mother nodded and her eyelids fluttered shut. "The beach." She was trying to hold on to the image like a life preserver.

Other than her mother thinking that Sophie was a nurse and Nelson a doctor, the ride to Sea Girt was uneventful. Her mother watched the scenery go by, sang some '50s songs, and then slept most of the way.

Rita and Anne Ramos, the nurse Aaron had hired, were waiting for their arrival. As Hallie expected, meeting so many new people had her mother confused for a while. But once she settled into her room, the Sea Star, she seemed a bit calmer. Aaron had made sure a hospital bed was brought in for her mother and a separate bed for the nurse. Sophie was in a private suite as well, called the Sand Dollar.

"I could get used to this," she told Hallie.

Rita had made a lovely lunch—a mix of butter and red leaf lettuces with grape tomatoes, crispy bacon, and thinly sliced red onions. Homemade honey mustard dressing crowned the shiny green leaves.

But as delicious as it was, Hallie's mother had trouble finishing the salad.

"Chew, Donna. Chew slowly and swallow," Anne encouraged her gently.

"I can't. I forgot how." Fright flickered in her eyes. "What do I do?"

"It's all right, Mom." Fear fluttered in Hallie's stomach as well. *Forgot how to chew?*

"Sometimes that happens." Anne tried to reassure Hallie. The nurse's explanation was lost on her.

On the nurse's request, Rita hurriedly fetched a small yogurt container from the refrigerator. Hallie was relieved that her mother found the yogurt easier to consume.

Though there were more clouds than sun, it didn't stop Hallie, her mother, and Sophie from enjoying Aaron's private beach. Sophie relaxed by the water with a book, while Hallie took her mother for a walk along the shore. The incoming waves tickled their toes, and the soft wet sand beneath their feet was spongy and cool.

"Are you enjoying yourself, Mom?"

"It's beautiful here."

Hallie breathed deeply, the invigorating air cleansing her lungs, filling her with expectation. But would the expectation be short-lived? She had sent a text to Aaron once they arrived at the house. There'd been no text back from him, so she called. No answer there either. Was he on his way? Would he be there at all?

Her comment about Lavelle being in love with him had stunned him, of course, but there was something else bothering him. She couldn't put her finger on it, but it was there—hovering, waiting to strike.

"Where is that nice man, Hallie? You said he would be here, but he isn't."

"Aaron? He'll be here later." She hoped.

"You promised he would be here." Her voice rose above the crashing waves.

"Don't get upset."

"I am upset. Your father's not home yet."

Hallie's ears perked up. Was her mother about to divulge something about her father? "Where is he?"

"He left. He left me. He's not coming back."

Was her mother's story based in reality? Or was it some fantasy she was spouting? "Why, Mom? Why isn't he coming back?"

"My sister took him away."

"Aunt Rosemary?"

"They ran away. They left me alone."

Had Rosemary and her father had an affair? "Mom, are you sure?" She was shocked at her mother's revelation. Hallie wondered if that could explain why her mother had physically hurt her that day in the nursing home.

The sound of the waves and the cries of the seagulls overhead couldn't drown out her mother's dread. Seeing tears in her eyes, Hallie regretted the pain her words had caused. But she had to know. "Mom, is my father alive?"

Her mother grabbed Hallie's arm. "Eddie left me. I want him to come back. Can you bring him back to me?"

"Mom?"

With the tears dried up, her mother, her brow puckering, looked at Hallie. "Where are we?"

Hallie sighed, grim thoughts crowding her mind. "We're at the beach, Mom."

Her mother smiled. "You're very kind to bring me here. Now are you a doctor or a nurse?"

****

Though every instinct warned him against contact with her, Aaron had directed Lavelle to meet him at the office. Except for a cleaning crew, the place was empty because of the holiday. They could discuss the matter in private. He had to know how she'd come across the information about his past. She was intelligent and resourceful. He wouldn't have wanted his assistant any other way. But this? What tricks had she used?

I want you.

Lavelle's explosive words tumbled around in his head. He had not been primed for that surprise. He'd always liked Lavelle, aside from her business savvy. But he thought of her as a friend—a good friend, and certainly not anything more. Apparently, she had other ideas. Had Hallie been right about Lavelle all along?

He glanced at his watch. He had called her an hour ago, but she hadn't picked up. He tried again, hoping she had gotten his first voice mail. Again, there was no answer. He didn't think it strange, just frustrating. Maybe she was embarrassed. Maybe she was nervous to face him. Whatever the reason, he had a feeling she wasn't going to show.

His phone suddenly vibrated in his hand. It was Lavelle.

"Did you get my message?" he asked, trying to remain aloof.

"Of course I did." Her tone was sharp and grated on his nerves.

"Well, where are you? We need to talk about this."

"Sorry, Aaron. I can't meet you. I'm on my way to Sea Girt. In fact, I'm almost there."

He struggled for control of his anger. "Lavelle, what are you doing?"

"I'm going to see Hallie."

"No. You can't do that."

"Don't get so upset. I'm not going to hurt her. At least not physically. I'm not a monster. I want to talk with her and explain my feelings. To tell her about us."

"There is no 'us,' Lavelle. Now turn the car around and come back to the office."

"I can't, but when I do get back, you'll be free of her. She's an intelligent woman. She'll understand. Bye, Aaron."

"Lavelle! She knows," he shouted into the phone, but she had already hung up.

Panicked, Aaron rushed to the garage and got in his car. Weaving his way through the city traffic, he came upon the ramp that would get him on the Garden State Parkway. The office, the city, everything after Lavelle's call was a blur. He knew he was driving too fast. If a good ol' Jersey-boy State Police officer stopped him, then he'd talk his way out of the violation or accept the fine. Either way, he had to get to Sea Girt to stop Lavelle from whatever she was planning to do.

How had everything gone downhill so quickly? It seemed just yesterday he was interviewing Hallie for the position at ARK. Now he was praying nothing terrible would happen to her. He wouldn't be able to forgive himself if she was harmed in any way.

He slowed at the tollbooth, his E-ZPass registering his amount. He stepped on the gas again once he cleared the stall. He needed to warn Hallie. His phone searched her number and rang. And rang.

"Pick up, Hallie," he mumbled, weaving around a car in the inside lane. "Pick up."

****

"She's resting," Hallie told Rita after the housekeeper asked about her mother. "I guess the ocean air did her in. Anne's with her." The two were in the kitchen, Hallie at the counter and Rita going through cabinets.

"You're a good daughter," Rita said.

"I'm only doing what I have to."

Rita nodded. "And what you're doing is caring for her. Where's your friend?"

"Sophie? Out by the pool. She's really enjoying herself."

"Then is it all right with you if I leave for a while? I have to go to the supermarket."

"Sure, Rita. You don't have to ask my permission."

Hallie, holding a bottle of iced tea, sat on the porch swing. She had a clear view of the street and the comings and goings of folks heading to or leaving the beach. Colorful pillows at her back, she kept one foot on the floor and rocked the swing slowly. She yawned. The relaxing motion was putting her to sleep, and she fought to keep her eyes open. She took a healthy sip of the tea. The heat from the late afternoon sun scorched the street and sidewalks. On the porch, the air felt cooler.

Hallie checked her watch. It was 3:35. Where was Aaron? Dragging her phone from the pocket of her denim shorts, she unlocked the screen and checked her messages. There was nothing recent from him. She thought about calling again but decided she'd wait. She didn't want to push him or make him think something was wrong—or that she was incredibly needy.

She replayed the Lavelle exchange with him over in her mind. Though he had kept his true opinion to himself, she suspected he was angry with her in blaming Lavelle for the messages. The ARK watermark was a telling sign—but Lavelle? Maybe it was a stretch. And to say the woman was in love with him? Maybe that was stretching her obvious infatuation a little too far.

Her thoughts focused on her own conundrum. Her mother. Learning her father hadn't died in an accident had come as a shock. Her mother could have been mistaken about her sister and her husband. Stage six of the damn disease was fraught with bouts of severe confusion and unwarranted fear. But there was something about the insistence of her mother's words, how adamant she was about the memory. If indeed Edward Cavanagh had deserted his family, she'd have to deal and come to terms with abandonment issues, not to mention her anger over how her father had treated her mother. And if he were still alive, if he and Rosemary were still together, that would conjure up another set of emotions. But would she ever know the true story?

The car in her vision drove by slowly as though searching for something. At first, Hallie became excited, thinking that Aaron had finally arrived. But the car wasn't his. Yet it turned and drove through the gates that Rita had left open. Hallie stopped the swing and squinted. Who was it? Nothing had been mentioned about company. Maybe the person behind the wheel was lost or delivering a package.

Or…

Hallie stiffened, her emotions running wild. If it was a package, would it be in the form of another threat? Bile stung the back of her throat. She had to stop these doom-ish images. What she and Aaron had to do was find the person responsible.

The car parked and the engine was cut. Who could it be? She didn't have to wait long. The driver emerged, and a startled Hallie gave a tiny squeak.

Lavelle.

Chapter Twenty-One

Hallie got off the swing and hurried down the porch steps. "Lavelle?" she called out.

Lavelle looked her way and then started toward the porch.

What was she doing here? Had Aaron invited her? Why? And then it came to her. What if Aaron wanted Lavelle here so he could prove to her she'd never hurt him in that way? Pretty extreme to go to such lengths. She'd just have to wait and see.

"Good to see you, Hallie." Her greeting was as carefree as the flower print sundress and sandals she wore.

"Hello, Lavelle. Don't tell me you're here on business. It's a holiday weekend."

Lavelle's laugh had a sharp edge. "No. No business today."

"Well, if you're looking for Aaron, you're out of luck. He's not here."

"I know. I just spoke to him."

Hallie bristled with surprise. The air between them was charged with tension that she couldn't explain. "You did? Is he on his way?"

Lavelle shrugged. "I came to talk to you, Hallie."

"Me? Why?"

"Can we go inside?"

Why had Lavelle called Aaron? Was she even

telling the truth?

"Sure." With a flicker of apprehension coursing through her, Hallie opened the door. "We can talk in here." Hallie showed Lavelle to the solarium at the back of the house.

Encased within glass walls, the solarium exuded relaxation. Robust plants bathed in the sunlight, and modern wicker furniture set the leisurely mood. The outside pool was off to the left. Hallie glimpsed Sophie stretched out on a chaise.

Lavelle took a seat. "I don't mean to bother you."

You are bothering me. I want you to leave. "Actually, I'm curious. If it's not about business, then why are you here? Did Aaron invite you?"

"You sound rather possessive, Hallie. No, Aaron didn't invite me. Coming here was my idea."

Hallie fidgeted in the chair, trying to relax her tense muscles. *Possessive? Her idea?* She threaded her fingers through her hair and managed to work up one of those simpleminded smiles that had no rhyme or reason.

Lavelle's concern marred her features. "Are you okay, Hallie? You seem a bit…jumpy."

"What do you want, Lavelle?"

Lavelle skewered Hallie with a look. "It's about Aaron and what's been happening to him."

"What are you talking about? Is Aaron all right? Is it something about ARK?" Was she alluding to the threats? The threats she might have sent? Hallie raised her chin, waiting for her confession.

"How are the two of us going to handle this?"

Hallie frowned. "Handle what? I don't understand." What *was* she talking about? Had Aaron told her about the court documents and the other messages? Maybe she wasn't the one behind the threats. Maybe she wanted Hallie's help to put a stop to them. Maybe she had Lavelle's motives all wrong.

Suddenly, agitated voices rolled in loudly from another part of the house, interrupting the women's conversation. Hallie recognized one in particular.

"You're making me late! Get away from me! You're making me late!"

"Please, Donna, slow down. You'll hurt yourself."

Warning bells went off in Hallie's brain. She got to her feet, her heart pounding. "Sorry, Lavelle, I have to take care of this."

"Is everything okay? Do you need any help?"

"I'll handle it." Hallie dashed to the foyer in time to see her mother coming down the main set of steps that led to the upstairs suites. "Mom, what's the matter?"

Anne looked distraught. "I'm sorry, Hallie. She woke up and jumped out of bed before I had the chance to stop her."

"It's okay, Anne. She can get feisty when she doesn't get her way." Hallie blocked the bottom of the stairs. Her mother tried to push her out of the way, but Hallie didn't budge. "Where are you going?"

"Let her go," Anne said. "It's better than restraining her. Just make sure the doors to the outside are closed."

Though Hallie stepped out of the way, her mother didn't move. Fear clouded her eyes. "Where am I? Where am I?" She repeated the question several times until Anne gently placed her hand on her shoulder.

"Donna, it's all right. You're with family and

friends. You don't have to be scared."

"But I am scared. I have no family. I'm all alone, and I don't know where I am."

Hallie blinked back the tears forming in the corners of her eyes. She hated this. She hated seeing her loving and hardworking mother reduced to a panic-stricken woman whose once vital mind was quickly making its way to a dark abyss. If only there was a magic pill or remedy to stop this horrible disease. If only she didn't feel so helpless, so powerless. But as helpless as she felt, she couldn't begin to imagine what her mother was dealing with.

"It's okay, Mom. I'll help you. We'll work this out together." Hallie held out her arms to embrace her mother, but this time, Donna, her eyes clouded with confusion, pushed her out of the way and took off through the house.

"Mom, come back. You're going to get hurt," Hallie shouted. She took off after her.

Anne was right behind. They followed Donna to the patio doors the moment Sophie opened them to come inside.

"What's going on? I heard some shouting—"

"Mom, no!" Hallie cried as her mother bolted through the opened door. "Stop her, Sophie!"

Sophie dashed back outside. "Donna, wait. Come back!"

Hallie rushed past her, her heart beating frantically. "Mom!" Her mother was headed straight for the pool. "Mom! Stop!" Hallie was too late. She watched horrified as her mother fell face down into the water.

Hallie didn't hesitate. She jumped in, but never having been taught how to swim, did her best to tread water as fast as she could. There was another splash, and someone skimmed her side and pushed her out of the way. Hallie tossed the wet hair off her face and saw Lavelle. She had dived into the pool and was already swimming back to the edge, dragging an animated and terrified Donna in her arms.

Lavelle lifted Donna out of the water and into the arms of Anne and Sophie. At last Hallie made it to the side. With Lavelle's help, she lifted herself out of the pool and ran to her mother.

"Mom, are you okay?"

Aside from shivering, her mother was fine. Sophie grabbed the towel she'd been using and wrapped it around her.

"Mom, please say something," Hallie begged, brushing back the wet gray strands of her hair. "Tell me you're all right."

Her mother looked at her. "The water felt wonderful. I feel so refreshed."

Though the situation could have turned tragic, Hallie shook her head while Anne and Sophie snickered.

Anne took over. "You need to rest now, Donna. Let's go back to your room."

"But I want to go in there again." Donna pointed to the pool.

"Plenty of time for that. Let's dry you off, change your clothes, and get you into bed."

Much calmer, Donna relented, and Anne guided her into the house.

Sophie put her arm around Hallie. "You okay? Can I get you anything? Xanax? Prozac? Zoloft?"

Hallie laughed. "How about all three?" She hugged

her friend. "I'm so glad you're here." Past Sophie's shoulder, she saw Lavelle, soaked to the skin, sitting on one of the chaise lounge chairs. She was leaning forward, elbows on her knees, her hands covering her face.

Breaking away from Sophie, Hallie asked if she wouldn't mind leaving her alone for a while.

Sophie turned and eyed Lavelle. "A friend of yours?" Sophie whispered.

"Not sure."

"Sounds intriguing. You're sure you want me to go?"

Hallie gently pushed her toward the house and then grabbed another towel from the rack by the patio door.

"Lavelle? Are you all right?"

Lavelle raised her head to look at Hallie. Her makeup was smeared; her eyeliner and mascara ran down her face like jagged prison bars. Her hair that had been styled so perfectly now hung in messy wet strands.

"Here." Hallie handed her the towel.

Lavelle thanked her, dried her face, and ran the towel through her hair. When done, she wrapped the towel around her shoulders. Hallie sat on the chair next to her.

"Your mother?" Lavelle asked.

"Yes." She wasn't thrilled Lavelle had witnessed something so personal, yet she was more than grateful the woman had saved her mother. "Thank you for what you did." She inhaled a shaky breath. "She has Alzheimer's."

Lavelle nodded. "It must be tough."

Emotion caused Hallie's voice to quaver. "Why did you go after her?"

"I just reacted. Isn't that what a good admin does?"

"Does a good admin threaten her boss as well?" Hallie took a much-needed breath. She was glad she'd asked the question. Glad it was out in the open. Whether it was true or not, at least she'd know.

Panic shone in Lavelle's eyes, and Hallie watched the blood drain from her face.

"You sent the court documents and those messages, didn't you?" Her tone wasn't accusatory, only curious.

"I shouldn't have come."

Hallie touched her arm. Her skin was cold and damp. "I'm not here to judge; I'm here to listen. Help me understand, Lavelle. Tell me the truth."

Her breath hitched a little. "How can you be like this, Hallie? How can you be so forgiving after what I've done? I don't deserve it."

"Watching my mother suffer with this disease, I've learned that life is too damn short. It's too short to be angry or miserable. Being angry solves nothing, but it can destroy everything. That's not what I want for you."

"I made some bad choices, foolish choices." She shook her head. "I'm so ashamed. I didn't mean for it to get this far." Tears formed in her eyes.

Hallie squeezed her hand gently. "How did you get Aaron's juvenile records and the article about his father's death?"

A look of surrender veiled Lavelle's face. Her shoulders sagged, and her body seemed to close in on itself. "It's been ten years since that night. Aaron had just hired me as his assistant. I worked for a company he bought, and while other employees from that company were being let go, I convinced him to keep me on. I had so much to prove. Working for Aaron Knight doesn't guarantee a permanent job."

Hallie didn't intend to smile at Lavelle's insightfulness, but she did.

Lavelle grinned back. "I was working late, and so was Aaron. Or at least I thought he was."

"Where was he?"

"He was in his office, but he…he was drinking."

"Drinking? You mean he was drunk?"

"For lack of a better word."

"Did you know why?"

"I didn't at first. Then I heard noises from behind his door. I knocked, but all I heard was him mumbling. The door was open, so I went inside." Lavelle's eyes widened. "I couldn't believe what I saw, Hallie. Aaron had practically trashed his office. There were papers everywhere."

"And Aaron? What was he doing?"

"He was sprawled out on the couch, holding an empty bottle of scotch. I didn't know what to do. Of course, I asked if he was okay and if I could help him in any way, but he yelled at me to leave." Lavelle looked past Hallie, her gaze clouded. "Then she came."

"Who?"

"Miranda Tybee. Do you know her?"

"I've met her. Once."

"I never trusted her, but she seemed to calm Aaron down from whatever was bothering him. She asked me to stay and straighten his office. She was going to take him to her place. He refused to go, but eventually Miranda won and got him out of the office."

"Did you ever find out what was wrong? Why he

was drinking?"

"Not until I saw the collection of newspaper articles. They were scattered all over, amid business proposals and contracts. I started reading them. They were about the Clark family, whom I'd never heard of, who had suffered a terrible tragedy. Why on earth would Aaron have these, I kept asking myself. Did he know the Clarks? Were they friends? Family members? Then I saw the court records. The name Michael Clark was written on the document. The date was August 15, 2003. I calculated quickly and realized that day was a ten-year anniversary of William Clark's death. There had to be some connection. I thought about it, and for some reason, it all came together. Aaron was Michael Clark.

"I don't know what possessed me, maybe I was insecure about my job, but I made copies of the records and articles. Just in case, I kept telling myself. I knew I'd never use them. I was curious. After I made the copies, I put them in a safe place and cleaned up the rest of his office."

"But Aaron values you. He's told me repeatedly how loyal you are, how trustworthy. When I insinuated you could be involved, he practically blew up. You're his right-hand...person. So why now, Lavelle?"

"It's because of you."

Hallie blinked. "Me?"

Lavelle pinched her lower lip with her teeth. Her expression withered like an empty balloon. "I'm embarrassed to even think about this." Tears thickened her voice. She wiped them away.

"It's all right." Hallie was aware of the tension stretching between them.

"I've seen women come and go in Aaron's life, but it's different with you. You're the one he wants. You're the one that's changed him, and he knows that." Lavelle's voice broke slightly. "You complete him, Hallie, whether you know it or not. He's a better man because of you."

"You're giving me too much credit. I didn't set out to change anybody. I needed this job so I could give my mother some quality of life."

"I know that, but things happen when we least expect them."

Lavelle was right. Hallie had never anticipated loving Aaron and him loving her back. "But that's a good thing, isn't it?"

"Not when I wanted him to need me for more than just a secretary."

"You're in love with Aaron." Hallie swallowed hard over the sudden lump of jealousy. "You wanted me out of his life so you thought using his past might scare me away."

"It was a stupid thing to do. I destroyed everything, but I know there'll be consequences for my actions. I'm sorry. That's all I can say."

"I can't speak for Aaron, but I accept your apology."

Lavelle stood, and Hallie followed. "It's time for me to leave."

"You're talking about quitting your job, aren't you?"

"Hallie, this is my mess. I made it, and now I have to find a way to clean it up. I can only do that if I leave ARK."

Hallie didn't waver. It was the right move for

Lavelle to make.

"Who knows? Maybe I'll meet my own Aaron someday."

"I'll miss you, Lavelle." Hallie grabbed her hands. "Promise me one thing."

"After what I've put you through, how can I not?"

"Promise me you'll forgive yourself."

Lavelle's mouth parted in surprise. "I'm not sure I can keep that promise. All I can say is maybe someday."

"Hallie?"

Both women turned. Aaron was standing on the patio. Hallie saw a glint of fear in his eyes.

"Hi, Aaron. Lavelle was just leaving."

"Goodbye, Hallie."

Hallie nodded and said the same.

Aaron had started toward them.

Squaring her shoulders, Lavelle met him head on and looked him straight in the eye. "You're a very lucky man, Mr. Knight. Don't mess it up." And with that, she made her way to the outside gate.

"Are you okay? I knew she was on her way here. I tried to stop her—"

"Everything's fine, Aaron." She stroked his arm. "I'm fine."

He gathered her in his arms. "Then what the hell was that about?"

She broke away, kissed him lightly on the lips, and took his hand. She heard Lavelle start her car and drive away. "Girl talk."

"What?"

"Let's go inside. I have a lot to tell you."

****

Lavelle had left her two weeks' notice on Aaron's desk but never showed up for work after the weekend. Everyone at ARK who knew Lavelle was curious, of course. When asked about her impromptu departure, Aaron only said it was her decision.

Hallie relayed the how, when, and why Lavelle had done what she did to Aaron. The woman's motives surprised him, but it made him better understand why she had to leave ARK. He would miss her, but he was also glad his past actions were still protected.

Though she'd tried, Hallie hadn't fully convinced him he wasn't responsible for his father's death. And as for forgiving himself, he'd promised her he would try his best to make it so.

It was the end of September, and the work grind at ARK was in full force. The city was once again crowded with its regular inhabitants while the out-of-state tourists had found their way back to their own routines. Though the nights were slowly growing shorter, the days were still warm. Aaron thought it a perfect time to head down to Sea Girt just for the weekend. The vacationers would all be gone, and he wanted Hallie to experience the "real" town.

"Do you think your mother would like to come with us again? With all that went on over Labor Day, I doubt you spent much time with her." They were in her office.

"She'd love it. She's been asking me about going back." She kissed him.

He kissed her back. "Aren't you afraid someone will see us?" His gaze was glued to the slightly opened door.

"What do you think?" She kissed him again, this

time lingering, savoring the moment.

*****

"How would you like to go back to the beach, Mom?" Hallie had scooted out of work early to tell her mother about Aaron's invitation. She thought the news would make her happy. Instead, her mother was listless and indifferent toward Hallie's surprise.

"I'm so tired, nurse." Her mother's voice was barely audible.

"It's me, Mom. It's Hallie. What's wrong?"

Her mother stirred slightly under the bedsheet, her gaze clouded with confusion. "I need my Eddie. He'll take care of me. You go home." Weak as she seemed, she still had some strength to shoo Hallie away.

Hallie didn't budge. "Eddie's not here, Mom. He went away."

"No. He's coming back. I saw him yesterday. He said he'd come back to me."

It was useless to argue. Still, Hallie felt this need to find out more about her father. Whether it was the truth or some fantasy in her mother's mind, she'd have to determine that herself.

"Where is Eddie?"

"He said he was coming back." She grabbed onto Hallie's arm. "Maybe he lost his way."

Maybe he did.

"I'm sure he'll be here. He would never leave me alone."

"What about Rosemary?"

Her mother's brow crinkled. "Who?"

"Your sister. Remember Rosemary?"

With her eyes narrowed, her mother fought to dredge up the memory. "Rosemary's gone, too. They're all gone."

Hallie couldn't decipher if her mother was speaking about her father and aunt going away together or if they were no longer alive. Perhaps she'd never know.

"Now it's my turn to go."

Assailed by a terrible sense of foreboding, Hallie quickly rebuked her mother. "Mom, don't say that. The only place you're going is the beach, okay?"

Her mother turned her head, a bright light in her pale blue eyes. "Eddie!"

Hallie touched her mother's hand. "Mom, he's not here."

"But I am."

Hallie looked up. Standing in the doorway was Aaron. Still dressed in his suit, he seemed a bit weary, but that weariness didn't take away from his content expression.

"What are you doing here?" Hallie asked.

He was holding a small transparent box.

"What's that?"

He walked over to the bed. "Mrs. Cavanagh, it seems we have some unfinished business to take care of."

Joy bubbled in her mother's giggle and shone in her eyes. "Hello, Eddie." As if on cue, she extended her hand.

He took it and helped her out of bed. "I have something for you, my sweet lady." He opened the box. Inside was a wristlet made of yellow tea roses and baby's breath.

"It's beautiful," her mother gushed.

"Let me put it on for you." He slipped the elastic

band over her hand and onto her wrist.

Though she was touched by his sentiment, Hallie worried her mother's erratic behavior might rear its ugly head. "This isn't a good idea, Aaron—"

"Music, Hallie."

"What?" She looked at him, confused.

"You must have some songs on your phone."

"Sure, but—"

"Good, then find something sweet and slow."

Hallie hesitated and then grabbed her phone from her tote bag.

"Don't keep us waiting, Hallie." Towering above her, he gazed down at Donna and winked. "I told you I'd be back."

Donna leaned her head against his chest. "Yes, you did, Eddie. You promised, and here you are."

Hallie scrolled through her bevy of songs and found a suitable playlist. She chose "The Way You Look Tonight." The artist was Frank Sinatra.

"Ah, Ol' Blue Eyes." Aaron nodded his approval. "Perfect." He stepped back from his partner, held her hand, and bowed. "May I have this dance, Mrs. Cavanagh?"

"Oh, yes."

As she watched the two of them move slowly around the room, Hallie blinked back sudden tears that threatened to fall. The look of happiness on her mother's face was priceless. His gentleness stole pieces of her heart, and her body flooded with want and desire.

But for now, he belonged to her mother.

The song over, he took a step backward and thanked her for the dance.

Her face still glowing with joy, she looked at him.

"I so enjoyed it..." She searched his face, and Hallie saw her eyes widen with recognition. "Aaron. Your name is Aaron."

"Why, yes, it is." He gazed at Hallie and smiled.

Hallie couldn't contain her excitement. "You remember."

"Of course I do." Her mother sounded mildly indignant. "Why wouldn't I? Help me into bed now. I'm very tired."

Hallie did as she was told. She fluffed the pillows and eased her under the covers. As she tucked her in, her mother's eyes grew sharp and assessing. Suddenly, she reached for Hallie, cupped her face in her small wrinkled hands, and studied her face. "Hallie," she whispered finally. "You're my daughter, Hallie."

She could no longer contain her tears. "Yes, Mom. I'm Hallie."

"You're beautiful. You're my beautiful daughter."

Hallie covered her mother's hand with her own. "Rest now, Mom. Aaron and I will be right here."

"I love you, Hallie." Her mother's voice was a bit weak, a bit fragile.

"I love you, too, Mom."

Her mother closed her eyes. Hallie got off the bed and joined Aaron. She wrapped her arms about his waist and leaned against his chest. He smelled so good. The scent of his cologne traveled along her nerve endings.

"She remembered me, Aaron. She remembered you." She looked at him. "She said she loves me."

He squeezed her gently. "I know, baby. I couldn't be happier for you."

"You made her happy, too."

"Well, I couldn't keep my promise to protect my mother, so I needed to keep my promise to yours."

A faint smile touched the corners of her mouth. For a while, they remained in each other's arms, a sweet silence enfolding them.

He stirred first. "Hallie."

Hearing the uncertainty in his voice, she raised her head and tilted her face toward him. "What is it, Aaron?" Her heart twisted with anguish.

She broke away from his hold and went over to her mother's bed. "Mom?"

She didn't move. She didn't open her eyes.

She's sleeping, Hallie tried to convince herself, her stomach clenching. *She's only sleeping. She said she was tired.*

With a crazy mixture of hope and fear churning inside her, Hallie watched the pink hue drain from her mother's cheeks, leaving her face pale and transparent. She sank deeper into the pillows, and her arm, the one adorned by the wristlet Aaron gave her, fell limply to her side.

"Mom?" She touched her face. It was warm but barely. "Oh, Mom." Tears flowed freely now, and sobs racked her body.

Aaron was right behind her. "I'll get the nurse."

She leaned against him, thankful for his strong presence in her life. "Please stay with me. Just for a little while longer."

Chapter Twenty-Two

Donna Cavanagh's funeral was a modest one. There was no family present except for Hallie. Joanne and Janet Pearson were there. So were Sophie, Rita, Nelson, and Anne. A few of the nurses and staff who cared for her were present as well. Hallie was surprised her coworkers were there, offering their support. Even Christopher, Aaron's doorman, made an appearance.

Aaron's gaze was as soft as a caress. "They're all here for you, Hallie. Every one of them loves you in their own way."

She wasn't sure why, but she had this feeling Lavelle might show, but she didn't, which was just as well.

Aaron was right by her side the entire time. He'd even offered to pay for the funeral, but Hallie refused. She needed to complete this final act of love for her mother on her own.

A few days after the funeral, Hallie went back to Golden Living to gather her mother's belongings. Sophie accompanied her, eager to help. There wasn't much. A few pieces of clothing, slippers, and the box of photographs. Whatever had happened to her father would remain a mystery. For now, the one photograph of him was all she had.

"Hey, what's happening out there?" Sophie asked.

Hallie joined her friend at the window. A small

group of men and women were gathering outside beyond the garden area. Over to the side was a woman holding a microphone and a man balancing a camera on his shoulder.

"Wait a minute," Sophie said. "Isn't that Aaron?"

Hallie's heart jumped. Sophie was right. There, in the middle of the group, was Aaron.

"Come on," Hallie said.

Sophie followed her to the courtyard.

Aaron, holding a large shovel with a golden spade, seemed surprised but happy to see her. "I've been calling you. Where have you been?"

During the last few days after her mother's passing, Hallie had had a tough time getting herself together. Aaron had recommended she take a few days off from work to relax and renew. She had taken his suggestion, but she only moped around her apartment, not paying attention to the world passing by her.

"I turned off my phone. I didn't want to be bothered. What are you doing here?"

Joanne, who was part of the group, interrupted her and Aaron. "We're breaking ground for a new wing." Her excitement was uncontrollable. "Thanks to a generous donation from Mr. Knight, we're building an up-to-date research facility exclusively for men and women suffering from Alzheimer's."

Hallie looked at Aaron. "Why didn't you tell me?"

"I wanted to surprise you." He waved his hands in the air. "Surprise!"

"I'm so glad you made it. I want you to join us." Joanne's face glowed. "After all, the center is being named after your mother."

Hallie's heart jumped. "My mother?" She looked at

Aaron.

"It's going to be named The Donna Cavanagh Center for Alzheimer's Research. You okay with that?"

"Okay? Oh, Aaron, it's wonderful. Thank you." She threw her arms around his neck, stood on her tiptoes, and kissed him.

"Let's go, people," the woman with the microphone said. "We go in five minutes."

"This is going to be on the news?"

"Of course." Aaron handed Hallie the shovel. "I think you should do the honors."

The others in the group flanked her, and the cameraman signaled to the reporter. "Stand by, folks. We go in five, four, three, two..." She turned to the camera. "Good afternoon, New York City. Today we're here at the Golden Living Nursing Home where Mr. Aaron Knight..."

Hallie wasn't listening. All she could think about was Aaron and the legacy he was creating for her mother.

He leaned into her. "You're up."

She poised the tip of the shovel above the ground and pushed it into the soil. "For you, Mom," she whispered.

After answering the reporter's questions, Aaron and Hallie snuck away from the crowd. Sophie volunteered to gather the rest of Donna's belongings.

"I'm so proud of you," she said to Hallie. She turned to Aaron. "And you. This is a great thing you're doing."

Aaron smiled.

"All right, you two get out of here," she told them. "And don't forget I'm your maid of honor."

"Is someone planning a wedding?" Aaron held the car door open for Hallie.

Her face heated up. "Sophie's crazy. Don't pay attention to her."

"Does she know something I don't?"

Finally, back at the penthouse, Hallie made herself comfortable on the couch. The sun, a glorious orange color, was setting slowly in the sky, bathing the buildings and Central Park with surreal light.

Aaron offered her a glass of white wine, which she took with a smile. He sat down next to her.

"I want to thank you for what you did today, Aaron. With the new wing and research lab, maybe someone will find a cure for Alzheimer's in our lifetime."

"A while ago, you told me I had to forgive myself for my past mistakes. Those were powerful words. Having you in my life taught me what's important—and it's not money or power." He held her close and kissed the top of her head.

When she looked at him, his eyes were wet. She cupped the back of his head and wove her fingers through his hair. "Forgiveness sets us free. And love..."

Instinctively, their lips found their way to each other's, their kiss as tender and light as a summer breeze.

Raising his mouth from hers, he gazed into her eyes. "And love," he continued for her, "love changes everything."

A word about the author...

Suzanne Hoos divides her time between teaching junior high English to future authors and her own writing career. *Love Changes Everything* is her sixth novel and her first contemporary romance.

~*~

Find Suzanne online at:
https://www.facebook.com/suzhoos
https://twitter.com/suzhoos

Thank you for purchasing
this publication of The Wild Rose Press, Inc.

For questions or more information
contact us at
info@thewildrosepress.com.

The Wild Rose Press, Inc.
www.thewildrosepress.com

To visit with authors of
The Wild Rose Press, Inc.
join our yahoo loop at
http://groups.yahoo.com/group/thewildrosepress/

Printed in the USA
CPSIA information can be obtained
at www.ICGtesting.com
LVHW052014031123
763001LV00010B/302